# RIDING
## *Godzilla*

# RIDING
## *Godzilla*

## P.S. FOLEY

**SEVEN LOCKS PRESS**

Santa Ana, California

Seven Locks Press
P.O. Box 25689
Santa Ana, CA 92799
(800) 354-5348

Individual Sales. This book is available through most bookstores or can be ordered directly from Seven Locks Press at the address above.

Quantity Sales. Special discounts are available on quantity purchases by corporations, associations, and others. For details, contact the "Special Sales Department" at the publisher's address above.

Printed in the United States of America

*Library of Congress Cataloging-in-Publication Data*
is available from the publisher
ISBN 1-931643-74-1
First Printing

Cover artwork by Kathy Foley
Cover and Interior Design by Heather Buchman

This book is a work of fiction. Names, characters, places, and incidents are either the product of the author's imagination or are used fictitiously. Any resemblance to actual events or locales or persons, living or dead, is coincidental.

To my daughters, Rowan and Storm—

May you be the heroes of your own stories.

# Acknowledgments

I would like to thank the following people for assistance with this book. First is my wife, Kathy, who served to inspire and guide me. If I dreamed a muse, she would be it. Technical advice was provided by the best horse person I know, Athena Foley, and my daughters' first riding teacher, Jenny Spooner. Early editors Patty Santry and Lisa Rojany Bucceiri provided accurate suggestions, as did early readers Luz Chavez, Ed Santry, Stephanie Leiter, Nona McConiville, Alexis Meadows and Marie Estocin. I'd also like to thank Peter Bogdanovich, who taught me the meaning of grief and, more important, about the courage to carry on, and Big Ed McNally, who teaches me every day about perseverance. The secrets of becoming a champion can be attributed to the fine coaches I've had: Mike Foley, Bill Pizzica, Bob Hailey, George Seifert, and Bill Walsh. Lastly I'd like to thank my mother, Norma Jean, who always told me her stories and taught me to tell a story well. The people who have touched my life are in my words, always, and forever.

*Chapter One*

It was ten in the morning and it was already hot. Texas hot. The kind of summer heat that beats down hard on the asphalt road causing heat vapors to drift toward the sky. Eleven-year-old Cassie Reynolds thought the vapors looked like lonely ghosts rising up to heaven. It left her feeling sad because she imagined one of those ghosts was her father.

Cassie's father had died on the Fourth of July. It was just after nine o'clock at night on the hospital's sixth floor when the nurse had come in and checked her father's pulse. The nurse had turned to Cassie and her mother and said, "He's gone to a better place." Cassie remembered hearing her mother softly crying. She looked out the window at fireworks off in the distance, knowing that for the rest of her life she would always remember this moment whenever she saw fireworks. The Fourth of July with all its fun and magic would always be associated with her father's death.

Three days had passed, and Cassie and her mother were on the way to the cemetery to bury her father. They rode in their old Plymouth van with an air conditioner that didn't work, and the van had an oil leak somewhere that caused a burning smell to seep into the passenger compartment. The day's heat, the oil smell, and the fact that her father was dead made this trip unbearable for Cassie. It was like some sort of nightmare she wished she could wake up from.

To make matters worse, their lives had been thrown into chaos by her father's illness. Cassie's father, Michael, had been sick for nearly a year, and his fight to live had depleted the family's savings. They were also deeply in debt. The fact was, they were penniless and the bank was repossessing the only home Cassie had ever known. They had three days to move, and Cassie's mother, Susan, had no idea where they would go. Things could not have been bleaker.

Still, Susan tried to keep the mood light. Susan was the eternal optimist, and no matter how bad things were she always tried to look at the bright side.

"Cassie," Susan said, "I know this is a hard day. But we should be thankful. Your father's in a better place. He's out of pain and with God now."

But her mother's words didn't help Cassie come to grips with her loss. Cassie had adored her father and part of her wanted to pretend he wasn't dead. She just wanted to go home and sit by her father's side and listen to one of his stories. Michael Reynolds had had a gift for making up stories, and Cassie especially liked the ones about courageous little girls who did extraordinary things in far-off places like India and China. Even during his long illness, her father had still managed to tell her stories. Now those stories were lost forever. Cassie just didn't want to believe he was gone.

"Mom, I really miss him."

"I know, sweetheart. I miss him too. We'll always miss him."

"No, Mom. It's like the world has died."

They gathered at the grave to say their farewells. Uncle Tommy had come, but he was the only member of Michael Reynolds' family who lived in Dallas. The remaining part of the family lived in Arkansas and couldn't afford the cost of travel to pay their respects. A few neighbors and a couple of people from his work had come, but Michael Reynolds had not touched many lives. When the priest said his final words, the only people who cried were Cassie and her mother.

The small group quickly dispersed to find some shade. Susan walked off to talk to Uncle Tommy for a moment, leaving Cassie alone at her father's grave. Cassie knelt down.

"Daddy," Cassie said, "I know you're in heaven, and I'm glad you're out of pain. But why did you have to die?"

It was hard for Cassie because she knew her father was right there inside the coffin, but he was still so far away. Alone in her grief, Cassie began to cry as she remembered the last conversation she had had with her father on the Fourth of July.

"Cassie, I'll always be with you," her father had said. "Just look up at the stars and know I'm there."

Michael Reynolds had closed his eyes for awhile. Then, he opened them and smiled. Cassie remembered looking into his eyes and thinking that he seemed to be at peace. Like he knew something that had set his mind at ease. Cassie remembered her father's final words—she closed her eyes and listened. It felt as though her father was right next to her speaking his words again.

"I know you'll make me proud, Cassie."

It was the last thing her father had said to her, and Cassie softly replied, "I will, Daddy. I will. I'll make you proud."

# Chapter Two

After her father's death, Cassie Reynolds' life was utter chaos. The bank took her home away, and she and her mother were thrown out in the street. For the first night, they slept in their car. They had to sleep sitting up because the rest of the van was filled with clothes and household items.

The next day they found a place to stay. It was a run-down motel called the Stumble Inn, and it was in a really bad section of the city. The room was filled with cockroaches, and outside, drug dealers lined the street. It was too dangerous for Cassie to go out alone. So when her mother went to work, Cassie stayed in the motel room all day and cried. Cassie was miserable and scared. She missed her father and she missed the home she had grown up in.

"It's only temporary," Susan said. "We'll find something soon."

But every night Cassie and Susan would search the city of Dallas for a home to live in. Nobody would give them a chance. The problem was they didn't have much money and their credit had been ruined by hospital bills, not to mention the recent foreclosure on their house. It was virtually impossible for them to find a place to rent. A couple of times they had come close, but they always lost out to someone else, and after three weeks, Cassie and Susan were very discouraged. Everywhere they went, the answer was no.

Then, as luck would have it, a friend at work told Susan she had a trailer for sale. The friend's mother had lived in the trailer for twenty years, but now she was in a nursing home. The friend wanted Susan to pay her a little money and move in to take over the rent payments. The rent was cheap. Cassie and Susan went to see it immediately.

The trailer was a single wide and in poor condition. The appliances were ancient, the carpeting was frayed, and the bathroom was falling apart. But the trailer park was in an excellent area, and the local middle school had a good reputation. The trailer also had two bedrooms. Being desperate, Cassie and Susan snapped it up immediately. They moved in the next night and were grateful to finally have a home.

However, when they were moving in their final belongings, a neighbor approached them.

"Hello there," the woman said. She was a woman in her seventies, plump, with a round face and large brown eyes that twinkled. Her skin was nearly flawless and it was the color of dark chocolate.

"Hello," Susan said, smiling.

"Are you relatives of Margaret's?" the woman asked.

"No," Susan replied. "I know her daughter from work."

"Are you moving in?"

"Yes."

"I hate to tell you this, but Margaret's daughter has made a mistake. I'm not surprised because she wasn't a very good daughter anyway."

"A mistake?" Susan asked.

"Yes," the woman said. "This park is only for people fifty-five or older. It's a senior citizens' park. I see you have a daughter and you don't look very old, so I'm afraid you can't live here."

Cassie and Susan looked at each other. They both started to cry.

"Now, now," the woman said. "It will be all right. You'll find another place."

"No, it's not all right," Susan said. "You see, my husband died a few weeks ago and the bank took our house. We have no place to go. Nobody will help us."

"It can't be that bad."

"It is," Cassie said. "We've been living in a motel with gangs and drug dealers."

"How do you plan to afford the rent here?" the woman asked.

"I'm working two jobs," Susan said. "We will make this work until we find another place. We have to make it work and we are good people. It's just that my husband's illness took all of our money."

The woman looked at them hard for a long moment. It was as if she was studying them and reaching into their souls. Finally, her expression changed.

"My name's Olivia Williams. I live next door. I'm not going to tell anyone that you moved in. But if someone should ask, just say you are related to Margaret and are visiting for awhile. The other residents can be kind of funny about younger people living here."

"Thank you so much, Olivia," Susan said. "We won't be any trouble to anyone. No one will even know we're here."

Olivia smiled, and Susan took a deep breath in relief.

"Welcome to the neighborhood," Olivia said. "If you have any trouble with your trailer, my husband, Henry, can help you out. He helps a lot of people around here."

"Thank you, Olivia," Susan said.

"Everyone deserves a chance." Olivia turned and walked back to her trailer, leaving Cassie and Susan with their work.

*Chapter Three*

The next night, Cassie sat at a card table set up in the living room while Susan lay on the floor. They were both exhausted. "Mom, I'm starving," Cassie said.

"I know, honey. I am too. But I don't get paid until tomorrow. I need our last two dollars for gas to get to work."

Suddenly, there was a knock on the door. Cassie answered. It was Olivia holding a tray.

"Just thought I would bring you some food," Olivia said. "I know how hard it is to move, and sometimes you forget to eat."

Cassie, mouth watering, took the tray. "We haven't had anything all day."

"Thank you, Olivia," Susan said.

"No trouble. You two enjoy the food. You can leave the dishes on my stairs."

Olivia started to walk away, but Susan followed her out.

"Olivia," Susan said, "I want to ask you something."

Susan stepped outside. "I know you don't really know us. But I'd like to ask a favor."

"A favor?"

"Yes. I mean, I can pay you. But I need someone to look in on Cassie. I mean, she's okay on her own. It's not like she needs supervision. It's just that with two jobs and all, I would just feel better if I knew there was an adult she could turn to in an emergency."

"Don't you have family?"

"Not much of one. We're kind of on our own."

Olivia looked at Susan for a long moment. Again, Susan felt as if

Olivia was studying her, measuring her as a human being.

"How much can you afford?" Olivia asked.

"Not much," Susan replied. "Maybe twenty dollars a week."

"Tell Cassie I'll be looking in on her."

"Thank you."

Olivia nodded and turned to walk away. Then she stopped and turned back to Susan.

"I hope you know you got a bargain." She walked back to her trailer and disappeared inside. Susan walked back inside her trailer and found Cassie already eating.

"Mom," Cassie said, "there's chicken and mashed potatoes and corn too. It all tastes so good."

"That's nice, honey. I also want you to know Olivia's going to check on you to make sure you're all right."

"I like her. She seems like a nice lady. But how did she know we were hungry?"

"I don't know. She just seems to know things."

*Chapter Four*

C assie and Susan settled into their new lives. Susan went to work and Cassie spent most of her days in solitude. The only kids nearby were at The North Dallas Riding Academy, just down the hill from the trailer park. Cassie could sit at her window and see the kids riding and jumping their horses. But that world might as well have been a thousand miles away because Cassie knew her mother didn't have money for riding lessons. Wishing for riding lessons was like wishing to be a princess. It was never going to happen. Still, Cassie liked to watch and dream of what it would feel like to ride and jump one of the beautiful horses.

Mostly, Cassie spent her days sitting around the trailer. She was still hurting from the grief of losing her father. Her terrible loss made her want to curl up in a ball, and she spent a lot of time doing exactly that. Cassie was lonely and in pain, and she had no idea how to make it go away.

With her mother always working, the only person aware of Cassie's situation was Olivia. One day, hearing a knock, Cassie went to her door with eyes swollen from crying.

"Have you been crying, child?" Olivia asked.

"No, Mrs. Williams," Cassie lied. "I'm just not feeling well."

"Would you like to come out and sit awhile? I have some lemonade."

"Not today," Cassie said. "I just don't feel up to it."

Olivia took note of Cassie's behavior and talked it over with her husband. "All Cassie did today was sit around that trailer and cry. That child is wasting away with grief."

"Have you talked it over with her mother?" Henry asked.

"Tried to," Olivia replied. "But she's not any better off than Cassie. She's working her own grief away. She works all day at a bank and then all night as a waitress. Susan says she has so many bills she can't afford to take a day off."

"Well, you tried, Olivia."

"What do you mean I've tried? That child needs help, and I'm going to do something about it."

"Now, Olivia," Henry said sternly, "that child is not ours to be responsible for. The mother's paying you to look in on her, not be her nursemaid. Besides, grief has its own way of working itself out."

Olivia's eyes darkened. "Henry Williams, don't you be telling me about grief. We've had our share. That child is in pain and we need to do something about it. If she were one of your horses, you'd be over there right now doing what you could to ease her pain."

Henry Williams knew better than to argue with his wife when she had her mind set on something. Fifty years of marriage had taught him that. So Henry accepted the fact that his wife was taking on a new project, and that the little girl next door would soon be part of their lives.

# Chapter Five

Olivia thought long and hard about what to do to help Cassie. After a day, she settled on a plan. She would share with Cassie the one thing that had helped heal her grief after her two sons were killed in the same week of the Vietnam War.

The next morning at nine, Olivia walked over to Cassie's trailer and knocked on the door. Cassie answered.

"Cassie, do you think you would be able to help me in my garden this morning?"

"I don't know, Mrs. Williams. I'm not really feeling good today."

"Oh, it won't take too long. I just can't clip my roses on account of my back hurting."

Cassie didn't know what to say. Today was a really bad day for her. She just wanted to lie in bed and cry.

"You would be doing me a big favor." Olivia added, "Today is the perfect day to clip roses, and I just can't do it by myself. If you can help me, I'll pay you some of the money your mother is paying me. I really need your help, child."

"Okay," Cassie said. "Just let me put some clothes on and I'll be over."

"The garden is on the other side of the trailer," Olivia said. "I'll be waiting for you there."

Olivia's garden was truly a special place. She and Henry had bought the trailer next door and removed it. This opened an entire lot for what was to be Olivia's masterpiece. She grew all kinds of vegetables and even had some fruit trees. But nearly half the garden was devoted to her roses, and Olivia knew everything there was to know about roses—when to water them, when to feed them, and when to cut them back. She cared for her roses with a loving heart and they responded in kind. They were magnificent.

Cassie was dressed in shorts and a tank top because it was early August in Texas, and that meant hot. She walked around Olivia's trailer and found a white picket fence. In the middle of the fence was an arbor with a gate. The arbor was covered with little pink roses. Past the gate was the prettiest garden Cassie had ever seen.

Olivia was sitting on a bench next to a birdbath. Her eyes were closed and she looked as if she was enjoying the sun.

"Mrs. Williams?"

Olivia opened her eyes and smiled. "Don't just stand at the gate, child. We got work to do. And from now on it's 'Olivia.' That 'Mrs. Williams' business makes me feel old."

Cassie walked in the garden and looked around. "This place is beautiful, Olivia."

"It's been years in the making."

"It looks like it was a lot of work."

"Yes, it was. But it was good work. When you're doing something you love, it doesn't seem hard."

Olivia stood and walked to the edge of her rose garden.

"Do you know anything about roses, child?"

"Just that they're pretty."

"Well, I'm going to teach you a little about roses. Everyone should know a little about roses."

"I remember my dad taught me that red means love. He used to take me to the florist with him on Valentine's Day. He'd buy a dozen for my mom and always bought one for me too. He said red roses were for people you love."

Cassie turned away and wiped her eyes. A memory had come flooding back and it was threatening to overwhelm her. Olivia saw this and just kept going on as if nothing had happened.

"That's true," Olivia said. "Your daddy sounds like he was a smart man because roses have been the preferred flower of women throughout history. Why, the Egyptian queen Cleopatra had huge rose gardens and demanded that her palace be filled with fresh-cut roses every day."

"Really?" Cassie said softly.

"Yes, and red roses became the symbol for love after Cleopatra covered Marc Antony's grave in red roses."

"Who was Marc Antony?" Cassie asked.

"Marc Antony was the love of Cleopatra's life. They loved each other so much that poets are still writing about them. When Marc Antony died, Cleopatra wanted to die too. But enough about death. We've got work to do."

So Olivia and Cassie went to work in the rose garden. Olivia started with the basics, and she was pleased to find that Cassie was a quick study. The only fault she could find with Cassie was that occasionally Cassie stared off at the riding school where some children were practicing their jumping.

"You seem interested in the horses," Olivia remarked.

"Yes," Cassie replied. "I like to watch the kids practicing."

Olivia and Cassie worked hard. Cassie cut some roses, weeded the vegetable garden, and pruned some trees. When it got toward noon, Olivia said, "I think that's enough for one day. Why don't we go inside for some lunch? It's getting hot."

"It's lunchtime already?" Cassie asked.

"Yes, it sure is. That's what a little hard work will do for you. It makes the time fly by."

They went inside. Cassie sat at the oak table in the front room while Olivia prepared lunch in the kitchen. However, when Olivia came out with a tray of tuna-fish sandwiches and lemonade, she saw that Cassie was crying.

"Why are you crying, child?"

"Today's my birthday." Cassie wiped her eyes on her shirt and tried to compose herself. "I'm sorry."

"That's nothing to cry about. Maybe when you get to be my age, you can cry. But not at your age. How old are you, anyway?"

"Twelve. My Mom says it's my last year of childhood. She cried before she left for work."

"Crying on a birthday? Who ever heard of such a thing? Birthdays are for celebration."

"I know," Cassie said. "It's just that ever since I was little my special celebration was with my dad. He would take me to a toy store and tell me to pick out whatever I wanted. It made me feel so special, and I felt like for just a little while I could have whatever I wished for."

"Yes," Olivia said, "when someone dies young, they leave an awfully big hole."

Cassie nodded.

"Say, child," Olivia said brightly. "If you could wish for anything, what would it be?"

"I'd wish I had my dad back."

"No. Pretend your daddy's right here. What would you wish for?"

"I don't know," Cassie said. Then she looked out the window at the kids riding horses off in the distance. "I think I'd wish for riding lessons."

"Then why don't you?"

"My mom can't afford them. I don't want her to feel bad about having to say no, especially on my birthday."

"Sometimes," Olivia said, "even without money your wishes can come true. The important thing is just to wish for them."

Cassie smiled. "Maybe you're right."

Olivia smiled back. She poured a glass of lemonade and handed it to Cassie. "Let's make a toast to wishes.

# Chapter Six

Every day for a week, Cassie helped Olivia in her garden. Cassie learned a lot about roses and worked hard on the tasks Olivia gave her, but every spare moment she would spy on the children at the riding academy. Olivia could see that Cassie was more interested in horses than in roses.

That night, when Henry came home from the academy, Olivia had a request.

"Henry, I've been doing some thinking about Cassie."

"Yes . . . " Henry replied wondering where this was headed.

"She's been doing great with the roses. And she's a real hard worker. And just so pleasant to be around. I'll tell you, Henry, there's something special about that girl."

"Yes . . . " Henry now wondered if this was going to involve him.

"But Cassie's heart isn't really into roses."

"No . . . ?" Now Henry *knew for a fact* that this was going to involve him.

"You remember, I told you about Cassie's birthday wish and how she wanted to ride."

"Yes . . . " Now Henry knew *how* it was going to involve him.

"I think it would really help Cassie if she could take some riding lessons."

"Those lessons are expensive. Cassie's mother can't afford them."

"You could ask Mr. Stanley for a favor."

"Mr. Stanley just built a new barn. He can't give away free riding lessons. Besides, the girls that are riding are about the worst snobs I have ever seen. They don't want to be riding with a girl that lives in the trailer park."

"Henry, I think riding would really take Cassie's mind off of her father. Now, you've worked at that academy for thirty years and you've never asked for a thing. I've never asked for a thing either, and I've never complained when you had to work weekends or stay out all night with a sick horse. I'm asking you to do this."

Henry rubbed his chin. He always did this when he was thinking. "Why are you so fond of this girl?"

"There's just something that makes me want to help her. I think she reminds me of myself when I was her age, and I remember someone who helped me."

Henry was surprised at this. After fifty years of marriage, he thought he knew everything there was to know about Olivia.

"Who helped you?" Henry asked.

"Mrs. Walsh."

"Wasn't she that woman your mother worked for cleaning her house?"

"Yes, she was. But when I was Cassie's age, my father left us and my mother had to work and take care of three kids. Mrs. Walsh knew we needed extra money, so she asked if I wanted to help in her garden. She's the one who first taught me about roses. I had the best summer of my life. I remember she always had plenty of lemonade too."

Olivia was quiet a moment. Then she looked Henry in the eye. "Kindness needs to be passed on, Henry. Working with Cassie reminded me of the kindness Mrs. Walsh showed me."

Henry could see in Olivia's eyes that she was not going to take no for an answer. "All right, Olivia. I'll ask Mr. Stanley tomorrow."

# *Chapter Seven*

The North Dallas Riding Academy sat on ten acres of land at the base of a gently rolling hill. With its forest green buildings and white trim, three riding arenas, and long white fences, it was one of the most charming riding schools in America. As a result of its charm, and the fact that several national riding champions had started there, The North Dallas Riding Academy had acquired a national reputation for quality.

The owner, Mr. Stanley, had inherited the academy from his father when he died. Mr. Stanley and his father were as different as night and day. His father had run the riding school out of a love of horses, children, and riding. In contrast, Mr. Stanley's primary purpose was to turn a profit, and this changed the atmosphere of the school since he had taken over five years ago. Henry and Mr. Stanley had numerous arguments over some of Mr. Stanley's decisions. Still, Mr. Stanley was actually a very nice man, and Henry, who had known him since he was a boy, liked him very much. It was just that Mr. Stanley placed profits at the top of his priorities. But as sometimes happens, when you chase money too hard, it finds a way of disappearing. Not that the academy was in financial trouble—it just always seemed to be short of cash.

Money was what Mr. Stanley was thinking about when Henry went to see him. Henry found Mr. Stanley behind his desk crunching numbers as usual. Henry knocked on the open door and Mr. Stanley looked up.

"Henry, come in. What can I do for you?"

"Well, Mr. Stanley, I'll get right to the point. I need to ask a favor."

Mr. Stanley paused. He knew that when someone started a conversation this way, it usually cost him money somewhere down the road. "A favor?" Mr. Stanley asked cautiously.

"Actually, it's for Olivia."

"Olivia wants a favor?"

"Yes," Henry said. "You see, my wife has started to care for a little girl who lives next door, and the little girl would like to take some riding lessons."

Mr. Stanley was relieved. "Of course she can have riding lessons. Just bring her over."

"She can't pay for them," Henry said quickly.

Mr. Stanley paused. His first instincts were right. A favor usually cost him money.

"That's a problem," Mr. Stanley said. "You know our teachers get paid by the rider, even in group lessons. I doubt they would be willing to take on a student for free."

"Maybe the academy could help out."

"Henry, you know money's tight with the new barn and all. Besides, I'd hate to start a precedent like that. If people knew someone was riding for free, and you know they find that stuff out, why, it would be a problem."

Henry nodded. "I told Olivia you would probably say as much."

"Sorry, Henry. If you think of another way, you know I would love to help."

"You know," Henry said, "I just thought of another way."

"What's that?"

"Well, you were saying just the other day that I could use a little help around here."

"Yes, that's true. You're seventy years old."

"Why don't we hire the girl? Olivia tells me she's a hard worker, and I could use the help cleaning out the stalls and getting the horses ready. Instead of being paid, she could get riding lessons. No money would have to change hands."

"I was thinking more along the lines of someone who could replace you when you retire."

"I knew what you were thinking. But I don't intend to retire anytime soon, and I could still use the help."

Mr. Stanley smiled. He knew that once again Henry Williams had gotten the best of him. "Henry Williams, you should be ashamed of yourself. I mean, did you plan that helper bit before you came in here?"

Henry smiled. "The thought had crossed my mind."

"Okay. You can tell Olivia her girl can have the riding lessons in exchange for work, but only on a trial basis. This girl needs to pull her weight so everyone knows she's not getting the lessons for free."

"Fair enough."

## Chapter Eight

When Henry arrived home that night, he immediately told Olivia about his conversation with Mr. Stanley. When he was finished, she smiled. "Henry Williams, you are a smart man. But don't think that's why I married you."

"Why did you marry me?"

"I married you because even after all these years you still make me laugh."

Olivia gave Henry a hug and kiss. He smiled.

"I want to go over and tell Cassie the good news," Olivia said. She started for the door, but Henry called to her.

"You make sure that girl knows that these lessons aren't for free. She's going to have to do some work."

Olivia walked to the Reynoldses' trailer and knocked on the door. After a moment, Susan answered.

"Oh, Olivia, I'm sorry I haven't paid you for last week. Could I pay you for two weeks this Friday?"

"Never mind about that," Olivia replied. "I have some news that both Cassie and you need to hear."

"Oh, all right."

Cassie came out directly. Because there was only a table with two chairs in the front room, everyone stood as Olivia delivered her news.

"Cassie, do you remember your birthday wish?"

Cassie looked at her mother, who frowned.

"Cassie," Susan said, "you told me that you didn't want anything for your birthday."

"I know, Mom."

"Susan," Olivia said, "Cassie's birthday wish was to have riding lessons down at the academy."

"Oh," Susan said sadly. "I'm afraid we can't afford riding lessons."

"That's the beauty of it," Olivia said. "Cassie can earn her own lessons. Henry needs some help, and the owner of the academy agreed to let Cassie have the lessons in exchange for a little hard work."

"But what about a horse?" Susan asked. "Doesn't she have to have a horse?"

"No," Olivia said, "she can just use one of the academy horses. That's what most people do when they start."

Cassie looked to her mom with pleading eyes. More than anything else, Cassie wanted to ride horses.

"Okay," Susan said, "but school is starting back up soon. I expect you to do all your homework and get good grades. If riding interferes, you'll have to stop."

"It's a deal, Mom," Cassie said, hugging her mom. Susan laughed.

"One other thing," added Susan. "Horses can be dangerous. I want you to promise me you'll be careful."

"I will," Cassie said.

Cassie turned to Olivia. "Thank you so much." Cassie walked up to her and gave her a big hug. Olivia smiled.

"Don't thank me, child. You need to thank Henry. But maybe you should wait until you see how much work he gives you."

"You know I'm not afraid of a little hard work. But what about your roses? I mean with your back and all?"

Olivia smiled. "You let me worry about the roses. If I get into a pinch, I'll just borrow you from Henry."

That night, Cassie was so excited she had a hard time falling asleep. She kept picturing herself going over jumps on a beautiful black horse. She just couldn't believe it: Her birthday wish was coming true.

# Chapter Nine

C assie sprang out of bed the next morning with the feeling that this day was the beginning of something good. She dressed and ate breakfast. When her mother awoke, she was surprised to see her daughter ready so early.

"It's not even six o'clock," Susan said. "What are you doing up?"

"I don't want to be late," Cassie replied.

"Late?" Susan asked. For a moment Susan thought she had forgotten something.

"Riding lessons, remember?"

"Oh, right."

Susan smiled and then went to get dressed for work. She was glad she had decided to let Cassie ride because she had not seen her daughter this excited about something in a long time.

After her mother had left, Cassie couldn't wait to go to the academy. She walked over and knocked on Henry and Olivia's door. After a moment, Henry answered. He was still in his pajamas.

"Hi, Mr. Williams," Cassie said. "I'm ready to go to work."

"Cassie, it's not even seven o'clock."

"It isn't?" Cassie replied. "What time should I come over?"

"Well," Henry said, "why don't you come over around ten. Olivia can walk you down."

"Okay. Ten. I'll be here."

"And from now on call me Henry."

Henry shut the door and smiled. He was a little superstitious when it came to some things, and he always looked for a magical reason behind the meaning of everyday occurrences, especially with new beginnings. He thought Cassie's anxiousness to work was a good omen.

At ten, Cassie met Olivia at her trailer and together they walked down to the academy. There was an ancient gate in the fence between the trailer park and the academy that Henry had made years ago, and the path was well worn by Henry's footsteps. About halfway down the hill, Olivia stopped and looked at Cassie.

"Cassie, the academy is a different world from any you've ever known. Many of the girls you'll be mixing with come from a different type of background. Sometimes they're not very nice to newcomers."

Cassie nodded.

"The thing to do is to just concentrate on your riding. If you become a good rider, they'll respect you. Then, when they get to know you, they'll like you. But don't expect them to be friendly right away."

Cassie knew that what Olivia had told her was important. She also appreciated the fact that Olivia cared enough to tell her this. "Okay, Olivia, I'll remember that."

The academy had a number of buildings and three riding arenas in the center of the property. On the outskirts of the property were horse corrals. And at the front of the property was a long driveway lined with ancient oak trees.

The riding arenas were filled with riders already practicing. The arena farthest from the buildings was for the beginners. The middle arena was for intermediate riders and people just starting to participate in horse shows. The first arena was the one closest to the buildings and was for the experts. It was the largest arena and the best-cared for. On one side, the arena had horse stalls that were reserved for only the best horses and along the other side were grandstands where people frequently gathered to watch the experts practice. Every young rider dreamed of being invited to the first arena. It was like making the varsity team.

Olivia and Cassie found Henry at the crossties, where the horses were groomed and saddled. Each crosstie is like a little stall with two metal posts at the front. The horses are chained at their halters between the posts so they can't walk away or move around very much. There were eight crossties, and three of them were filled with horses of different sizes and colors. Henry was just throwing a saddle on a large brown horse when Olivia and Cassie walked up.

"Henry," Olivia said, "I brought Cassie down to start work."

"That's good. Just let me get the saddle on Ol' Dapper Dan here, and I'll be right with you."

Henry worked quickly. You could tell just by watching him that he was good with a horse. There were no false moves or pauses in his actions, and he had the saddle on and cinched before Olivia could answer back. Once done, Henry turned and smiled at Cassie. "So are you ready to learn about horses, child?"

"Yes, sir," Cassie quickly replied. "I sure am."

It was the type of answer Henry hoped to hear. He didn't know Cassie very well and his only knowledge of her had come from Olivia. Henry liked her ready enthusiasm and that was another good omen.

"I'll be headed home then," Olivia said. "Your momma's working late tonight, Cassie, so plan on having dinner with us."

"All right, Olivia. Thanks."

Henry looked at Cassie. "So tell me, child, have you spent any time around horses?"

"Not really. My dad used to take me to the pony rides over at the park. But I've always loved them."

"I'm either going to teach you everything I know about horses or nothing. In about a minute we're going to know which it is."

"It will be everything," Cassie said. There was conviction in her voice. Henry liked that too.

"The first thing you need to know,"Henry said, "is that horses are not like us. They're herd animals and have been prey for about a million years. This means that their first impulse is to view us as a predator. So instinct tells them to run away or kick or bite to protect themselves. That's why when you approach a horse, you do so slowly, calmly, and precisely. Now, I want you to come over here and rub Dan's neck."

Cassie walked up to Dan with a confidence that surprised even Henry. She moved slowly and calmly, gently rubbing the side of Dan's neck. The horse looked over at Cassie and didn't seem the least bit threatened. Henry was surprised.

"That's fine, Cassie," Henry said.

"He seems like a real gentle horse," Cassie replied.

Henry didn't respond, for he knew that "gentle" was not how he would describe Dapper Dan when he was in the crossties. "Skittish" was the proper word, but Dan had remained calm. Henry wondered why.

For the remainder of the day, Henry had Cassie follow him around the academy while he did his work. Along the way, Henry began teaching Cassie both about the job and the horses. He was pleased to find that Olivia was right: Cassie was a quick study. By the end of the day, Cassie knew most of the horses' names and what stalls they belonged in. She also learned the fine art of mucking. In other words, Cassie was cleaning up horse poop. But she didn't mind. To Cassie, the first day inside the academy was a dream come true.

That night, before they fell asleep, Olivia asked Henry how he really felt about Cassie.

"You know," Henry said, "it was the darndest thing. That horse I was saddling when you walked up?"

"You mean Dapper Dan?" Olivia said.

"Yeah, Dapper Dan. Well, I had planned for him to be in the crossties for when you both showed up."

"Why?" Olivia asked.

"I wanted to teach Cassie her first lesson about horses, which is you need to be careful around them until you get to know them."

"I don't understand."

"Well, I'm the only person I know of that can get near that horse in the crossties. If anyone else gets near Dan, he starts jumping around and tapping his hoofs like he's Sammy Davis Jr. He scares people to death."

"Henry Williams, you should be ashamed of yourself. Scaring that poor child on her first day."

"That's just it," Henry said. "Dapper Dan just stood there calm as day when Cassie petted him. It was like Cassie had known him for years. At first, I thought there was something wrong with Dan so I asked someone else to pet him. Sure enough, he did his tap dance."

Olivia laughed. "You've always been full of tricks, Henry Williams, and I'm glad this one didn't work. I told you there was something special about that girl."

Henry searched his mind for the reasons Dapper Dan had been so calm around Cassie. Finally, he said, "I don't know what it means. But it means something."

*Chapter Ten*

There were two weeks left before summer vacation was over, and Cassie spent nearly every waking moment at Henry's side or taking riding lessons. Henry had Cassie paired with who he thought was the best riding instructor at the academy, Linda Flemming. Linda was a very nice woman in her late thirties who had once had a successful career on the professional riding circuit. But what Henry liked most about her was that Linda's philosophy of horses was similar to his own.

"Cassie," Henry said, "horses are looking for leadership. They don't care who the leader is, but someone has to be it. That's because they're herd animals and instinctively they need a leader. If the horse doesn't trust you to be a good leader, the horse will do what it thinks it needs to do to be safe—not what you want it to do."

"Do horses really think like that?" Cassie asked.

"Partially they do. But they are also driven by instinct. So you're dealing with not only their thoughts but also impulses. But horses learn quickly whom they can trust."

Later that afternoon, Cassie was talking to Linda after her lesson.

"Cassie," Linda said, "your body language is extremely important for building trust in your horse. The way you sit in the saddle, the way you lean, the way you touch your heels to their sides, every movement is being felt by the horse and conveys information about what you want your horse to do. If you're precise and consistent with your horse, he'll learn to trust what you're telling him."

"Henry says they need to trust you before they'll let you be the leader," Cassie said.

"That's right," Linda replied. "And the way you build that trust is with precise and consistent movements."

At the end of the day, Henry and Cassie were walking past the first arena, where the expert riders practiced. A young girl about the same age as Cassie was yelling at her horse and yanking on his reins.

"Starfire! Will you wake up? We're jumping today. Remember?"

The horse's ears were pinned back. Henry noticed and pointed that out to Cassie.

"See that horse's ears? The ears tell you everything. They point in the direction the horse is focused on. Except when they're back like that. When they're back, the horse is mad and you don't want a horse mad at you."

The horse started backing up and the girl hit him hard with her crop. "No!" the girl screamed. "What's gotten into you? We're jumping today!"

The girl hit the horse several times on its rear and she kicked his sides hard. The horse ran forward and then left its feet. The horse and rider easily cleared the jump.

Henry just shook his head.

"Remember, horses never forget and a really bad experience can ruin a horse. They're a lot smarter than we give them credit for."

"Do you think that will ruin that horse?" Cassie asked.

"No," Henry replied. "They're not as fragile as that. But you can tell by the way the horse was reacting that it was only doing it because it was being told to do it. Starfire made that jump because he's afraid not to make it."

"That rider is dominating her horse, not leading it," Cassie said.

"That's right. You want your horse to perform because the horse wants to please you, not because it's afraid of you. You have to be firm, but there's a big difference between dominating and leading."

Cassie looked over at the girl and the horse. The girl appeared to be a very good rider.

"Henry, who is that girl?" Cassie asked.

Henry looked over at the girl. "Her name is Rebecca Simms."

"She looks like she is a really good rider," Cassie said.

"In her age group, Rebecca is one of the best. But that doesn't make the way she treats her horse right. She thinks that forcing your horse to perform is a sign of strength. It's a mistake a lot of riders make. Real strength is being patient and firm and learning to make your horse want to do something. If you can learn to do that, you'll become not just a good rider, but a great one."

At the end of two weeks, Henry was impressed with how far Cassie had come. He also began to suspect that she had a gift for horses. When he ran into Linda Flemming at the soda machine, his suspicions were heightened.

"Hey, Linda," Henry said. "How's Cassie coming along with her riding?"

"Really well. She's posting well and she has great balance in the saddle. But you know, it's kind of an amazing thing. It just seems like the horses enjoy being ridden by her. They just do anything she asks."

When Henry got home that night, he told Olivia what he thought. "I don't know. The way Cassie is around horses, she's gentle and firm at the same time. The horses just seem to respond to her. I'm wondering if she has a gift."

"I told you there was something special about that girl, and I'm glad we've helped her. You don't seem to mind either. The way she just keeps asking you questions about horses and you answering as best you can. If I didn't know you so well, I would think you were having fun teaching her."

Henry laughed. "Well, she is a good worker. Mr. Stanley's happy. And she's been a big help."

"And the best part," Olivia said, "is that she's not sitting in that trailer crying all day."

# Chapter Eleven

T he first day of school is always a little scary. But for Cassie it was doubly so. Not only was it the first day of middle school, but it was a new school where Cassie didn't know a single soul. Some kids from the academy would be there, but Cassie had been so busy helping Henry and learning to ride, she hadn't really been able to meet many of them. She took care of their horses, and to most of the kids she was just another hired hand like Henry.

So Cassie was surprised when on the bus to school she saw a picture of Rebecca Simms with her horse on a billboard. Rebecca's smiling face was looking down on the people who passed, and on Starfire's bridle was a big blue ribbon. There were words above them that read: "At Blue Ribbon Auto Mall Everyone's a Winner." Cassie was impressed.

But her excitement at seeing Rebecca's billboard soon turned to dismay between first and second periods. Cassie stopped in the bathroom and found four girls already there. The girls were standing in front of the mirror checking their makeup. Cassie had seen these girls riding at the academy, and one of the girls was Rebecca Simms. Rebecca noticed Cassie when she walked in.

"Haven't I seen you at the academy?" Rebecca asked.

"Yeah," Cassie stammered.

"Why do you go there?" Rebecca asked and the other three girls turned to look at Cassie.

"I'm, ah, working and taking riding lessons."

"Do you work for Henry?"

"Ah, yes. Yes, I do."

"Where do you live?" another girl asked.

"Next door to Henry."

"You mean in the trailer park," Rebecca said and the way she said it made Cassie cringe.

"Yeah," Cassie answered.

The girls all looked at each other. A couple of them rolled their eyes.

"Oh," Rebecca said coolly and then added, "you can go now."

But Cassie just looked at them a moment too long. She so badly wanted to know these girls and have friends. Rebecca noticed and frowned.

"Let's go," Rebecca said to the other girls and they all walked out without saying goodbye to Cassie.

Cassie stood there by herself. She looked in the mirror and saw what Rebecca had seen. She hated that her clothes were shabby and that she was poor. To Rebecca and her friends, Cassie wasn't worth knowing, and in less than thirty seconds, Rebecca had made her feel like dirt.

The rest of her day went all right, and Cassie tried not to let Rebecca and her friends ruin her day. But when the bus passed Rebecca's billboard on the way home, she decided she didn't like her very much. She didn't like the way Rebecca had treated her horse, and she didn't like the way Rebecca had treated her.

# Chapter Twelve

Cassie quickly settled into a routine of going to school, where she thought about riding all day, and then coming home and rushing through some of her schoolwork as quickly as possible so she could get to the academy. Once there, Cassie would work hard, even doing things that weren't asked of her until it was time for her riding lesson.

After her lesson, she would help Henry some more, and on many days, she would not finish until after dark. In the evenings, she would usually have dinner with Olivia and Henry because her mother was working her second job. After dinner, Cassie would try to do some homework, but she was frequently too tired and would just go to bed. She didn't have any free time and she didn't care. If she had free time, she would have just spent it at the academy.

Yet, everything was far from perfect. Cassie was still in terrible pain. At night, before she went to sleep, and in the morning just after she woke, Cassie would think of her father and feel a deep sense of loss. The only thing that would make the pain bearable was to think of riding. When she did this, the pain would lessen, but it did not go away. It stayed with her waiting to be reignited by a thought or memory, and she carried the weight of it around with her every waking moment. Still, riding served to get her up in the morning.

Then, on Friday, something happened that would change the course of Cassie's life. She arrived at the academy to find Henry searching in the tack room for something.

"Did you lose something, Henry?"

"I seem to have misplaced my keys."

Henry stopped and rubbed his chin. "You know, I may have left them at Godzilla's shed. Will you go behind the barn and see if they're there? They'll be on a barrel next to the door."

"Sure," Cassie said and started off. Then Henry called to her.

"Child, whatever you do, don't open the door to that shed."

"Okay," Cassie said.

Cassie had never been behind the barn, and she was surprised to find another small building she had never seen before. It looked like a large shed, and it had signs posted on it that read: "Keep out. Danger."

Cassie quickly found Henry's keys on the barrel by the door. She picked them up and started to walk back. But then she stopped to look at the building again. It was all closed up and there weren't any windows. Cassie wondered what was inside. For some reason, Cassie sensed a great sadness and she knew that whatever was inside was hurting. It was like the pain she was living with. She was tempted to look inside, but she remembered Henry's warning. So Cassie ran back to Henry intending to ask him about it.

But when Cassie returned to the crossties, she found Henry had another problem on his hands. Rebecca Simms was yelling at him.

"I told you yesterday! My horse needs to be ready when I get here! I don't have time to wait around!"

Cassie couldn't believe it. She hated the fact that someone was yelling at Henry. Especially Rebecca Simms.

"It was my fault," Cassie said loudly.

Rebecca Simms turned and saw Cassie. There were two other girls, the same ones from the bathroom, standing with Rebecca.

"Henry asked me to check the schedule, and I forgot," Cassie said.

"It better not happen again!" Rebecca yelled. "My father pays a lot of money to this academy, and if you want to continue riding for free then you better not make any more stupid mistakes. Now get my horse ready!"

Rebecca and her friends glared at Cassie. But Cassie ignored them and walked away.

Rebecca's horse, Starfire, was a magnificent animal. But as Cassie got him ready, she wondered if Starfire liked being ridden by Rebecca Simms. She guessed this horse probably hated it.

Cassie walked Starfire out to the first arena, where Rebecca was waiting.

"The saddle better be on right," Rebecca said. Cassie just handed the horse over and walked away.

It was after dark when Cassie and Henry headed for home. They walked together up the path to the trailer park.

"Henry, why do you think Rebecca Simms acts like that?"

"I think Rebecca Simms likes to make people feel bad so she feels better about herself. It's kind of sad, really. By the way, why did you take the blame for her horse not being ready? I didn't tell you to check the schedule."

"I know. I just didn't want her yelling at you. She's so dumb. But it's her loss."

"How do you mean?"

"Because you're probably one of the best teachers in the world. She could learn so much from you, and instead she yells at you. Now that's stupid."

Henry smiled because Cassie's words had just taught him something. He realized why people become teachers in the first place: It is one of the best feelings in the world to know that your knowledge and experience are valued by your student.

"Thank you for saying that, child."

"You don't need to thank me for what's true."

Cassie and Henry walked a little farther up the trail in silence. But Cassie still had something on her mind.

"Henry, what's in that shed behind the barn?"

"That's Godzilla."

"Godzilla? What's Godzilla?"

"Godzilla is a horse who at one time was one of the best jumpers in the country."

"Why is he in that shed?"

"It's a long sad story."

"I'd like to hear it, if it's all right."

"Sure. Well, Godzilla had a sweetheart. A filly he had grown up with since he was a colt. Her name was Sunny. They were trained together and they learned to jump together. Godzilla and Sunny were two peas in a pod. If they were away from each other, they weren't worth a nickel. It was like they were joined at the hip."

"Joined at the hip?" Cassie asked. "Does that mean they were sad when they were apart?"

"Yeah," Henry said, "but it was more than that. It was like neither of them wanted to live without the other."

"Really? And they were both jumpers?"

"Yes, Sunny was a good jumper, but Godzilla was great. But it was a problem. We soon realized that Godzilla only did his best when Sunny was nearby. It was like he needed her to watch him. But sometimes that's how horses are. They become very attached to each other."

"What happened?" Cassie asked.

"Godzilla and Sunny used to practice together, and one afternoon Sunny took a terrible fall on a jump and broke her leg in about three places. It was a mess, and there was nothing anyone could do."

"That's terrible," Cassie said.

"It gets worse. Sunny was in pain and screaming. So to stop her pain, Mr. Stanley came out with his rifle and shot her. The only trouble was, we had forgotten Godzilla was still in the arena. Godzilla went crazy. He tried to kill Mr. Stanley and he chased everyone out of the arena. Then he stood guard over Sunny's body. He wouldn't let anyone get near her. For a whole day and an entire night, Godzilla stood there."

"What did they do?"

"The next morning they shot him with a tranquilizer and then put him in his stall. When the tranquilizer wore off, he just went crazy. Knocked down the stall door and ran to the arena. But by that time, Sunny's body was gone. Godzilla was crazy. He went after everyone that tried to get near him. Even me, and I had known him since he was born. So they shot him with another tranquilizer and put him in that shed. He's been there ever since. Won't let anyone in. I feed him and try to clean his stall, but every time he goes after me. He's really scary to be around. Ears back all the time like he's just waiting for the chance to kill me."

"Hasn't anyone tried to do anything?" Cassie asked.

"Mr. Stanley's tried everything. He's had vets out and horse whisperers. He even brought in an old Indian from New Mexico that was supposedly some kind of healer. Nothing's worked."

"I knew there was something sad in there."

"Yep," Henry replied. "What's in that shed is the worst kind of grief. Brokenhearted grief that don't want to live and doesn't want life around it. Mr. Stanley's talking about destroying him and that's probably what should be done. But Godzilla was once worth a lot of money. More than half a million dollars, and the memory of what he was is all that keeps Mr. Stanley from putting him down."

"There must be something someone could do," Cassie said.

"I wish there was," Henry replied sadly. "We've all pretty much given up, and that's something I hate . . . giving up."

Cassie and Henry walked the rest of the way home in silence. Cassie's mind was trying to wrap itself around the story of Godzilla.

That night, Cassie lay in bed awake for the longest time thinking about Godzilla. She kept feeling that he was in pain just like her. She hated thinking of a horse locked up in a shed by himself, lonely and desperate, just waiting to die. And her last thought before she went to sleep was that there must be something she could do.

Chapter Thirteen

When Cassie awoke early on Saturday morning, she was still
thinking about Godzilla. She decided that she just had to see
him that very day. Maybe after she saw him, she could figure out a way to help him. But she couldn't let Henry know because he
would forbid it. She didn't like sneaking around, but she knew what
Godzilla was feeling. She was living with grief every day too.

Cassie went to the academy at nine and found Henry already there.
She spent an hour and a half mucking some thirty stalls. Then she had
her riding lesson with Linda. The whole time she was thinking of
Godzilla. Even Linda noticed.

"Cassie, you seem distracted today."

"I'm sorry. But Henry told me the story of Godzilla last night. I can't
stop thinking about it."

"Oh," Linda said. "Isn't that just the saddest story? I don't know
what will become of him."

"It's like everyone has just given up on him."

"Well, people have tried everything they can think of to help him.
Even I've tried. You know I rode him in one of my last shows. He was
probably the best horse I've ever ridden."

"There must be something someone can do."

"A lot of smart horse people have spent a lot of time trying. I tried
to lead him out of the shed. You know, he tried to bite me and kick
me. He's one big scary mess."

In the afternoon, Cassie waited until Henry had gone to the office
to talk to Mr. Stanley. After he left, Cassie went to the tack room and

got a carrot from the refrigerator. She looked around, and seeing that there was no one watching, she walked to the shed.

When she got there, Cassie looked at the signs reading: Keep out. Danger. For a moment, she thought she was just being foolish. Who was she, anyway? She'd worked around horses for only a month, and she had been warned: Godzilla was extremely dangerous.

But then Cassie sensed the sadness that was hidden behind those walls. Her heart went out to Godzilla, and she knew that if someone didn't help him, he would be put down.

Cassie stepped up to the massive door and undid the latch to the top of the Dutch door and pulled. The door was extremely heavy because the shed had been built to keep stallions away from mares when they were in season. Stallions had been known to kick through their stall walls in an effort to visit their girlfriends. Godzilla wasn't a stallion. He was a gelding. But just the same, Mr. Stanley felt safer with Godzilla locked behind these thick wooden walls.

The inside of the stall was large, and even though there was a sky-light that let in light, the edges and corners of the shed were dark. It took a moment for Cassie's eyes to adjust to the light changes before she could see Godzilla. He was standing along the edge of the shed in the darkest place he could find. Cassie was surprised at how big he was. He was the largest jumper she had ever seen. His coat was jet black and his neck was muscular and powerful. But he hung his head down low like an animal that had been beaten into submission. He had been defeated by his grief.

"Hey, there, Godzilla," Cassie said gently.

The horse's ears went back, but he did not move. Cassie saw there were sores on his legs, and she noticed for the first time how badly the shed smelled. It was like a dungeon. Cassie felt tears fill her eyes.

"Godzilla, I know how much it hurts to lose someone you love. I felt the same way when my dad died. I hurt so badly I just wanted to give up. I think you need a friend who knows how that feels, and I'm going to try and be your friend. I know how it feels to be this sad."

Cassie saw that Godzilla's ears twitched, and she took this as a good sign. She was not the least bit afraid of him or worried that he would suddenly attack her. All she felt was his pain.

"Nobody knows I've come here, and I would probably get into trouble if they found out. But I'm going to come here every day and spend a little time with you. I think you need me to be your friend."

Godzilla didn't respond or act as if he heard Cassie. But that didn't matter to Cassie. Something inside her made her feel as if he was listening.

"I've got to go back now. But I've brought you a carrot."

Cassie held the carrot out for Godzilla, but he made no movement toward it. Cassie wasn't even sure if he saw it. She threw it to him and it landed at his front feet. Cassie waited to see if he would pick it up. But Godzilla just stood there.

"Oh well, maybe you'll eat it later. 'Bye, Godzilla, I'll see you tomorrow."

Cassie stepped back and pushed the massive door shut. She latched it and started to walk away. Then she stopped and looked at the shed.

"Maybe everyone's given up on you," Cassie said to herself, "but I'm not going to. I'll be here every day, Godzilla. You'll see."

*Chapter Fourteen*

For most of September, Cassie made time for visiting the terrible horse Godzilla. She even went on Sundays, when the academy was closed. Cassie always brought "a big, delicious, juicy carrot." Although Godzilla wouldn't take it from her, it was always gone the next time she came.

Cassie worked hard to keep these visits secret, and both Henry and her mother had no idea she was going to visit what many people considered a dangerous animal. She was surprised that people were scared of Godzilla because he never once showed any sign of aggressiveness toward her. The big horse would just stand there, quietly listening, as Cassie poured out her heart to him.

Cassie began to tell Godzilla about her life. She told him about crying herself to sleep at night thinking about her father, and how sometimes when she woke up in the morning she forgot he was dead. She always sprang to her feet thinking she would see him, but when she landed on the floor she remembered he was gone from her life. The realization hit her so hard that she would just climb back in bed and cry. Sometimes she cried so hard and for so long that she nearly missed the bus for school.

"I can't tell my mom how I feel," Cassie added. "She has enough to worry about, and the last thing I want is for her to worry about me."

When Cassie finished telling Godzilla this, she realized that for the first time the horse was looking directly at her. What's more, his ears were pointed forward in her direction, meaning his focus was on her. But Cassie didn't react. Instead, she decided this was the time to tell Godzilla something that had been weighing on her mind.

"You know, I'm not going to call you Godzilla anymore. I've been doing some thinking, and you just don't seem like a Godzilla to me. Now my real name is Cassandra, but everyone calls me Cassie. I thought about Godzilla and decided that the shortened version should be Dillie. So from now on that's what I'm going to call you, Dillie. You just seem more like a Dillie than a Godzilla."

Cassie wasn't sure, but she thought Godzilla seemed to like this idea. His ears stayed focused on her and he seemed to relax.

After Cassie started calling the big horse Dillie it seemed to change things between them. He would look up when she arrived and watch her almost the whole time she spoke. It also made Cassie feel closer to him. Then a funny thing began to happen. Cassie started to tell the big horse her secrets, things she wouldn't dare tell anyone.

"I hate school," Cassie blurted out one day. "It's just so hard to do my homework. My dad used to help me, and every time I sit down to do it I think of him. I don't know why I do that, but I do. Then I just start hurting so bad I just can't work. I'm falling behind and I don't know how to catch up."

She poured her soul out to the horse, telling him about her fears and her grief.

"You know, Dillie, I don't have any friends at school. Ever since my dad died, we've been real poor, and my mom can't afford to buy me any nice clothes. Most of my clothes are too small since I grew over the summer."

Cassie looked down at her clothes and grimaced.

"I think I must look kind of weird because no one seems interested in being my friend. But it's okay because most days I just go to the library and read. They have lots of great stories about horses."

Cassie grew quiet as a tear welled in her eye.

"I don't know, Dillie, I just feel so different from everyone else. It's like I don't fit in and there's something wrong with me. Ever since my dad died that's how I've been feeling. All alone. If it wasn't for the academy, and Henry and Olivia, I'd be . . . "

Suddenly, Godzilla let out a snort and Cassie paused, wondering what it meant. It was the first time he had ever done anything like that in front of her. Then Cassie smiled because she thought she knew why.

"Dillie, you talked to me. You thought I was leaving you out. Not on your life. You want to know what the very best part of my day is? It's coming to see you. I look forward to talking to you because I think you know what I'm feeling."

Then toward the middle of October, something magical took place. It began when Cassie had a run-in with Rebecca Simms at school. Rebecca had decided Cassie should leave the academy because she felt threatened by her. Cassie had been riding for only a couple of months, and she had already been promoted to the second arena. She was starting to jump and Linda Flemming was very impressed with her. Unfortunately, Linda chose to tell Mr. Stanley what she thought right outside his office.

"Stanley, I think you'd better make room on that wall of yours for another champion."

"Who? Brittany Thurman?" Mr. Stanley asked.

"No, Cassie," Linda replied.

"You mean little Cassie? Henry's helper?"

"You'd better believe it. The girl's a natural. Great balance. Determination. I've never seen a young rider make so much progress so quickly."

"Well, what do you know! Glad to hear it."

The academy was a little world where rumors ran rampant, so of course the conversation started a rumor. A girl named Kelly Clark had heard the conversation, and she was a lifetime member of the Rebecca Simms riding posse. Of course, Kelly ran as fast as she could and reported to Rebecca that people were saying Cassie was going to be the next champion. Rebecca, who hated any competition, vowed right then and there to get rid of Cassie Reynolds. The next day at school, Rebecca and her friends cornered Cassie in the hall between classes.

"You little piece of trailer trash!" Rebecca hissed at Cassie. "We don't want trash like you at our academy. Nobody wants you there so you better not be there today, or we'll make your life a living hell."

Cassie, who had been totally caught off guard by Rebecca's outburst, was mortified. People were staring at her, and that made it even worse. Cassie tried to say something but couldn't. So she just burst into tears and ran away.

"You'd better run, trailer trash!" Rebecca yelled after her.

Then Cassie got her progress report at school. The students were required to take them home to be signed by their parents. Cassie got hers and cried again. Her report showed she had C minuses in most of her courses and a D in English. She feared her mother was going to be really mad. So mad she might even take riding away, and that might mean Godzilla too: the two things in Cassie's life that were holding her together.

But her problems were not over. Cassie arrived at the academy to find Henry in the tack room rummaging through the refrigerator. He seemed angry.

"Where are they?"

"Henry, I'm here."

"Cassie!" Henry yelled.

"Yes," Cassie replied. "What do you need, Henry?"

"I need some carrots is what I need. Where are all the carrots?"

Cassie cringed. She had been bringing a carrot to Godzilla every day and forgot to keep track of how many were left. Now they were gone.

"I've been giving them out," Cassie said.

Henry grimaced. "I told you not to be giving them out all the time. The horses will start expecting them. We only use them on special occasions. We don't want the horses spoilt."

Cassie's eyes welled with tears. Henry softened.

"Never mind. It's all right, child. I'll just tell Rebecca Simms we don't have any left. I hope you gave them all to her horse anyway. It would serve her right to have a spoilt horse. Now go get your work done."

Cassie hurried through her work, and then she had her riding lesson. Rebecca Simms saw Cassie and gave her a dirty look. Cassie was clearly having a hard day.

"What's wrong today, Cassie?" Linda asked after the lesson.

"I don't know," Cassie said. "Just an off day, I guess."

"Well," Linda said, "we're all entitled to a few of those."

But when Cassie was done and had put her horse away, she saw that Henry was on the other side of the arena working on the fence. So Cassie headed straight for Godzilla. When she got to the shed, Cassie opened the door and just started crying.

"I had the worst day, Dillie! Rebecca Simms called me 'trailer trash' in front of everyone. I got a D and Mom's going to kill me. Henry's mad. And I don't have any carrots."

Cassie buried her head in her hands and sobbed. If she hadn't had her face covered, she would have noticed that Godzilla was watching her. She also would have noticed when he walked in her direction. But she definitely noticed when the big horse came and rubbed his face gently against hers. Cassie was still crying when she threw her arms around Godzilla's neck and said through her tears, "I love you, Dillie."

## Chapter Fifteen

Cassie knew something special had happened between the big horse and her, and this had lightened her spirit considerably. But that night, she was forced to deal with the mess she had made with her schoolwork. Her mother was working late so Cassie had dinner with Olivia and Henry. Between the main course and dessert, reality came crashing down.

"How was school today, Cassie?" Olivia asked.

"Not too great."

"Why not, child?" Olivia asked.

"Because I got my progress report. It wasn't good."

Henry stopped eating and set his fork on his plate. He looked at Cassie and his face was serious. "Where is it?"

Cassie suddenly felt as if she was in real trouble. "In my backpack."

"Go get it," Henry said.

Cassie obeyed and went to get the report, but she was worried. Henry was her most trusted teacher, and for this reason, she dreaded showing it to Henry, even more than her mother.

Cassie returned and handed the report to Henry. He immediately began to study it. His face showed disapproval and Cassie cringed.

"Cassie, you're getting a D in English?"

"Yes, sir."

"Why?" Henry asked.

"I don't know. I got an F on my last paper because it was about horses. Mr. Wakeman wrote on it in huge letters: 'No more stories about horses.' "

"And Cs or C minuses in the remainder of your courses. This is not good. You haven't been doing your homework, have you?"

"No, sir."

"Cassie," Olivia said, "don't you know that an education is the most important thing in the world? Why, an education means freedom. It gives you choices, child."

"I'm just into riding. That's all I think about."

"Riding comes second to your education," Henry said. "If you want to ride, you have to do well in school. That was my understanding of the agreement you made with your mother."

"We're going to have to talk to your mother," Olivia said.

"What do you think is going to happen?" Cassie asked.

"What do you think should happen?" Henry asked.

"I think I should start doing my homework."

"I think you're right," Henry said. "But to ensure that you do, I'm going to suggest to your mother that you don't ride until you get your grades up."

"What!" Cassie said. The thing she was most afraid of seemed to be happening.

"You need to do your homework," Olivia said. "You're better than this. I'm going to suggest the same thing. I think the academy should be off-limits for awhile."

"No, please!" Cassie said. "That's all I've got. Riding and Dillie."

"Dillie?" Henry asked. "Who's Dillie?"

Cassie didn't know what to say so she just kept her mouth shut. Henry and Olivia looked at each other.

"You better get home," Olivia said, "and do your homework. We'll talk with your mother."

Cassie stood to leave. "I'll get my grades up. You don't have to take riding away."

"We're not taking anything away," Henry said. "You made a bargain with your mother, and you haven't lived up to your end. Now get home and do some work. The sooner you start working, the sooner you can start riding again."

"You're right," Cassie said.

Cassie left and went back to her trailer. Once she was gone, Henry and Olivia turned to each other and smiled.

"Who would have thought it?" Henry said. "Cassie sharing our lives like this. You meet her at the bus every day, and she works all afternoon with me. She practically has dinner with us every night because her mom is always working, and now we're like a couple of grandparents agonizing over her schoolwork."

"I suppose you're right," Olivia replied. "We sure have grown fond of that child."

"How's Susan doing on the rent?" Henry asked.

"She hasn't been able to pay. She told the management company that the IRS cleaned out all of her accounts and that she's not sure if she'll have the money until next month. Maybe we should tell the management company to forget the rent. We don't need the money."

"No," Henry said thoughtfully. "Susan's a smart girl. She'll put two and two together and figure out we own the park. No telling where that might lead. Besides, Susan's a proud woman and determined to make it on her own. She doesn't want a handout. We know that feeling, Olivia, and it's always served us well."

*Chapter Sixteen*

When Cassie got home she was very upset. She felt as if she would die if she couldn't see Dillie and ride. Those two things were the most important part of her life, and she did not want to give them up.

Then, Cassie got angry at Olivia and Henry. What right did they have to take riding away? They weren't her parents. Her mother should be the one to decide the punishment. Cassie began throwing a fit and started hitting her pillows until she finally got tired. Then she just lay there and cried.

She thought about Dillie. He would be expecting her in the afternoon, and she knew he'd miss her if she didn't show. She didn't want him to feel abandoned. She was the only thing he had in life too. Cassie needed Dillie and he needed her.

Cassie got even angrier. *It wasn't my fault,* she thought. She couldn't help it that every time she sat down to do her homework she thought of her father. He had always come home from work and sat with her while she did it. Cassie lay back on her bed and thought about her dad. She remembered him with his flashcards, quizzing her on her multiplication tables. He had always made the work fun, and if she worked hard, there had always been a little reward. Maybe a trip to the zoo or to the ice cream parlor. But now he was dead, and he wasn't there to help her.

The memory of her father's hospital room popped in her head. She could still remember the coldness of it and how her father was struggling to live. Cassie remembered her father saying, "I'll always be with you. Just look up at the stars and know I'm there."

Slowly, she understood why her father had said these words. It was for times like this.

Cassie ran to the front door. She stood looking up at the sky. It was a beautiful night with the stars blazing bright.

"Daddy, I need help. Help me do my homework."

Cassie waited for some kind of answer. Suddenly, a shooting star made its way across the sky, arcing toward the earth in a mighty flash. Cassie felt as if it were an answer from her father. He was there to help.

Cassie returned to her room and sat down at the desk. She decided to do the difficult work first. She opened her math book. She started working, only this time she felt as if her father were right next to her helping her. She found it didn't hurt so much. It actually felt kind of good.

"Thank you, Daddy," Cassie said at one point.

After about an hour, Cassie heard her mother pull up outside and then she heard Olivia and Henry talking to her mother. She couldn't hear what they were saying, but Cassie knew she was in for it.

Cassie didn't know it, but her mother was having a very hard day too. In addition to the Internal Revenue Service cleaning out her savings account, Susan had a tire blow out on the way home from work. Luckily, a couple of teenage boys had stopped to help her, but they said it looked as if she needed four new tires. Susan had no idea where she was going to find the money.

The last thing Susan had wanted to hear was that Cassie was doing poorly in school. She had assumed that Cassie was doing fine. Susan had even been feeling thankful that at least that part of her life was working.

A few moments later, Cassie heard her mother walk through the door.

"Mom," Cassie called, "I'm still up."

Susan Reynolds walked in. She looked angry. "What happened with your progress report?"

"I didn't do so great."

"That's what I hear. Henry says you need to give up riding until you get your grades up."

"I know," Cassie said. "I don't know what I'm going to do without riding."

Susan's face softened and she walked over and sat on Cassie's bed. Cassie turned to face her mother and she thought for the first time her mother looked beaten. This wasn't the buoyant mother Cassie knew.

"You really love riding, don't you, sweetheart?" Susan said.

"Yes, I really do. Mom, when you go over a jump it just feels like flying."

"Cassie, we might have to move."

"Why?"

"Some things have happened, and we can't afford to pay the rent this month."

"Where will we move to?" Cassie asked. "It has to be someplace close to the academy."

"No, honey. We'll have to move to Grandma and Grandpa's."

"In Arkansas?"

"Yes."

"But Grandma and Grandpa are poorer than us."

"Not anymore, and they have a house. If the landlord kicks us out, we won't have anyplace else to go."

Cassie could sense that her mother was scared, and Cassie was frightened too. In one short day, her world had come crumbling down again. Still, Cassie knew her mother needed her to be strong at that moment. She reached out and hugged her mom. Susan began to cry.

"Don't worry, Mom," Cassie said gently. "We'll find a way to make this work. We'll do it together."

# Chapter Seventeen

The next day was Saturday, and Cassie could have slept in. Instead, she got up early to say goodbye to her mother. But when she saw her, Cassie knew she was still feeling discouraged.

"Mom, we'll get through this."

Susan smiled and hugged her daughter. "I don't know what I would do without you." She walked over and put on her coat. "I'll be home late. But maybe tomorrow we can go to a movie."

"Can we afford it?" Cassie asked.

"I've had twenty dollars hidden in my room for if we ever got desperate. I say we go out for hamburgers and a movie."

Cassie smiled. She knew her mother was starting to bounce back.

"Okay," Cassie said. "I'll find a paper and see what's playing."

"It's a date," Susan said. "I'd better get going. The bank's considering me for a promotion, and I don't want to be late."

After her mother left, Cassie headed straight for her bedroom. She opened her books and worked until she was done. She now felt as if her father was next to her trying to help.

Afterward, Cassie walked over to Olivia's trailer and knocked on the door. Hearing gospel music, she knew that Olivia was in her garden. She walked around the trailer to the gate. Olivia was sitting on her bench enjoying the sun.

"Hi, Olivia."

Olivia looked over at Cassie and smiled. "Come in and sit for awhile."

Cassie walked through the gate and sat on the bench next to Olivia.

"Have you been doing your schoolwork?" Olivia asked.

"Yes, I pretty much have it all done. I even went back and did some assignments from last week. I'm hoping the teachers will accept them and raise my grades."

"That's great, Cassie. If you show your teachers you're trying, they will help you. You'll be back at the academy in no time."

Cassie was quiet a moment, and Olivia waited for Cassie to reply. Olivia was good that way. She always allowed you time to think before you spoke.

"Olivia, do you know a lot of people in the park?"

"I'd say so. Henry and I have lived here nearly forty years."

"Do you think some of them could use some help? I mean I could do cleaning and yardwork. You know me. I'm not afraid of a little hard work."

"Why do you want to work, child?"

"Because my mom's been working so hard and that just isn't fair. I need to help. Otherwise, we might have to move to Arkansas."

Olivia was quiet a moment. Cassie could see that Olivia was digesting what she had said and that her mind was working on the answer.

"You're twelve years old. You need to concentrate on your schoolwork. *That's* your job. If you really want to help your mother, then that's what you should do. Once you start working for money, then that's what you'll do for the rest of your life, and you have plenty of time for that. Besides, I think the rent will take care of itself."

"Maybe if I get back to the academy I could just get paid something instead of taking so many riding lessons."

"And give up the thing that makes you feel alive? You have a right to do what you love, and you've earned that right. My advice is to concentrate on your schoolwork and everything will take care of itself."

Cassie spent the rest of the afternoon reading *The Old Man and the Sea* for her English class. She admired Santiago for his struggle and not giving up. But she felt really bad when the sharks ate his fish.

That night, Cassie had dinner with Olivia and Henry. She was careful, but she inquired about Godzilla.

"Still mean as ever," Henry said, "but I've noticed a change. It takes him a few moments before he comes after me. It's like he wants to make sure it's me."

As Cassie walked home she thought of Godzilla. She decided that she was going to go see him that night. She waited up for her mom. Susan was in good spirits when she arrived, but was really tired so she went straight to bed. Cassie waited awhile, then she got the flashlight Henry had given them. She also grabbed some apples from the refrigerator and put them in a bag.

When Cassie stepped out of her trailer, she studied Henry and Olivia's trailer. The lights were off, and Cassie was certain they were asleep. She switched on her flashlight and made her way down the well-worn path to the academy.

Cassie enjoyed her walk. The night air was crisp and the stars were blazing in the sky. When she looked up at them, she felt close to her dad, and that feeling made for a very pleasant walk. Once she got to the academy, it was just a short distance to the shed behind the barn.

Cassie undid the latch and pulled the heavy door open. She could barely make out Godzilla, who was standing in the shadows. Instinctively, the horse's ears went back. Cassie switched off the flashlight, leaving the glow of the full moon as the only illumination.

"Hey, Dillie, it's just me."

Godzilla relaxed his ears and walked over to where Cassie stood at the door.

"Brought you something. I didn't have a big, juicy, delicious carrot, but I do have these."

Cassie took an apple from the bag and held it out for Godzilla. The horse immediately took it, and as he chewed, Cassie took one for herself. But Godzilla quickly finished his apple and then tried to bite Cassie's.

"Oh, you like apples, do you?"

Cassie gave Godzilla the rest of her apple and then began to stroke his face. Cassie became a little sad.

"Dillie, I'm afraid I have some bad news. The government took all our money because we didn't pay our taxes last year. So we can't pay the rent. Mom says that if they kick us out, we'll have to move away."

Godzilla finished his apple, but he didn't shy away. He stayed close to Cassie as she stroked his face.

"I've also gotten in trouble because I did poorly in school. Now I can't come to the academy until I get my grades up. So the only way to see you is to sneak out and come down here at night. If I get caught I'll be in even more trouble, but I don't care. I just have to see you at least once a day."

Godzilla pulled away and then went for the bag of apples Cassie had in her hand.

"Looks like someone's hungry tonight."

Cassie pulled an apple from the bag.

"Last one, Dillie. I'll split it with you."

Cassie took a large bite and then broke the apple in half. She gave Godzilla his half and then took a bite of her own.

"This is a good apple," Cassie said.

But Godzilla quickly finished his half and then wanted the rest. He reached over with his mouth and tried to bite the apple.

"Hey, this is mine. You had yours."

Cassie pushed his head away. But Godzilla came back and tried to bite Cassie's again. Finally, Cassie laughed.

"All right, you can have it."

She gave the horse the apple and he began to chew it up.

"Dillie, I don't know how things could be any worse."

Godzilla let out a snort and Cassie paused. "You're right. Nothing could be worse than watching my dad die. If I could make it through that, I guess I can make it through anything."

Godzilla finished his apple and then rubbed his face against Cassie's. Cassie wrapped her arms around his neck and they stood snuggling together against the chill of the autumn night. Cassie was content not to say anything more, and the big horse did not move or shy away for the longest time.

# Chapter Eighteen

Sunday morning brought rain, and the sound of the drops hitting the bedroom window woke Cassie up. It was still early so she just lay in bed feeling blue. She was thinking of riding. For a moment, she grew angry again. But slowly she realized that it was her own fault she wasn't riding.

Cassie went to her desk and thought about what work she could do. But she had finished all of her schoolwork the day before.

Then Cassie remembered her father had taught her to set goals. They would sit at the kitchen table and dream about outstanding accomplishments. Some dreams were so huge they were almost outrageous, like becoming an Olympic champion or the president of the United States. Other dreams were smaller, like simply being an honest person.

She and her father would write these dreams down and then he would ask, "What do you need to do to accomplish these dreams?" Cassie had replied, "I have no idea." Her father smiled and simply said, "It's easy, Cassie. You just start with baby steps. The baby steps lead to larger steps, and before you know it, you're making giant leaps. But to ensure those baby steps get started, you have to set goals."

With her father's illness, Cassie's big dreams had faded away and the memory of those moments at the kitchen table brought a feeling of sadness. But Cassie also felt her father was next to her helping to sort it all out. She took out a piece of paper and began writing down some of her dreams. She had heard that equestrian jumping was an Olympic event so she wrote down "Olympic champion." Next to it she wrote down "A student." She quickly saw that the two were connected so she wrote down her first goal. "I will be riding again in one week." Then, she signed her name to it. By writing her goals down and signing it, she had given it the power to come true. Cassie sat back and smiled.

"Thank you, Daddy."

Cassie then mapped out everything that was to happen in school the next week. In science, she had a quiz on botany. In history, the class was learning about Texas. In math they were starting algebra, and in English, the dreaded class that had been most responsible for the loss of her riding privileges, they had a paper to write on *The Old Man and the Sea*. It wasn't due until next Friday, but Cassie decided to write it that day.

By afternoon, Cassie had finished her paper and she and her mother went to the movies. They saw a movie called "Racing Stripes," and Cassie liked it immensely. After having hamburgers at McDonald's, she and her mom had $3.33 left. She asked her mother to stop at the store to buy some carrots.

"Carrots? What do we need carrots for?"

"They help me study," Cassie said. "I'm always hungry when I study."

"That's good. I like it that you're eating healthy."

"Especially after McDonald's," Cassie said with a smile.

After buying the carrots, Cassie and her mom headed for home. On the way, they passed the billboard with Rebecca Simms and her horse.

"Look, honey," Susan said. "Isn't that the girl from your riding school?"

"Yes," Cassie replied.

"She looks nice. She must be a really good rider to be up on a billboard like that."

"She's not very friendly. And the reason she's on the billboard is because her dad owns the business. He's really rich. But she is a good rider."

But that was all Cassie said. Cassie knew her mother had enough troubles without having to hear about Cassie's problems with Rebecca Simms. She was also afraid that if she told her mom about how she was being treated at school then that would just be another reason to move to Arkansas. She did not want to move.

By the end of the night, Cassie couldn't wait to see Godzilla and tell him about her goals. Susan went to bed early, enabling Cassie to leave sooner than usual.

Cassie assumed Henry and Olivia were asleep too. The lights were off in their trailer, and Cassie knew they always went to bed early.

But Henry was up getting a drink of water. He happened to look out the window and saw Cassie's flashlight floating toward the academy. At first, Henry thought it was a ghost. He once thought he had seen one of his sons walking down the same path Cassie was on, and being superstitious, he thought it was possible that his son's ghost had returned. But on closer inspection, Henry saw that it was Cassie.

"What the . . . ?" Henry exclaimed.

Henry immediately went to his bedroom and started getting dressed. This woke up Olivia.

"What is it, Henry?"

"It's Cassie. She's out walking in the night."

"For heaven's sake, why?"

"I don't know. But I intend to find out."

"I hope it's not some boy named Dillie."

Henry slipped out of the trailer and headed for Cassie's light. Henry watched closely and saw the light disappear behind the barn.

By the time Henry got to the barn, he could hear Cassie's voice.

"Hey, Dillie. I brought you a big, juicy, delicious carrot."

This confused Henry because he had no idea who she could be talking to. He thought maybe it was indeed some boy so he quietly walked behind the barn. But what he saw stopped him dead in his tracks. Cassie was feeding a carrot to Godzilla. At first he was alarmed, and his instinct told him to run and pull Cassie away. But then he heard Cassie speak.

"It's the strangest thing, Dillie. When I remembered my dad teaching me to set goals, I got really sad at first. But then I realized that the memory was there to help me. It's like those memories are little gifts from my dad."

Henry was stunned as he watched Godzilla rub his face against Cassie's. When Cassie began to stroke the horse's face, Henry knew she was not in danger. Astonished, he whispered, "Cassie's got the gift."

Henry stayed in the shadows watching and listening to Cassie and Godzilla for the entire time they were together. Henry learned so much about Cassie's life. He learned of the trouble Cassie was having at school with Rebecca Simms and how Cassie was so worried they were going to have to move. But most of all, Henry learned how deeply Cassie still grieved for her father. It made him feel like he just wanted to go over and hug her.

But Henry almost fell over when he saw Cassie walk in to clean Godzilla's bedding. He himself had been too afraid to even get near the horse. Every time he did, Godzilla had either tried to bite him or kick him. But Cassie just talked away while she walked in and out. The horse followed her around like a puppy, and Henry knew that the meanest horse he had ever known had finally accepted someone in his life.

"A twelve-year-old girl. Who would have thought it?" he said to himself.

When Cassie's visit came to an end, Henry stayed in the shadows. He heard Cassie say, "I love you, Dillie," and he smiled when he heard Godzilla whinny as Cassie started back to her trailer. He checked his watch. It was nearly one o'clock.

By the time Henry got home, he was both amazed and worried. He also wasn't surprised to find Olivia waiting up.

"Henry, you were gone for so long. Is everything all right?"

"It's the darndest thing, Olivia. I don't think I would have believed it if I had not seen it."

"What's the darndest thing?"

"You know where Cassie went?"

"Where?"

"She's been sneaking out at night to care for Godzilla."

"Godzilla?" Olivia asked with alarm. "Isn't that the horse you're so afraid of?"

"I may be afraid of him, but Cassie's not. And around her he's as gentle as can be. That horse has accepted her."

"Really?"

"It's just unbelievable, Olivia. She even cleaned his stall. Last time I tried, Godzilla came at me so fast I thought he was going to kill me for sure. But he just follows Cassie around like she's owned him for years."

"You're kidding."

"No, I'm not. Cassie's got the gift. I don't know where it came from but she's got it. I'm just glad I found out about this tonight, though."

"Why's that?"

"Mr. Stanley just called me this morning. He was planning on sending the vet out tomorrow morning to put Godzilla down. They want to do it early in the morning so no kids are around."

"What are you going to do?"

"I'm going to tell Mr. Stanley about Cassie. Hopefully, he'll reconsider."

# Chapter Nineteen

The next day was Monday. It was the day Cassie declared war. Not on any person, group, or institution, but on the problems she was facing in her life. Cassie intended to deal with them head-on.

In class, Cassie participated in all the discussions. Then, after each class was finished, she waited until she and her teachers were alone. She approached them to ask why she had received the grades she did on her progress report. She took full responsibility for her poor performance and said, "I intend to change it immediately." Her teachers were impressed by the change of attitude. Mrs. Porter, her science teacher, was amazed

"Cassie," Mrs. Porter said, "you spoke in the class discussion and your ideas were so well thought out. I had a feeling you weren't living up to your potential. Let's just hope we keep it up."

"You don't have to worry about that, Mrs. Porter. I intend to."

After English class, Cassie confronted Mr. Wakeman about her grade on her last paper. The confrontation became an intellectual argument.

"You gave me an F on my last paper." Cassie said. "I worked really hard on that paper, and you didn't even grade me on my writing."

"Cassie," Mr. Wakeman said, "all your papers have been about horses or horseback riding. The writing is good. But I told you that I didn't want any more papers on horses. You went ahead and did it anyway. That wasn't fair to me."

"The assignment was to write about something you know that takes skill. Well, I know riding so that's what I wrote about. Besides, you're the one who always says that good writers write about what they know."

"That's not the only thing you know. I want you to explore other areas of your life. As your teacher, I need to make you stretch."

"Fair enough," Cassie said. "Can I write about something else and try for a better grade?"

Mr. Wakeman liked the determination Cassie was showing and decided it should be rewarded.

"Okay," Mr. Wakeman said, "you can write about anything except horses, and the grade you receive will replace the F I gave you. But the paper on *The Old Man and the Sea* is still due on Friday."

Cassie smiled. "I already wrote it." She took her paper from her notebook and handed it to Mr. Wakeman.

Mr. Wakeman was surprised. He took the paper and read the opening sentence. He had to smile.

"That's great, Cassie," Mr. Wakeman said.

In Cassie's quest to achieve her goal, she was finding strength that she didn't know she had. That's the magical thing about a goal. It was giving her the courage to act boldly when she needed to.

Another magical thing about goals is that they make the minor inconveniences in life seem insignificant. When Rebecca Simms and her friends cornered Cassie in the hall, Cassie stood her ground.

"Hey, trailer trash!" Rebecca yelled. "Didn't see you at the academy on Saturday. That's good. Keep it that way."

Cassie looked Rebecca Simms in the eye. "First of all, Rebecca, I like where I live, and second, I'll be back within a week."

Cassie walked away. She didn't have time to waste worrying about Rebecca Simms, her friends, or their opinions. Her goal had freed her from the trivial nonsense of Rebecca Simms.

At lunch, she went to the library, but instead of reading *Black Beauty* or *Sea Biscuit*, she wrote a new paper for English class. Only this time her subject was her father and goal-setting. Her opening sentence was, "A goal can change your life."

She went on to write about her day and how it had unfolded, how she had met with each of her teachers and how they had been so willing to help. She also included her run-in with Rebecca Simms and how it had made her that much more determined to meet her goal. Finally, she ended the paper with a quote from her father: "Nothing is more powerful than a person with a goal."

When the school day ended, Cassie was surprised. The day had seemed to fly by. She took a moment to think about everything she had accomplished in one day. Then, another magical thing happened. Cassie felt good about herself. She had only one last thing to do to complete her day. She had to deliver the paper to Mr. Wakeman. On the way to her bus she stopped by his class.

"Finished already?" Mr. Wakeman asked.

"Yes," Cassie said. "It pretty much just wrote itself and there's only one mention of horses."

Mr. Wakeman smiled. "All right, I'll have it back to you on Friday."

"Thanks, Mr. Wakeman. I really needed a second chance."

"I understand, Cassie. I've had plenty of second chances myself."

As Cassie rode home on the bus, she was already thinking about the things she needed to do to complete her goal of riding again in one week. She had lots of homework to do and she had to study for her quiz on botany. Cassie was still studying when the school bus pulled to a stop in front of the trailer park.

Olivia was waiting for her.

"Olivia, you were right. All my teachers wanted to help me."

"That's great, child."

"I want to go straight away and do my homework."

"You can't," Olivia said. "Henry needs to see you."

"About what?" Cassie asked.

"I'm not sure. I think it has something to do with a horse."

# Chapter Twenty

Cassie found Henry at his usual afternoon spot. He was at the crossties grooming and saddling horses for the day's lessons. "Hi, Henry. Olivia said you wanted to see me?"

Henry gave Cassie a severe look. She knew she was in some kind of trouble.

"Go clean Godzilla's shed, and when you're done, you can feed him too."

"What?" Cassie whispered. She was caught. Her face turned red.

"You heard me right. Go take care of Godzilla."

As Cassie walked away toward Godzilla's shed, her mind was racing. How did Henry Know? Cassie was afraid she was in serious trouble. This was definitely not good.

When Cassie opened the shed door she saw that Godzilla's ears were back. The horse hadn't been expecting Cassie, but when he saw that it was she, he relaxed his ears and walked over to her. She rubbed his face.

"Hey, Dillie. I think we're in trouble. Henry knows about me coming to see you, and I think he's mad. But at least he sent me to clean your stall. That's a good sign."

Cassie went to work immediately. Because it was daylight and she didn't have to sneak around, she was able to clean the stall thoroughly, something she had been meaning to do. Then, after a few moments of working, she heard voices. It was Henry and Mr. Stanley.

"If I hadn't seen it with my own eyes," Henry said, "I wouldn't have believed it."

"How long do you think this has been going on?" Mr. Stanley asked.

At the sound of Mr. Stanley's voice, Godzilla became agitated. His ears went back and he moved to the front of the shed. Godzilla looked out, and when he saw Mr. Stanley, the big horse reared up and started trying to knock the door down. Cassie ran to his side and tried to settle him down.

"That horse really hates me," Mr. Stanley said.

"Horses never forget," Henry replied.

Mr. Stanley and Henry watched with amazement as Cassie was able to soothe the big horse. She rubbed his neck, and the horse began to quiet down.

"Easy, Dillie boy. I'm here with you. Everything's all right."

Mr. Stanley and Henry looked at each other and Henry shrugged. "I can't explain it."

"Amazing," Mr. Stanley said. "I'd better check my insurance. I think I have to put Cassie on the payroll to make sure she's insured. Tell her to come to my office when she's finished."

Mr. Stanley started to walk off, then stopped and looked at Henry.

"You were right. After everything we've tried, it was a twelve-year-old girl who got through to him. Who would have thought it? And to think I was going to put him down this morning. It's just amazing."

After Henry and Mr. Stanley left, Godzilla stayed close to Cassie. It was as if he knew something had changed and just wanted to be near her. Cassie finished cleaning his stall and made sure he had plenty of water and food. When she was finished, she just stood next to the big horse and hugged him. She was still scared and could sense that Godzilla was too. Finally, Cassie said, "I don't know what any of this means. I just hope they let us stay together."

After awhile, Cassie heard Henry's voice.

"Cassie, are you finished in there?"

"Yes."

"Then meet me at the tack room."

Cassie gave Godzilla a kiss. "I'll find out what's going on and let you know. Don't worry."

Cassie went straight to the tack room. She took one look at Henry's angry face and knew she was in big trouble. But she spoke first. "Henry, I'm sorry."

"Cassie, what you did was wrong. And it was dangerous too. You also broke a trust I had in you."

"Henry, I'm sorry," Cassie said and her voice cracked with emotion. "I just wanted to help Dillie. He's never been mean to me. Not once."

Cassie had tears in her eyes and Henry softened.

"It's all right, child. If you hadn't gotten close to Godzilla he would have been put down. So you can feel good about knowing you saved his life. But you have to promise me that if that horse ever turns on you, even once, you'll stop taking care of him. He's an unpredictable animal. He could seriously hurt you."

"I promise," Cassie said.

"And then there's the sneaking-around part."

Cassie cringed. "I'm so sorry," she said quickly.

"Sorry's not good enough," Henry said sternly. "You have to promise me you'll never do anything like that again."

"I promise."

"If you break this promise, Cassie, you won't be able to work with me again. I have to know I can trust you. Understand?"

"I understand," Cassie said, wiping a tear away.

"Good," Henry said. "Now you need to go see Mr. Stanley and when you're finished there you need to go do your homework. Except for Godzilla, the academy is still off-limits until you get your grades up."

"Yes, sir." Cassie started away.

"Hey, Cassie."

Cassie turned to face Henry.

"At least now I know where all the carrots went," he said.

Henry smiled at her and she felt much better. That was the great thing about Henry, Cassie thought. She always knew where she stood with him. If he was angry, he always told you flat-out and that was it. He never held a grudge. But Cassie knew that Henry had meant every word he had said to her. If she ever lied to him again he would fire her.

Mr. Stanley was all smiles when Cassie arrived at his office. This was because he felt as if Christmas had just come early. His most valuable horse had just been saved and now he had great hopes that Godzilla might make a comeback. Those hopes rested on Cassie's shoulders.

For Cassie, it was odd to be in Mr. Stanley's office. She had hardly said hello to him during the three months she had been at the academy, and he had never really acknowledged her. Now Mr. Stanley was acting about as warm as a person could be toward her.

"Cassie, have a seat."

She sat down across the desk from Mr. Stanley. The chair was made of black leather, and Cassie felt small inside the arms of the big chair. She looked around the room at the pictures on the walls. They were photographs of horses and riders, and each picture had the word "Champion" at the bottom with a date. Some of the pictures were very old.

"How long have you been working with Godzilla?" Mr. Stanley asked.

"I haven't really been working with him. We just kind of meet and talk."

"Talk?" Mr. Stanley asked. "What do you talk about?"

"Nothing really," Cassie said evasively. She didn't know Mr. Stanley very well. Plus she didn't think that her conversations with Godzilla were any of his business. To Cassie, those conversations were private.

"Well," Mr. Stanley said, "whatever you're doing, it's working. I'd like you to keep it up."

"Okay," Cassie said. "I'd like that."

"Good. Now did you know that Godzilla is a real valuable horse?"

"Henry told me he was once a great jumper."

"Yes, he was. About a year back he was the best horse I had ever seen. Do you know the story of what happened?"

"Yes, Henry told me."

"Good. Anyway, Godzilla is worth somewhere around five hundred thousand dollars, and it's real important to the academy that he makes a comeback. So I have a business proposition for you. I will pay you, say, fifty dollars a week if you will help me to get him jumping again."

"I'm not sure if Dillie wants to jump, Mr. Stanley."

"Dillie? Who's Dillie?"

"That's what I call him."

"Oh, well maybe you could just help me to get him going. You work with him and keep me posted on how he's doing, and I will put you on the payroll. Deal?"

Mr. Stanley stood and stuck his hand across the desk for Cassie to shake. Cassie shook it.

After Cassie left, she felt a little upset. As far as she was concerned, she didn't need to be paid to take care of Godzilla. She did that because she loved him. Still, fifty dollars a week was a large amount of money for Cassie, and she and her mom could use the extra cash. She decided that working with him meant only taking care of him. Any progress with jumping wasn't her department.

Before going home to do her homework, Cassie stopped by to see Godzilla. She told the big horse about the meeting with Mr. Stanley and how he was going to pay her to take care of him. Then she gave Godzilla a big hug.

"This is great. Now I can come see you any time I want, and I can stay as long as I want.

Godzilla rubbed his face against Cassie's.

"You're right, Dillie. This does change things. I'm going to miss the way it was before when it was just you and me. Now everyone expects me to report on how you're doing. I guess my dad was right. He said that with every good thing that comes, you usually have to give something up."

# Chapter Twenty-One

That night, Cassie waited up for her mother. A thunderstorm was passing through the Dallas area, and as Cassie sat up preparing for her botany quiz, she enjoyed hearing the sound of the rain tap-tap-tapping against the roof of her trailer. The roof had some leaks, and Cassie had placed bowls in various areas to capture the water falling from the ceiling. But even with the leaks, Cassie felt safe, cozy, and happy. It had been a memorable day. Everything had gone according to plan at school, and even better, things had worked out well at the academy.

However, there was one last hurdle. Henry had told Cassie that she needed to tell her mother everything and that she had to get her approval before she could officially be Godzilla's keeper. This was why Cassie was waiting up.

Susan came in the door, and though it had been a long day, she was in great spirits too.

"Cassie, I've got some great news."

"I do too, Mom.

"You first," Susan said.

"No, Mom," Cassie said. "You said it first."

They both laughed.

"Okay," Susan said. "The property management company and I talked. They said I could make payments on the rent, and that they won't be evicting us."

"So we don't have to move?"

"Looks that way, honey. I also got the promotion at work so I'll be making more money. Not a lot more, but I think I have a future there."

Cassie got so excited she leapt up and hugged her mom. They both started jumping up and down saying, "Isn't this great" and "I love you" to each other. After a moment, Susan pulled back.

"Things will still be tight, Cassie. But at least they're looking up."

"This is so great, Mom."

"I know. So what's your news?"

"I got a job."

"A job?"

"Yes," Cassie said. "I'm going to make fifty dollars a week taking care of a horse called Dillie. Mom, he's such a great horse."

"Fifty dollars a week?"

"Yes. So now I can help pay for Olivia and some of the rent too."

"That's amazing."

"But Henry says I need to tell you a few things."

"What things?"

"Well," Cassie said trying to buy some time to think, "Dillie is a real valuable horse, but he was real sad. He loved another horse but that horse died. Afterward, he wouldn't let anyone near him. I'm the only person he'll let take care of him."

"Is the horse dangerous?"

"Well . . . " Cassie said, buying time again. She knew what she said next might be the deciding factor in her mother's decision. If she got it wrong, her mother might easily say no.

"Dillie has never been mean to me, and I've been taking care of him for two months."

"Two months? Why haven't I heard about this before?"

"Because I was afraid that if everyone knew, then I wouldn't be able to take care of him."

"I'd better talk to Henry."

"Mom, there's something else."

"What?" Susan asked.

"I've been sneaking out to take care of Dillie."

"You mean at night?"

"Yes," Cassie said. She cringed because she knew this was going to be the worst part. But Henry had told her that she had to tell her mother everything.

"Cassie, this is not good. I'm very upset with you. I want you to go to bed right now. We'll talk about this in the morning after I talk to Henry."

"But . . . "

"No buts. You get in bed right now. And don't you ever sneak out of this house again."

Cassie obeyed her mother and went to bed, but she couldn't sleep. Her night was filled with fear that her mother would say no. If the answer was indeed no, then Godzilla would be all alone again, and so would she. It was a miserable night.

The next morning, Susan woke up early. She knew that Olivia and Henry were early risers, so Susan walked over at six. Olivia and Henry were up and, over coffee, Henry told Susan the story of Godzilla. He was honest and didn't sugarcoat it.

"Susan, that horse is the only horse I've ever been scared of."

But then Henry told Susan about hearing Cassie's conversation with Godzilla, and how she had poured her heart out to the horse. Henry told Susan about Cassie's trouble with Rebecca Simms, how she was so afraid about moving and, most important, how much she still missed her father.

"I can't explain why the horse has accepted Cassie. The only connection I can find is the grief. Godzilla was hurting and Cassie was hurting too, and I think they just needed each other. There's a healing taking place."

"But will the horse hurt her?" Susan asked.

"I can't say. All I can go on is what I've seen. Godzilla is a completely different horse around her. He's gentle as a lamb. I'll tell you something, Susan, and I don't say this lightly: Cassie has a gift when it comes to horses. It's something that can't be explained or understood. It just is."

When Susan returned to her trailer, she found Cassie waiting for her answer. "Cassie, I have to think on this. I can't give you an answer right now."

"Mom, let's go down to the academy right now. Let me show you how gentle Dillie is."

"I can't," Susan said. "I have to go to work, and you have to go to school."

Cassie walked up to her mother and looked in her eyes.

"Mom, I need you to do this for me."

Susan saw that Cassie did in fact need her to do this. There was something in her daughter's eyes, the way they pleaded for her mother to give her this chance.

"Okay," Susan said, "let's go see this horse."

When they arrived at Godzilla's shed, the first thing Susan noticed were the signs: Keep out. Danger. The warning made Susan nervous and she wanted to turn back. But then Cassie walked right up and opened the shed door.

"Dillie, it's me," Cassie said.

The big horse looked at Cassie, but then he saw Susan and his ears started to go back.

"Dillie, it's all right. This is my mom and she wanted to meet you. Mom, this is Dillie."

Cassie walked in the shed. It worried Susan to see her daughter next to this huge horse because she seemed very small next to Godzilla. But Cassie was so calm, and Susan watched how the horse walked up to Cassie and rubbed his nose against her daughter's face.

"Hey, Dillie. We brought you a big, juicy, delicious carrot. And I brought my mom to meet you."

Cassie put her hand under Godzilla's chin and walked the horse over to where her mother stood. Susan backed up. She had never really been around horses, and her first impulse was to flee.

"Don't be afraid, Mom. You weren't part of Sunny's death so I don't think you have to worry. Here, give him this."

Cassie handed her mother the carrot and Susan looked at it, not knowing what to do.

"Just hold it up to his mouth," Cassie said. "He'll take it from you."

Susan was scared, but she held the carrot out to Godzilla. The horse reached over, and in one mighty bite, took the carrot from Susan's hand. Susan quickly pulled her hand away. She was thankful that Godzilla had taken only the carrot and not her whole arm.

"What are those sores on his legs?" Susan asked.

"Those are there because nobody was taking care of him. I put some medicine on them yesterday. I think it hurt him, but he let me do it. Dillie knew I was trying to help him."

Cassie gave Godzilla a kiss on the nose and then patted his neck.

"See, Mom. Dillie's just a big pussycat."

Susan was thoughtful. Then she remembered Henry telling her: "I think that horse needs Cassie and I think Cassie needs Godzilla. There's a healing taking place."

"All right, Cassie," Susan said. "I'll support your decision to take care of this horse as long as he never hurts you. If he does something even once, then you have to stop."

"Don't worry, Mom. Dillie will never hurt me."

"One more thing," Susan said.

"What's that?"

"If you ever sneak out again, you'll be forbidden to care for this horse, and you'll never ride again. In other words, Cassie, your life will be over. Got it?"

"I got it Mom. It won't ever happen again."

Cassie stepped over and hugged her mom, and Susan hugged her back. But Susan wasn't prepared for when Godzilla stuck his nose between them. Susan quickly backed away and Cassie laughed.

"Mom, you don't have to be scared. Dillie just wants a group hug."

# Chapter Twenty-Two

The rest of Cassie's week went exceedingly well. She attended classes, where she was very focused and participated in all the discussions. She always made sure that she was prepared. In the afternoons, she took care of Godzilla and then did her homework. After her homework was completed, she would walk back down to the academy and visit with Godzilla some more. If Henry saw her, he would always ask, "Is your homework done?"

The only thing missing from her life was riding. She had grown to love the sport, and even though she wasn't riding, Cassie would lie on her bed and picture herself going over jumps. She had found a way to keep practicing without actually doing it.

By Friday, her planning and work had paid off. Cassie got an A on her botany quiz, and her English teacher, Mr. Wakeman, had another nice surprise. He gave her back her paper on goal-setting and, written on the front was "nice job" with a big A circled. When Cassie saw the grade she nearly did a back flip.

"Mr. Wakeman, you really liked it that much?" Cassie asked.

"Yes, Cassie," Mr. Wakeman said. "I wouldn't have given you the grade if I didn't. Your paper showed good creative thought, but the best part was how you incorporated it into the context of your life. It was an excellent piece of writing."

"Does this change my grade?" Cassie asked.

"Sure. I would say you are now a solid B in this class. You might even have a shot at an A."

Cassie smiled. "Mr. Wakeman, if it wouldn't be too much trouble, do you think you could write me a note saying that? I have someone I need to show it to."

"Will you keep up the hard work?"

"Of course. I intend to ace your class. It's my favorite subject."

"Then I'll write the note."

When Cassie got home on the bus, she saw that Olivia was waiting for her. She couldn't wait to show her Mr. Wakeman's note. When Olivia read it she let out a little holler.

"Wow! Now that's more like it, Cassie girl. You need to go straight away and show this to Henry. Maybe he'll let you ride today."

Cassie headed straight to see Henry. When he read the note he smiled.

"You went from a D to a B in one week. And it says here that he thinks you are capable of an A. That's outstanding."

"I was hoping to start riding today," Cassie said.

"I'd like to say yes, but we still need to get your mother's approval. Your bargain was with her, not with me. Besides, the vet is here. Mr. Stanley's been waiting for you so the vet can check out Godzilla."

Cassie was disappointed about not riding, but she was happy the vet was going to see Godzilla. She wanted to make sure he was in good condition. She walked to the shed and opened the heavy door. Godzilla saw it was Cassie and walked over. She scratched the big horse behind the ears.

"Hey, Dillie. The vet's coming to see us. I want you to behave because it's important we make sure you're okay."

A moment later, Cassie and Godzilla heard voices outside the shed. It was Mr. Stanley and Dr. Tom Dillingham, the vet. At the sound of Mr. Stanley's voice, Godzilla's ears went back and he looked toward the door. Cassie rubbed Godzilla's neck to try and settle him down.

"Godzilla is a different horse around this girl," Mr. Stanley was saying. "I don't think you have to worry."

"All I know is that last time, he drew blood," the vet said nervously.

The two men stood at the door and looked in. Godzilla started toward the door and the two men backed up.

"Mr. Stanley," Cassie called, "I think you should move away. Dillie doesn't like you very much."

"Ah, good idea," Mr. Stanley said and moved away from the door. The vet stood there wondering what he should do. He wanted to move away too.

"Hi, I'm Dr. Tom. I'm the vet."

"Yes, I know," Cassie said. "How are you?"

"I'm a little tentative. Do you think he'll be all right?"

"I think so. Why don't you come in and we'll find out."

Dr. Tom walked in slowly. He watched Godzilla and saw that his ears were still back. Cassie began to rub the horse's neck, and he started to relax. The vet moved forward and walked around Godzilla, but he made sure to give the horse a wide berth.

"Last time I saw him," Dr. Tom said, "he had really bad thrush because nobody could get in here to clean his stall. But it looks like it's starting to clear up."

"I've been keeping his stall extra clean. And I've been putting some ointment on his sores," Cassie said.

"That's good. How about his hocks? There's still some sores there from lying on the hard ground."

"I've been trying to keep his bedding soft. The sores were much worse."

"Yes," Dr. Tom said. "They are better than I remember. I'll give you something to put on those as well."

Dr. Tom walked around Godzilla again. "He seems to be in such good shape considering he's been abandoned for nearly a year. How long have you been caring for him?"

"We've been together a couple of months. But it took awhile before he really let me care for him. I'd say it's been about a month I've actually been able to do anything about his sores."

"Well, you're doing a great job. Can I see his teeth?"

"Sure," Cassie said, and she walked up to Godzilla. She parted his lips so the Dr. Tom could see his teeth.

"They look fine, he said. "How about exercise? Has he had any?"

"No, I've thought about it. But I just don't know how he'll do in the ring."

"You should try. He is a jumper. The sooner he starts exercising, the sooner he can come back."

"Okay," Cassie said.

"Good," said Dr. Tom. "You've done a great job caring for him. I never thought he'd make it. Call me if you have any questions."

"Sure," Cassie said.

The vet walked out to give his report to Mr. Stanley. Cassie heard the word "amazing" in the conversation. She patted Godzilla on the neck.

"You did great, Dillie."

Cassie turned her back, and Godzilla walked toward the front door of the shed. The bottom part of the Dutch door was closed, but unfortunately for Mr. Stanley, the top part was open. Mr. Stanley just happened to be near the door listening to Tom Dillingham give his report, and was smiling as he heard the good news. But his smile quickly disappeared as Godzilla stuck his head out of the door and grabbed Mr. Stanley by his shoulder. Mr. Stanley's screams were heard across the academy. Godzilla, teeth locked on Mr. Stanley's shoulder, tried to shake his owner. But Mr. Stanley slipped from the big horse's grasp and fell to the ground in a heap.

Mr. Stanley lay on the ground in a daze rubbing the place where Godzilla had bit him. Henry had heard the screams and came running. Several more people arrived as well.

"Are you hurt?" Dr. Tom asked.

"What happened?" Mr. Stanley asked.

"Godzilla bit you on the shoulder and shook you. You're lucky he didn't break your neck."

"Godzilla?" Mr. Stanley asked.

Mr. Stanley got to his feet and turned to see Godzilla standing in the doorway looking back at him with a blank stare.

"You, you!" Mr. Stanley stammered. His face went red in anger. "You stupid horse! If you weren't worth a half a million dollars, I'd sell you for dog food!"

Godzilla just stood there looking at Mr. Stanley mockingly. The vet walked up and looked at Mr. Stanley's shoulder. His shirt was torn, and blood was seeping through the material.

"It broke the skin, Stanley," Dr. Tom said. "When was your last tetanus shot?"

"Oh, everyone just leave me alone. Come on, Tom, let's go to my office. Stupid horse."

Mr. Stanley and the vet walked off toward the offices. Henry looked at Cassie, who was now standing next to Godzilla in the doorway.

"Are you all right?" Henry asked.

"I'm fine," Cassie said.

Henry just shook his head and went back to work. Cassie stood next to Godzilla with a worried look on her face. Mr. Stanley's anger reminded Cassie that Godzilla didn't belong to her and that as soon as he could, Mr. Stanley would sell him. Now that Godzilla had attacked Mr. Stanley, the sale would more likely be sooner than later.

Cassie turned to the big horse. She patted him on the neck and gently said, "Dillie, that wasn't nice. Not nice at all."

# Chapter Twenty-Three

During the next week, Cassie concentrated on her riding. She had missed it terribly, and now that she was back, Cassie practiced so hard that Linda Flemming's hopes for Cassie grew. Linda saw that Cassie had talent, but more importantly, that Cassie had determination. The kind of determination that it takes to be a champion.

It also helped that Cassie loved riding more than any sport she had ever known. Hard work becomes easy when you love what you are doing, and Cassie worked hard, loving every moment of it. After she finished her riding lessons, she quickly got her chores done. Afterward, she would sit on the fence of the expert ring and study those riders practicing. By watching the experts, Cassie was able to learn much more about her own riding. She learned not only from their successes, but from their mistakes as well. At night, Cassie got into the habit of reviewing everything that Linda had taught her that day. She would picture herself riding and incorporating Linda's instructions. The magic of practicing in her mind enabled Cassie to make giant leaps with her riding.

Godzilla was also doing very well. His sores were healing nicely, and he was eating regularly. He allowed Cassie to groom him, and he looked like a different horse. Godzilla held his head high and he seemed to be alert and calm. Cassie felt that Godzilla might even be happy—his spirit was returning.

At the end of the day on Saturday, Cassie sat outside the tack room admiring the sky. There were little wispy clouds just starting to turn pink. Cassie felt thankful as she looked up at the fading light of the big Texas sky. It had been a great week.

"Hey, Cassie."

Cassie looked over and saw Henry smiling.

"Work's all done," Henry said. "We can head for home."

"I think I might just sit here awhile and look at the sky."

"It is beautiful."

"You know," Cassie said thoughtfully, "I'd like to share it with Dillie. I think I'll bring him out for some exercise."

"Now?"

"Yeah, why not? I think he'll like it."

"I'm going to stick around then. I'd like to see this."

From the tack room, Cassie picked up a halter, and she and Henry walked to Godzilla's shed.

Cassie walked in the shed, and Henry could hear her talking to Godzilla. It still amazed him how this young girl had been able to connect with this unpredictable horse. Henry thought he had Godzilla figured out: The horse had given up and wanted to die. But then Godzilla had chosen Cassie, and the surprise of this choice threw everything Henry thought he knew into confusion.

"Dillie," Henry heard Cassie say, "we're going out for some exercise. I don't want you to be scared. And we won't go to the ring where Sunny died. We'll go down to the beginners' ring."

A moment later, Cassie came out of the shed with Godzilla in tow. The horse was excited, and Henry quickly backed away.

"Henry," Cassie said, "you don't have to be afraid of Dillie. I had a long talk with him about you, and he knows you're on our team."

"Are you sure?" Henry asked.

"I'm sure."

Henry stepped a little closer as they walked out past the barn. But just the same, Henry kept a close eye on Godzilla, ready to jump out of the way at any sign the horse was going to turn on him.

When they got past the barn, Godzilla stopped. The arena where Sunny had died was right in front of them. It was the first time Godzilla had seen the place in nearly a year. Cassie tugged on the rope, but he wouldn't move. So she stepped close to Godzilla and rubbed his face gently.

"Don't worry, Dillie. It's just you and me and Henry. You're safe. We won't let anything happen to you."

After these words, Cassie pulled gently on the rope and Godzilla followed. Henry shook his head in disbelief.

"Do you think he understands your words?" Henry asked.

"No. I don't think he understands the words, and the words aren't really important. It's the feelings behind the words that matter. He understands what I'm feeling and I understand what he's feeling."

They arrived at the far arena and Cassie opened the gate. Henry climbed up on the fence. Cassie walked Godzilla in and took off the halter. But Godzilla just stood there. It was as though he didn't know what to do.

"It's safe here, Dillie," Cassie said. "You can run if you want."

Cassie left Godzilla standing in the arena and went to where Henry was sitting on the fence. She placed the halter on a fence post and climbed up and sat.

"Go ahead, Dillie," Cassie called. "Have some fun."

Godzilla looked over at Cassie. Then he took a step forward. Then another. Soon he was walking. He went a good distance. Then, suddenly, Godzilla broke into a run. He ran from one side of the arena to the other. He would stop sometimes and look for Cassie. Then he would break into a run again. Godzilla was having fun, as if he was happy to be alive.

"Whoa!" Henry said. "Look at him go."

Godzilla galloped back to where Cassie was sitting and stopped in front of her.

"It's okay, Dillie," Cassie said. "I love watching you run."

Godzilla whinnied at her, then turned and galloped across the arena.

"Do you want to ride him, Cassie?" Henry asked.

"I don't know. We sort of have this friendship based on trust. If I ride him, it will be like I'm telling him what to do. I'm not sure he would like that."

Henry looked at Cassie. "You don't really mean that, child,"

Cassie was quiet and looked away.

"Why don't you want to ride him?" Henry asked.

Cassie decided to tell Henry the truth. "The real reason is that if I start riding him, and he starts jumping again, then Mr. Stanley's going to sell Dillie the first chance he gets."

Henry was quiet. He knew this was probably true. "It's my guess that Godzilla won't let anyone ride him but you."

"Maybe not," Cassie replied. "But I don't want to risk losing him."

"It is a risk, child, but Godzilla is a jumper. That's his destiny. You owe it to him to bring him back. He's the best jumper I've ever seen."

"It still scares me, Henry. I need Dillie."

"You know," Henry said, "there's something that's always helped me. I look at the horses that have come and gone in my life, and I think of them like they're my children. You raise them up, you take care of them, and you do everything you can do to make them reach their potential. But in the back of your mind, you know that you are only doing this so that one day they can leave you to fulfill their destiny."

"It's just so hard. I don't want to lose him."

"I know how hard that is. When my boys wanted to join the Marine Corps I knew something bad could happen. But I raised them to have courage, and I was proud when they decided to join. They joined because they loved their country and thought they could help. Looking back, I sometimes think I should have stopped them, but I know that wouldn't have been right. I had raised them with such care so they would be able to choose what they wanted. I'm proud they grew into men who could make such a choice."

"You really loved your sons."

"Just like you love Godzilla."

Godzilla walked back and put his head in Cassie's lap. She stroked his face and realized that with every step of progress Godzilla made, it was one more step toward losing him. Then the big horse suddenly broke away and tore to the far side of the arena again. Cassie smiled. She was glad she had brought him out for some exercise.

"Cassie," Henry said. "Isn't today Halloween?"

"I think it is," Cassie replied.

"Aren't you supposed to be meeting friends to trick or treat?"

Cassie looked across the arena at Godzilla running.

"Seeing Dillie running tonight was the best treat I could ever have. That and talking with you."

## Chapter Twenty-Four

All through November, Godzilla continued to improve as Cassie was exercising him four times a week. Mr. Stanley took a keen interest in these exercise sessions. Cassie would see Mr. Stanley watching from a safe distance with a big smile plastered across his face. She suspected he was thinking of the ways he would spend the half-million dollars once the horse was sold.

Mr. Stanley also frequently sought out Cassie to inquire about Godzilla's progress. "How's our little project coming?" Mr. Stanley would ask.

"Fine," Cassie would reply.

She never wanted to say too much. But Mr. Stanley would not give up; he was after one thing.

"Don't you think you should start riding him?" Mr. Stanley would ask.

"I don't think he's ready."

"Well, you need to start him jumping. The sooner the better."

"All right, Mr. Stanley. I'll talk to him about it."

Then Cassie would worry for the rest of the day about losing Godzilla. It was all very stressful.

One thing in Cassie's life that was going well was her riding. Linda had taken a special interest in Cassie because she liked how hard she worked. Linda suggested they have two riding lessons on Saturdays, and Cassie immediately agreed. Cassie was never too sore or tired to say no to extra practice.

At the end of November, Linda had some news for Cassie.

"There's a little show coming up in a couple of weeks, and I think we should enter it."

"A show?" Cassie was excited. She often heard the other girls talking about their shows, and she longed to see what they were all about.

"Yes," Linda said. "It's a C show. You know, for beginners. But it would be a good place to start. I think you're ready."

"Okay," Cassie said, "thanks, Linda." Cassie walked away very excited. She couldn't wait to tell her mom, Henry and Olivia. But mostly, she wanted to tell Godzilla.

Then doubts started to enter her mind. Horse shows were expensive. There were the entrance fees and the cost to transport the horse. Cassie would also have to ask Mr. Stanley if she could even use a horse. She had been riding a horse named Hobbs for her practice sessions, but he was always in demand because he was good with the little kids.

Another problem was what to wear. Cassie had a couple of old pairs of riding pants and some old boots that Henry had found somewhere, but they weren't appropriate for a real show. She didn't want to look stupid in her first show, and a riding outfit could cost hundreds of dollars. Cassie knew her mom couldn't afford it. The next day she talked to Linda.

"Linda, I don't think I can do the show."

"Cassie, you can do it. You've been jumping great. You're ready."

"It's not that. My mom and I have been having a tough time with money. I couldn't ask her to pay for something like this."

"Oh," Linda said, "I didn't think of that."

Cassie thought the matter was closed. She was disappointed, but there was nothing she could do. Riding was expensive, and she was glad she got to do it at all.

The end of November was rainy and cold. Olivia and Henry invited Cassie and Susan to Thanksgiving Day dinner. It was a hard day for

Cassie. She remembered that her father was still alive last Thanksgiving, and Susan, Cassie, and her father had spent the day cooking the feast together. Even though he was sick, Michael Reynolds still found a way to make the day fun. He spent the day telling Cassie stories about growing up in Arkansas. There were lots of stories, and they were very funny, like the time he and his nine-year-old brother tried to drive the family car and crashed it into the tractor. "It wasn't funny at the time," Michael Reynolds said. But when her father had told the story, Cassie and her mother thought they would nearly die from laughing. It was stories like this, stories about her father's history, that were now etched in Cassie's memory forever.

Henry seemed to be having a tough day too. Henry was rather quiet and he seemed sad. Then a curious thing happened during dinner. Henry's nephew Mark Sinclair called and spoke to Olivia. Afterward, the nephew wanted to speak to Henry. But Henry didn't want to talk to him.

"Henry," Olivia said, "it's Mark, and you need to speak to him."

"Tell him I'm sorry. I just don't feel up to it."

"Henry Williams! You talk to your nephew right now. You're going to ruin his Thanksgiving."

Henry got up from the table and went to the phone. Henry spoke for a minute and then came back. But he didn't sit down to finish his meal. "I'm sorry, everyone," Henry said, "but I need to go for a walk."

Henry left, and Susan and Cassie looked at Olivia.

"Grief is always there," Olivia said. "Sometimes it just shows up, and there's nothing you can do."

# Chapter Twenty-Five

Henry was depressed the next day too. He was quiet and sub- dued when Cassie and he walked down the hill to the academy. All he said was, "It sure is funny how a holiday can make you blue."

It was still raining, and the day's lessons had been canceled. So Cassie and Henry took advantage of the day to do some extra work on the horses' stalls and tack. They cleaned and fed the horses, and by the end of the day, Henry seemed to feel better. As they started back up the hill toward home, Henry suddenly turned to Cassie. "Olivia wants you to come to dinner again tonight."

"You do realize I eat dinner at your house more than I do my own."

"Well, tonight's kind of a special occasion."

"It's not Olivia's birthday or something, is it?"

"No," Henry said, "but it's something important. In fact, it's so important I almost forgot to do something. Go on ahead. I'll meet you at the trailer."

Henry turned around and walked back toward the academy. Cassie continued up the hill and was surprised to see her mother's van parked at the house. There was also another car that she didn't rec- ognize.

Cassie went to her own trailer first and called for her mom. There was no answer so she headed for Olivia and Henry's trailer.

When Cassie walked in, she saw her mother and Linda seated at the dinner table. The table was set with Olivia's special china, and everyone looked at her and smiled. Cassie was confused.

"Mom, Linda. What are you doing here?"

Just then, Henry walked through the door. Cassie saw him wink at her mother.

"All right," Cassie said. "What's the secret?"

"Never mind about that," Olivia said. "Let's eat and then we'll have the surprise."

Olivia brought out the food. It was mostly leftovers from Thanksgiving.

"Leftovers on china," Susan said. "You sure know how to make the little things in life seem special, Olivia."

This confused Cassie even more, and as everyone ate, she was surprised that Linda and her mother acted like they knew each other. Finally, dinner was finished and Cassie looked at each person at the table.

"Okay," Cassie said, "will someone tell me what's going on?"

Henry looked at Linda. "It was your idea, Linda. You should be the one to tell her."

"Yes," Susan said, "you're the one who made it all happen."

"Okay," Linda said. "Cassie, after you told me you couldn't ride in the show, I talked to Henry. We both went to Mr. Stanley and explained how hard you've been working and that you deserved this chance. Mr. Stanley liked the idea because he said you're going to have to ride Godzilla in a show some day and that you'd better get some experience. So the academy is going to pay your entrance fee."

"He also agreed," Henry said, "that I could take the day off to go with you. He's going to let us borrow a trailer, and I can pull it with my truck."

Cassie smiled. "Will he let me ride Hobbs?"

"Yes," Henry said.

But then Cassie remembered she didn't have any riding clothes. "But what will I wear? All the other riders will have the right clothes. I just have an old pair of pants and boots. I don't even have my own helmet. I just use the old one from the academy."

"It doesn't matter what you wear," Henry said. "It only matters how you ride. It's not a fashion show, Cassie."

"But it matters to me. I don't want to look silly."

Everyone smiled and looked at each other. This made Cassie angry. "I'm not going to a show dressed in my old clothes and boots. Everyone will laugh."

"Why don't you go down and talk to Godzilla," Henry said. "Maybe he can straighten you out."

"All right," Cassie said, "I will. At least he understands." She stood up and walked to the door. But when she got there she stopped and turned to everyone. "I really appreciate everything you've tried to do. But I'm not going to look stupid."

Everyone laughed. Cassie just looked at them as if they were crazy and left the trailer in a huff.

By the time she got to Godzilla's shed, she was really angry. It was as if they were laughing at her just because she cared how she would look. She didn't want to seem ungrateful, but she was definitely not going to look stupid. She opened the shed door and started raving to Godzilla.

"Dillie, you won't believe what just happened . . . "

But as the door opened, something caught her eye. There were some clothes on a hanger on the inside of the door. Cassie couldn't believe it. There were two pairs of riding pants, two white blouses, and a beautiful black riding jacket. She looked on the ground. There was a black velvet helmet and a box with some boots. The clothes looked brand new and expensive.

"Are these for me?" she asked and then looked at Godzilla. The horse walked over to her and she hugged him.

"They are for me, aren't they?"

She bent down and tried on the helmet. It fit. She took it off and then tried on the jacket. It was a little big but it was close enough. Then she looked at the box with the boots and checked the size.

"Women's eleven. These must be for me too."

She gathered up the clothes in her arms. Then she stopped and looked back at Godzilla.

"Dillie, I'm going to be in my first real show. Can you believe it? This is so cool."

The horse came up to her again and Cassie kissed him on the nose.

"This means I have to do it. I can't back out now. I just hope I don't make an idiot out of myself."

By the time Cassie got back to Olivia and Henry's trailer, she was so excited she could hardly keep from jumping up and down. She walked in and everyone smiled.

"You really had me, Henry. Thank you so much, everyone. But where did you get this stuff? It all looks so expensive."

"I called an old friend," Linda said. "She has a daughter who dropped out of riding, and she had hung on to her things. She said we can use them for as long as we need to."

"But the boots look brand new and they're my size. I know you didn't borrow the boots."

Everyone was quiet and they all looked to Susan. Finally, Henry said, "Susan, I'm going to tell her. We tried everywhere to find you some boots. But Cassie, you got big feet, girl, and we couldn't find any. So your mother met Linda at the store and bought you new ones. She didn't want you to know because they were expensive on the account of your feet being so big and all."

Everyone laughed and Cassie blushed. She walked over and hugged her mom.

"Thanks, Mom."

Cassie went around the room and gave each person a hug and a "thank you." Once Cassie was finished, Susan stood up.

"I've got to go back to work," she said. "Thank you, Olivia. That was another great dinner."

Olivia smiled. "You're always welcome, Susan."

"I'll walk you out, Mom," Cassie said.

Cassie and Susan stepped outside and they stood on the driveway.

"Mom, thank you so much. But can we really afford them? I mean . . . "

"No, Cassie. Don't worry. It's worth every penny. I want to see you fly."

# Chapter Twenty-Six

The following Saturday was a beautiful winter day. The sun was shinning, and it was unseasonably warm in Dallas. Henry and Cassie woke up early. Henry had the truck and trailer hitched and ready to go by seven. Afterward, Cassie met Henry and they went down to the academy, where they cleaned the horse stalls and made sure all the horses had water.

"We'll feed tonight when we get back," Henry said.

Henry posted a note on the tack room door that read: "Gone to a horse show. If you want to ride, you have to get your own horse ready." Cassie read the note and smiled.

"Rebecca Simms won't like that very much," she said.

"She's gone too," Henry said. "There's a big show over in Austin. She took her horse and went there."

Cassie gathered up everything she needed from the tack room. She grabbed her favorite saddle and bit that Hobbs seemed to like. Out of habit, she also started to grab a helmet, but then she remembered she had one that was almost brand new in the truck.

The last task was to load Hobbs into the trailer. Hobbs was an experienced and gentle horse who had been to a lot of shows. He didn't give Henry and Cassie any trouble about getting in the trailer. Once he was inside, Cassie gave him a carrot and he munched away happily.

"I guess we're ready to go," Henry said.

"I have one last thing to do," Cassie said. "I'll be right back."

Cassie ran behind the barn to Godzilla's shed. She opened the heavy wooden door, and when the big horse saw her he approached.

The horse nuzzled his face into her chest, and Cassie scratched him behind the ears.

"Wish me luck, Dillie. It's my first horse show. Can you believe it? I'm so nervous."

Cassie kissed Godzilla on the nose.

"When I get back, I'll come straight away and tell you how I've done."

Cassie closed the door. Than she took a deep breath. The realization that she was going to her first show had finally sunk in. Cassie had done nothing but think about the show for the entire week and now, almost suddenly, it was here. Cassie was scared, happy, and excited all at the same time. The combination of feelings was a little overwhelming. Cassie took another deep breath and then ran to where Henry was waiting.

"Are you ready?" Henry asked

"I think so."

"Nervous?"

"Yeah."

"Don't be. Just pretend it's another day of practice and you'll do fine. I have a feeling this will be the first of many shows for you, Cassie."

They climbed in the truck and were off. As they drove off the academy grounds, Cassie knew there was no turning back.

The horse show was at the Dallas Fairgrounds, only a half-hour drive from the academy. Before Cassie had a chance to gather her thoughts, they had arrived.

Cassie was surprised that there were so many people already there. People were grooming and preparing their horses, and there were several kids already dressed in their riding outfits.

"I have to change," Cassie said in a panicked voice. She had on her old boots and jeans.

Henry laughed. "Don't worry. We have plenty of time for that. The first thing we need to do is unload Hobbs and find Linda to get you checked in."

Henry quickly found a parking spot and pulled the truck to a stop. Afterward, they unloaded Hobbs and tied him to the side of the trailer. In contrast to Cassie, Hobbs seemed perfectly relaxed and calm. Then Linda walked up.

"Hey, Cassie," Linda said, "are you ready for your first show?"

"I'm kind of nervous."

"Don't worry. Everybody's nervous their first time. Just look around and have fun. Don't worry about how you do."

"Okay," Cassie said. Linda's words seemed to help.

"Come on," Linda said. "Let's get you checked in, and then you can change."

While Cassie went off with Linda, Henry spent his time getting Hobbs ready for the show. When Cassie and Linda returned, Hobbs was ready and so was Cassie. She even had on her new riding helmet. Henry smiled.

"You look like a rider," Henry said.

Cassie felt like a rider. She had seen herself in the mirror and the clothes had transformed her. She was still nervous, but at least now she felt as if she belonged.

Cassie had four events, or classes, as they're called in equestrian competition. Her first three classes were strictly riding classes in which riders are judged on their technical skills. Judgments were made on things like posture in the saddle and how the reins are held. The riders are also judged on how well they change the gait of their horses from walking to trotting to cantering. It's very important that they keep their balance through these changes because the judges want the changes to look smooth and controlled.

In the first class, Cassie was so nervous she made several mistakes. She didn't keep her heels down when Hobbs was cantering, and when she changed his gait, she didn't put her proper foot forward. As a result, Cassie did poorly and managed only ninth place out of twelve riders. She was very disappointed. But luckily, Linda was right there to give her encouragement.

"Cassie, it was your first class and you were nervous. It's hard to do well in a technical class when you're nervous."

In her next two classes, Cassie did better, but not much. She took seventh and fifth, respectively. Linda watched Cassie closely. Her mistakes were common ones and came from inexperience. But Linda noticed something more. Linda wondered if Cassie wasn't more of an athlete than a technical rider. There was something restrictive and confining in the technical classes, which Cassie was weaker in. Cassie liked the freedom of riding and jumping where technical skill is not judged.

After her third class, Cassie went and sat next to Henry and Linda in the stands.

"Cassie," Linda said, "your last class is a jumping class. You don't have to worry about keeping your heels down and which foot goes forward. You can free your mind and just ride."

A few moments later, Susan and Olivia showed up. Cassie was happy to see them. She had wanted her mother to come to her first show, but because she had done poorly, she was embarrassed. Linda came to her rescue when Susan and Olivia asked how Cassie had done.

"She did really well for her first show," Linda said. "But I think her last class will be her best performance."

"Oh good," Susan said. "I'm glad I'll get to see it."

Cassie, freed from thinking and worrying about each specific movement, quickly got into the zone. The zone was a special place that athletes find inside their minds where their mind and body function perfectly together. There isn't any wasted thought or movement. It's almost as if every choice the mind makes, the body already knows the thought before it's finished. This is when peak performances occur. Cassie rode her best. She cleared every jump without a miss, and when the class was finished, Cassie had won.

Everyone in the group was ecstatic with her performance, and they gathered around to congratulate her. Her mother gave her a big hug. Cassie, with a big smile plastered across her face, couldn't contain her excitement.

"Mom," Cassie said, "did you see me fly?"

"Honey, you were unbelievable out there. This is your sport, babe."

Cassie hugged her mom tightly, thinking that her mother's words rang true. She had indeed found her sport.

Word spread quickly around the academy that Cassie had won the jumping class in her show. It had only been a C show, but when the news reached Rebecca Simms, she was livid. It had taken Rebecca over two years of riding to win her first jumping class. Cassie had done it in her first try.

The situation between Rebecca and Cassie was made worse when Linda moved Cassie up to the expert ring for her practice lessons. This forced Rebecca to watch Cassie practice, and she did not like what she saw. Cassie was a hard worker, much harder than she. Cassie also accepted instruction easily and was able to make the adjustments required quickly. Rebecca Simms wanted to be rid of Cassie once and for all.

Cassie had no idea why Rebecca hated her so much. When Rebecca and her friends cornered Cassie in the hall the next day at school, she tried to find out why.

"Rebecca, what have I ever done to you?" Cassie asked.

Rebecca gave Cassie a dirty look and spit, "We don't want you at the academy."

"But I can't leave," Cassie replied. "I have no place else to go."

"You can go back to your trailer park," Rebecca hissed. "You don't belong at our academy, trailer trash."

Cassie walked away baffled because it seemed to her that Rebecca had everything. She was pretty, popular, and rich. She was also a very good rider. Cassie just couldn't figure out why Rebecca had chosen her to be mean to.

Over Christmas break, things with Rebecca got really bad. Henry was sick so Cassie was running the stables by herself. After Rebecca finished her lesson, she brought her horse, Starfire, to the crossties for Cassie to take care of.

Henry had taught Cassie to take care of the horse that was first in line. Rebecca usually didn't pay any attention. She would just leave Starfire and then walk away with her friends. But, on this day, Rebecca stayed behind to see if Cassie took care of Starfire right away. When Cassie took care of the horses that had gotten to the crossties first, Rebecca yelled at Cassie.

"You stupid idiot! Why are you taking care of those other horses first? Starfire is worth a hundred thousand dollars."

Cassie was so busy she didn't have time to deal with Rebecca Simms.

"Rebecca," Cassie said, "if you're so worried about your horse, why don't you take care of him yourself? It would probably do you some good."

Rebecca didn't have a reply for Cassie. But she did go straight home and tell her father how rude Cassie had been to her. She also made sure to tell her father how Cassie was always mean to her at school. As a result, William Simms took his daughter's side and wanted Cassie gone too. He called Mr. Stanley and complained and requested that Cassie be fired. Since Mr. Simms was a big supporter of the academy, Mr. Stanley listened. If it hadn't been for Godzilla, Cassie would surely have been fired. Instead, Mr. Stanley came out and had a talk with Cassie.

"You have to be respectful of the riders. You work for the academy and represent us. Now, the Simms family pays a lot of money for us to take care of their horse and you need to take care of him first. If you don't think you can do that, then you can't work here."

This scared Cassie deeply because the most important things in her life were riding and Godzilla. She did not want to lose them.

"Yes, sir," Cassie said.

"The next time Rebecca brings in her horse, I want you to apologize."

That afternoon, Rebecca Simms brought Starfire over to the crossties and waited for Cassie to see him. Luckily, Cassie dropped the horse she was tending to and took care of Starfire first. Rebecca was disappointed. She had hoped Cassie would have let Starfire go and then there would be a scene and Rebecca could get her fired. But Cassie was careful around Rebecca. Still, Rebecca tried to antagonize her.

"Isn't there something you want to tell me?" Rebecca asked.

Cassie bit her lip. She wanted to tell Rebecca she was a spoiled brat, but she kept that thought to herself. "I'm sorry for not taking care of Starfire first."

"It better not happen again or you'll be out of here." Rebecca walked away. Cassie didn't know it, but she had won that round. There was nothing Rebecca could do to get Cassie fired that day.

When Henry returned, Cassie told him what had happened.

"It's just politics, child. It's part of life. Everywhere you go you're going to run into it. People have hidden agendas or they try to single you out to make you look bad. The only thing you can do is try and stay true to yourself and do your best."

But later that day, Henry decided to play a little politics of his own. He saw that Rebecca was standing with a group of her friends near the soda machine. He knew this would be a perfect time for him to throw a little support Cassie's way.

"Good afternoon, ladies," Henry said. "Have you heard how Cassie saved Godzilla's life?"

Everyone knew the legend of Godzilla, and there had been rumors about Cassie getting close to Godzilla swirling through the academy. But they hadn't heard Henry's version.

"How did she do that?" one girl asked.

"Mr. Stanley was planning to put him down. But then Cassie started taking care of him to show Mr. Stanley he wasn't a lost cause. If she hadn't done it, Godzilla would be dead. Almost everyone here at the academy has tried to do something for that horse, but only Cassie was able to save him."

"That's really cool," one girl said, and some of the others nodded in agreement. Henry glanced at Rebecca Simms and saw that she looked particularly unhappy.

There was nothing Rebecca could do to make Cassie look bad for saving Godzilla. After Henry left, Rebecca tried to say something mean about Cassie. But now the girls were reluctant to join in. Rebecca's friends had begun to think that if Cassie had saved Godzilla, she couldn't be all bad. What's more, the kids all went home and told their parents about Cassie.

The next day, a girl named Clara actually went up to Cassie. She knew she was risking the wrath of Rebecca Simms, but she decided she wanted to get to know Cassie.

"Cassie, what you're doing with Godzilla is really great," Clara said.

Cassie was surprised. She had expected Clara to say something mean.

"Thanks," Cassie replied. "He's really starting to come back. He's a really good horse."

Cassie smiled at Clara and she smiled back. Cassie was finally making a friend at the academy.

# Chapter Twenty-Eight

Christmas Day started out as a sad day for Cassie. She thought about her father a lot and was reminded of the times they had gone out on Christmas Eve to get their tree. It had been a family tradition. They would all pile into his old truck, Sir Stinky, and drive to the railroad tracks to get a fresh tree right from the trains. Then, they would drive home and spend the evening decorating the tree. When Cassie woke up the next morning, she would find lots of presents and goodies underneath. This year, Susan and Cassie didn't even have a tree, and when Cassie woke up, it didn't feel like Christmas at all.

Moreover, her mother had to work two shifts at Denny's and Cassie would be spending Christmas alone. But she got up early with her mom, and they exchanged presents. Susan gave Cassie a fifty-dollar gift certificate to Ross Dress for Less, and Cassie gave her mom two passes to the movies. They hugged, and her mother said she would call between her shifts.

"I'm sorry I have to work on Christmas," Susan said. "But I have tomorrow off. Maybe we can use the passes to see a movie."

After her mother left, Cassie took a walk to see Godzilla. She brought her favorite horse a Christmas present. Actually, she brought two. A big, juicy, delicious carrot and a crisp, clean apple. After Godzilla gobbled them up, she cleaned his stall and made sure the big horse had plenty of food and water. Then she hugged him for a long time and cried.

"It's Christmas, Dillie, and I miss my dad."

When Cassie returned to her trailer, she saw that Olivia was working in her garden. She got excited and ran to her trailer to get Olivia's present. She had it all wrapped and tied with a bow. She ran back to Olivia's garden and stood at the gate.

"Hi," Cassie said, "can I come in?"

Cassie always asked for permission before entering Olivia's garden. To Cassie, it seemed like the right thing to do, sort of like asking for permission from a saint before entering a church. Olivia liked that Cassie always did this. It showed respect for how personal and private this place was for Olivia. She looked over and smiled.

"Of course, child," Olivia said. "You're always welcome here."

Cassie walked in the gate. "I got you something for Christmas." Cassie held out her gift, and Olivia's eyes opened wide. "For me?" she said.

"Yes, and I think you should open it here in your garden."

Olivia went to her bench and sat. She opened the present and found a long metal piece, sort of like a pair of tongs, with two claws on the end. She studied it for a few moments.

"What is it?" She asked.

"It's a thorn remover. I had my mom take me to the garden store, and the man said it was newest thing in roses."

"Well, what do you know? Let's see if it works."

Olivia walked over to her roses and cut a stem. She walked back and picked up the thorn remover. But she wasn't sure how it worked.

"Like this, Olivia," Cassie said. She took Olivia's hands and placed them so the thorn remover was properly on the rose stem.

"Now just pull," Cassie said.

Olivia pulled and all the thorns came right off. Olivia looked at the thorn remover as if she was surprised it had worked.

"Don't that beat all," she said. "That's a fine invention."

"I bet even Cleopatra didn't have one of these."

Olivia smiled and she gave Cassie a hug. "Thank you for my gift," Olivia said. "It was very thoughtful."

"Merry Christmas, Olivia."

Tears welled up in Olivia's eyes. "And Merry Christmas to you, Cassie."

Cassie also had a present for Henry and she went to look for him. She found him at the front of the trailer park building a new mailbox stand for the residents. When she saw him working so hard, she was surprised.

"Why are you fixing the mailboxes on Christmas?" Cassie asked.

Henry smiled sadly. "I always feel blue on a holiday. And I found if I keep busy then I don't feel so blue."

"I feel sad too," Cassie replied. "But I brought you a present." Cassie held out her present. Just like Olivia's, the gift was wrapped and had a big bow.

Henry put down his shovel and took the present. He unwrapped it slowly and found a box. He opened the box to find a beautiful pocketknife with a mother-of-pearl inlay on the handle.

"How did you know my other knife had gone dull?" Henry asked.

"You said it last week at the academy. You were trying to cut a piece of leather and you complained."

Henry looked at the knife and smiled. "That's a mighty fine knife. Thank you."

Henry put the knife in his pocket and turned back to the mailbox.

"Can I help you with the mailbox?" Cassie asked. "I don't want to go home and sit in the trailer."

Henry looked at Cassie knowingly. "Sitting around by yourself is about the worst thing you can do when you're depressed," Henry said and picked up a white plastic bucket. He held it out for Cassie to take. "Go fill this bucket with water and bring it back. I think Mrs. McNally'll let you use her faucet. Just tell her it's for me."

Cassie took the bucket and ran off to Mrs. McNally's. A moment later, she returned with a bucket full of water.

"Here," Henry said and handed Cassie a trowel. "After I pour the cement in the hole, you pour in some water and start mixing."

Cassie did as she was told, and she proceeded to follow Henry's orders for nearly four hours. Their only break was when Olivia came out with some lemonade.

"Cassie's doing fine work, Olivia," Henry said.

"I can see that, Henry, but don't work her too hard. I have Christmas dinner cooking."

Henry and Cassie went back to work setting posts, hammering nails, and securing mailboxes. At one point, Cassie stopped and looked at Henry. "A little hard work sure helps to get rid of the blues."

"It sure enough does."

"Do you think it will ever get easier for me, Henry? Holidays, I mean."

Henry stopped his work. "Cassie, you're missing what once was and you have your whole life to replace what's missing with new memories."

"But you still get sad, and it's been nearly thirty years since your sons died."

"That's true. But I'm missing what might have been. When it comes to Christmas, I start thinking of what my sons would have grown to be, and that's a hard thing for me. You'll always feel blue, Cassie, when you think of your dad, but you're going to have lots of Christmases to build new memories to fill up what you lost."

When they were done, seventeen residents had new mailboxes. Cassie and Henry stood back and admired their work.

"That should last another thirty years," Henry said. "You did a good job, Cassie."

"I'm going to always remember this Christmas, and it's because I spent it with you building a mailbox stand."

Henry smiled. "You know, I'm not feeling so blue. I say we clean up and go see what Olivia has cooking for dinner."

"Yea," Cassie said. "I'm hungry too."

They quickly cleaned up the tools and carried them back to Henry's trailer. They sat down and had a great Christmas dinner, and when they were done, Henry and Olivia gave Cassie a Christmas present. It was a new pair of riding gloves, and Cassie loved them.

# Chapter Twenty-Nine

The first two weeks of January brought more rain, and the academy was closed. But Cassie still used the time to practice. Linda Flemming brought in videotapes of championship riders, and Cassie sat next to Linda watching the tapes every day. Linda would point out the good choices riders had made and also their mistakes. Cassie learned a great deal from watching these tapes. Linda was training her mind as well as her body.

Cassie's work with Godzilla was also going extremely well. Even though it was raining, Cassie still took the big horse to the far arena to exercise every day. Godzilla seemed to love the rain, and anyone who knew Godzilla could see he was growing stronger under Cassie's care. Mr. Stanley was particularly pleased. His half-million-dollar payday was growing closer.

However, Mr. Stanley was always trying to find a way to hurry it along, and he approached Cassie with the same question almost every day.

"Say, Cassie. Godzilla looks like he's doing great."

"Yes," Cassie replied, "he seems happy."

"When do you think you'll start riding him?"

Cassie knew why Mr. Stanley always asked the same question. He wanted his money. Cassie, of course, wanted to prevent Godzilla from leaving the academy. But she was running out of excuses, and Mr. Stanley was losing patience.

"I'm not sure Dillie wants me to ride him," Cassie would always say.

This answer always made Mr. Stanley angry. Finally, Mr. Stanley's patience wore out, and he took matters into his own hands. He came up with an idea to help move Godzilla along.

On the last Friday in January, Mr. Stanley walked up to Cassie in the late afternoon.

"Cassie, I think we should move Godzilla to a different stall."

"Really? Which one?"

"One of the premium stalls along the expert arena is open. Let's move him there. I think if he sees the other horses jumping, Ol' Godzilla may get inspired."

Cassie became alarmed. "I don't think Dillie will like it there. He'll be looking into the arena where Sunny died."

Mr. Stanley's face turned red. "Godzilla is my horse, and you're being paid to get him jumping again. So do what I tell you to do. Move him there today."

"Yes, sir," Cassie said.

Mr. Stanley walked away, leaving Cassie very worried. He had given her a direct order, and she had to follow it. She went to check out the open stall. It wasn't in very good condition. It had been vacated by a horse that had been sold because the woman who owned it didn't have time to ride anymore.

It was late afternoon, and even though Cassie was tired from working all day, she decided to clean the stall from top to bottom. First, she got a broom and knocked down all the cobwebs and rinsed the feeders thoroughly. Next, she took out all the old bedding and replaced it with new. Cassie knew Godzilla was going to have a tough time with this move, because horses were creatures of habit. She wanted to make sure that her smell would be inside the stall so that at least Godzilla would be familiar with that.

But what worried her the most was the fact that the stall overlooked the first arena, the place where Godzilla's best friend, Sunny, had died. Cassie knew this place represented the worst memory in

Godzilla's life, and she wasn't sure how he was going to react to being in this stall. She was pretty certain it was going to be hard for him.

Cassie worked for an hour, and when she was almost done, Henry walked up.

"I've been looking for you," Henry said. "What are you doing?"

"Mr. Stanley says I have to move Dillie here today."

"Why?"

"Because Mr. Stanley thinks that if Dillie sees the other horses jumping, then he'll want to jump too."

Henry just shook his head. "Utter stupidity. That man forgets everything he's ever learned about horses when money's involved."

Cassie didn't say anything. She went back to work preparing the stall. Henry stood watching her for a moment.

"How much longer do you think you'll be?" Henry asked.

"I don't know," Cassie said. "I'm about ready to bring Dillie over. I might have to stay with him awhile."

Henry knew that "awhile" might turn out to be a long time. He had often spent time with a sick horse, and it always took longer than he expected, and Henry knew Godzilla was sick. Not in the normal way you think of sick, but sick in his spirit. Henry knew that Godzilla's spirit had been close to breaking.

"I'll bring you down some dinner."

Henry walked off and Cassie finished her work on the stall. When she finished, she took a deep breath. It was time to bring Godzilla over.

It was nearly dark when Cassie walked to the tack room to get a halter. The sky still had some red left on the western horizon, but dusk was quickly surrendering to the night. The academy was deserted.

Cassie walked behind the barn. The top door to the shed was open, and Godzilla had his head out waiting for Cassie to come close it up and to say goodnight. When Godzilla saw the halter, he thought they were going out for exercise. The big horse became excited.

"No, Dillie," Cassie said. "We're not going out for exercise. We're moving to a new stall. Mr. Stanley's ordered me to move you."

Cassie opened the bottom part of the shed door and walked inside. She stood next to Godzilla and rubbed his neck. "This is going to be a big change for you, but don't worry. I'm going to be with you."

Cassie slipped the halter over Godzilla's head and led him out of the shed. They walked past the barn using the same path they always used when they went to exercise. But when they reached the first arena, Cassie stopped.

"Dillie, we need to walk along the fence here to your new stall."

Cassie turned and began to walk along the fence to the first arena. At first Godzilla followed, but Cassie could sense he was becoming nervous. Then he just stopped.

"It's all right, Dillie. Don't be scared. I'm with you. I'm always with you."

Cassie's words helped calm the big horse. He followed Cassie along the fence, but he was looking out into the arena. Godzilla let out a noise that sounded like a whimper.

Cassie had left the door open to the new stall. But when she tried to lead Godzilla in, the horse wouldn't follow. She pulled harder on the rope, and Godzilla began to pull back. Soon, the horse pulled back so hard that he pulled her to the ground. She fell hard and let go of the rope. But the horse didn't run away. When he saw that he had pulled Cassie to the ground, he walked over and stood close to her. She sat up and the big horse lowered his head and rubbed his face against hers.

"Dillie, I know you don't want to be in this stall. I don't want you to be in this stall. I know every time you look out, you're going to see the place where Sunny died. But Mr. Stanley's in charge, and he says you have to move here. If we don't do this, Mr. Stanley might take you away from me. So we either do this, or we go back to the shed knowing Mr. Stanley might not let us be together."

Cassie got to her feet. She took the halter rope in her hand and looked at Godzilla for a long moment. Then she reached out and rubbed his face. "It's up to you, Dillie. I'll do whatever you want me to do."

Cassie pulled on the rope. The horse hesitated, then he followed her into the stall. She took the halter off and stepped outside the stall and closed the door. She stood watching.

Godzilla began to pace around the stall like a tiger in a cage. It didn't help that this stall was much smaller than the shed. But the worst part was its proximity to the first arena. Godzilla paced and then suddenly stopped and looked out the door. He let out a whinny, but the sound was so sad it brought tears to Cassie's eyes. She knew Godzilla was reliving the memory of Sunny's death.

"It's going to be okay, Dillie. I'm here with you. We'll get through this together."

Then Cassie had an idea. "Dillie, I'll be right back."

She ran to the tack room and went straight for the refrigerator and grabbed a carrot. She ran back as fast as she could.

But when she returned, she saw that Godzilla wasn't pacing anymore. He was facing the back of the stall with his head down in the corner. He looked like the horse she had seen that first day, broken and defeated.

Cassie knew the carrot wasn't going to help. She opened the stall door and walked inside, throwing the carrot in the feeder. Then she sat next to where Godzilla was hanging his head. She tried to sit as close to him as she could, and she reached out and rubbed his face.

"Dillie, I know how hard this is for you. When I remember my dad lying in the hospital bed dying, I just want to curl up in a ball and die too. It's like the memory is so fresh, and the worst part is that there's nothing you can do to change it. There's no way to fix it. You just have to go on. You can't give up."

Cassie then became quiet. She just sat close to the big horse feeling his pain. She would rub his face now and then to let him know she was there.

After about an hour, Henry arrived. He wasn't surprised to see that Godzilla was having a hard time.

"Cassie, I brought you down some food."

Cassie got up and walked to the door. She took the plate from Henry and set it in the corner.

"How's he doing?" Henry asked.

"Not good. I think I'm going to stay the night. When my mom gets home, could you tell her I'm here?"

"Sure, I'll bring you down some blankets and a pillow."

"Thanks, Henry."

Cassie sat down next to Godzilla. Henry watched for a moment, but he knew there was nothing he could do so he returned to his trailer. When he walked in the door, Olivia wanted an update.

"The horse looks broken," Henry said. "But if anyone can save him, Cassie can."

Around eight, Henry headed back down to the academy. His arms were loaded down with blankets and a pillow. He also had a flashlight. When he arrived at the stall, he saw that Cassie was still sitting close to Godzilla.

"Cassie, I brought you some blankets and a pillow."

"Thanks, Henry. I'll get them in a little while."

Henry noticed the food plate in the corner. "You need to eat something," Henry said.

"I'm not hungry right now," Cassie replied. "I'll eat when Dillie eats."

Henry knew there was nothing he could say. Something was going on between Cassie and Godzilla that couldn't be explained or understood. It was as if their spirits were connected, and Henry knew he couldn't interfere. This was like a fever. It had to run its course.

Henry walked back up the hill to wait for Susan. On his walk he thought about Godzilla. It had been his experience that horses did in fact feel a sense of loss. He had read about horses in the wild staying close to a dead horse for some time after the death. He also had seen elephants experience the same thing on the Discovery Channel. But he had never known the sense of loss to be so strong or last as long as it had with Godzilla. With human beings, it was different. Henry knew grief could last a lifetime. Maybe it was the same with Godzilla.

Susan arrived home around midnight. Henry met her on the driveway. She became worried when she saw Henry walking up.

"Henry? Is everything okay?"

"Yes, " Henry said, "everything's fine. But Cassie asked me to tell you she's staying the night with Godzilla. He's sort of having a tough time."

"I better go down and check on her."

"I'll walk you down," Henry said.

Susan went into her trailer and dropped off her purse. She also got a warm coat because the night air had turned chilly. She met Henry in front of her trailer and they walked down to the academy. Along the way, Henry told Susan what he thought.

"Susan, what's happening between Cassie and Godzilla can't be explained. You just need to accept the fact that the horse needs Cassie tonight, and she knows this. You need to trust your daughter's wisdom."

When Susan and Henry arrived at the stall, they saw that Cassie had gotten up for a blanket and had wrapped it around herself. She had also fallen asleep. Susan became alarmed when she saw her young daughter sleeping next to the big horse.

"Henry, is she safe?"

"Yes," Henry answered, "Godzilla won't hurt her."

"Are you sure?"

"Yes, I'm sure. Godzilla and Cassie are working something out. They need to do this together. Susan, you need to trust that Cassie knows what she's doing because I believe tonight is Godzilla's only chance to make it. If you stop it now, Cassie will always blame you if Godzilla doesn't get past this."

Susan was thoughtful. She knew how much the horse meant to her daughter. Cassie had to see this through on her own terms.

"Will you be checking on her?" Susan asked.

"Absolutely," Henry said. "I'm going to stay down here too. I'll be nearby in the tack room all night."

"Okay," Susan said, "I just hope Cassie's horse is all right."

At just after three in the morning, Godzilla walked quietly to the stall door and looked out at the arena. Cassie awoke, and when she saw Godzilla staring out she walked over to his side. She reached out and rubbed the horse's neck. They stood there for a long time. Then Cassie thought of something.

"Dillie, will you show me where it happened?"

For some reason, Cassie thought this might help. She opened the door to the stall and they walked out into the chilly night. She decided not to put on a halter because she felt she didn't need it. Not for this.

Godzilla knew where they were going. He led the way to the gate to the arena and waited while Cassie opened it. They entered the arena and Godzilla stopped.

"Show me where it happened, Dillie."

Godzilla led Cassie past some jumps. When they reached the center, the big horse stopped and pawed the ground.

"It happened here almost a year ago?"

Cassie's voice woke Henry in the tack room. He climbed out of the cot and walked to the door and looked out. He thought he was dreaming for a second. Cassie and Godzilla were standing together in the center of the arena. Cassie was hugging the big horse, then she pulled away and turned to face him.

"Dillie, there's something I want to show you."

The horse followed Cassie out of the arena. Henry hid in the shadows and watched them pass.

Cassie and Godzilla walked along the side of the fence of the first arena until they reached the road that ran through the academy. There, they turned and headed toward the academy entrance.

The academy road ran a long distance, but Cassie and Godzilla walked only a short way. They stopped at a plot of ground just beyond the offices. It was the horses' graveyard.

"Dillie," Cassie said, "they buried Sunny here."

Cassie and Godzilla walked in the graveyard and made their way through the headstones until they came to Sunny's grave.

"Dillie, this is the place. See, they even have a marker. It says, 'Sunny, a good horse.' "

Godzilla seemed to understand. He pawed the ground and then reached his head down and touched the grave with his lips.

"Nobody wanted Sunny to die, Dillie," Cassie said. "It was just an accident."

Cassie and Godzilla stood together in the cold night. Cassie cried a little and then gave Godzilla a hug.

"I remember when my dad died," Cassie said. "I felt so helpless, and that's how things like this make you feel. Helpless and sad and angry, and there's nothing you can do about it. But I remember the prayer from his funeral. It says, 'God, grant me the strength to change the things I can and the courage to accept the things I can't change.' Some things just happen, Dillie, and they can't be changed. But my dad wanted me to go on. He made sure I knew that, and I know Sunny wanted you to go on too. Sunny wouldn't have wanted you to give up."

Henry was spellbound by what he was watching, and Cassie's words brought a tear to his eye. It was like magic was unfolding right before him. The magic of healing. Godzilla was being healed by Cassie's words, and in speaking her words, Cassie was healing herself. Together, this young girl and this big horse were healing each other.

Godzilla and Cassie stood at the grave for a long time. Then Godzilla turned and rubbed his nose against Cassie's cheek. Finally, the big horse turned to leave. Cassie and Godzilla started to walk back up the road toward the stall. Along the way, they passed other horses. The horses all began to whinny at Godzilla and Cassie. It was as though the horses knew something special had taken place too. When Henry heard Godzilla whinny back, he smiled. He knew Godzilla was going to be all right.

# Chapter Thirty

The rest of the weekend went well for Godzilla. He seemed to be adjusting to his new stall and surroundings. Cassie was also surprised to find that Mr. Stanley seemed to be right. Godzilla was watching the horses and riders practicing in the arena. It made Cassie think that he might be ready to jump again.

On Sunday afternoon, Cassie and Susan walked down to the academy and took Godzilla out for some exercise. They walked around the property and then let the horse loose in the far arena. He ran and jumped in the air. Godzilla would return to Cassie and Susan for a moment, and then he would turn and tear across the arena to the far end. He was acting like a young colt, happy to be alive.

Something had also changed for Cassie. The pain of losing her father was turning into acceptance. She still missed him, but the blackness that had engulfed her spirit was lifting. She walked to the fence and stood next to her mother. "I think I'm starting to feel better about Dad."

"That's a good thing, honey. It was the main thing that worried your father before his death. He knew it was going to be hard for you because you two had been so close."

"Dillie's helped."

"You do love this horse, don't you?"

"Yeah."

"It's so amazing to me how life always keeps you guessing."

"How do you mean?" Cassie asked

"Look at you, Cassie. You've become this great rider and you have this beautiful horse. Six months ago we never knew this could have happened."

"But Dillie's not mine."

"Maybe not legally. But Henry says you saved his life."

"Yeah, and now I'm afraid of losing him too."

"That's a risk you always have in life. If you love something there's always the possibility of losing it. But it's a risk you have to take to live a full life. I mean, look at Dillie. You must feel so proud knowing that your love saved him. That's what you have to remember."

"Do you miss Dad very much?" Cassie asked.

"Sure. I miss him every day. I miss coming home and knowing he's there. I miss the way he would call me "babies" in the middle of the night. But I wouldn't change a thing. Even with the pain I feel for having lost him. The feeling of having loved makes it all worth it. Because that's hard to find. That's what I hold onto."

"I guess if Dillie gets sold, that's what I'll have to remember," Cassie said thoughtfully.

# Chapter Thirty-One

The following Monday afternoon, Cassie arrived at the academy and found that Henry had gotten most of the horses ready. So all she had to do was muck about twenty-five stalls. She stopped by Godzilla's stall to say hello and then got right to work. It took about an hour and she finished in time for her four-thirty lesson.

As usual, she had Hobbs reserved for the lesson. She walked him into the arena and climbed up in the saddle. Then she rode Hobbs into the arena to start her practice session. This was a mistake.

Suddenly, there was the biggest ruckus you ever heard coming from the premium stalls. Everyone looked and saw that it was Godzilla going berserk. He was screaming and kicking the stall door, making more noise than a roaring tornado.

"Cassie," Henry called, "I think you've got a problem."

Cassie did indeed have a problem. She quickly dismounted and walked Hobbs back to the crossties. Henry was standing there, smiling.

"Henry," Cassie said, "can you take care of Hobbs?"

"Sure," Henry said. "Looks like you'll be riding a different horse today."

Cassie walked to Godzilla's stall. But when she got there, Godzilla turned away from her and faced the back of the stall. Cassie found herself staring at his butt. Cassie smiled.

"So what's the problem?" Cassie asked.

Godzilla ignored her.

"You're jealous."

Godzilla still ignored her.

"All right," Cassie said, "if that's how you feel about it, I'll just ride you. I have to get my lesson in."

Suddenly, Godzilla turned and walked over to Cassie. He rubbed his face against hers and Cassie knew the time had come.

Cassie walked to the tack room and grabbed a halter. Everyone in the arena was watching. People began looking at each other asking, "Is Cassie really going to try to ride Godzilla?" Word began to spread. By the time Cassie was walking Godzilla to the crossties, people from the offices and barn were coming out to see if it was true. Parents, who had been sitting having a cold drink or coffee at the academy café, left their conversations to watch the young girl ride the horse with the nasty reputation. But the person who was most excited at the news was Mr. Stanley. He ran from his office to watch. The whole way he had a big smile on his face.

When Cassie and Godzilla got to the crossties, they passed Hobbs. Godzilla reached out and tried to bite Hobbs. But Cassie pulled him away, and Hobbs moved quickly to avoid Godzilla's teeth.

"Dillie!" Cassie yelled. "You stop that. It's not his fault. If you want to bite someone, then bite me."

When Godzilla got in the crossties, he was a perfect gentleman. He let Cassie do everything she needed to do. He stood perfectly still as Cassie put his saddle on and even lowered his head to make it easy for Cassie to put on his bridle. Cassie unchained him from the crossties and led Godzilla to the arena. When she got there, she noticed a lot of people sitting on the fence waiting to see what would happen. Cassie smiled.

"I guess we'll be riding in a fishbowl today, Dillie."

Dillie snorted. It sounded to Cassie like, "Let them watch."

"Don't get carried away with yourself, Dillie. It's your first day back. Let's not overdo it."

Cassie entered the arena and walked Godzilla over to the mounting blocks. He was such a big horse that even with the blocks Cassie had to stretch to climb on. Once on, Cassie reached down and patted Godzilla's neck.

"Okay, Dillie. Let's have us some fun."

Cassie turned Godzilla and they started off. At first, they just walked a little ways. Then Cassie just barely touched her boots to his sides and he went into a trot. They went around the arena several times and not once did Cassie have to work to keep him in his trot. But what surprised Cassie was that his trot was so smooth. It was almost effortless to stay in her post.

Cassie decided to do some turns. She just barely pulled his reins and leaned with her body ever so slightly, and Godzilla turned. Again, the big horse stayed in his trot and his gait was even and smooth. Every turn was perfect, and Cassie was impressed with how he responded to her commands.

"Cassie, you're looking good, girl!" Linda Flemming yelled.

Then, Cassie touched her boots to his sides again and Godzilla broke into a canter. The ride was so smooth that Cassie found it was easy to keep her form. The big horse covered ground quickly, and before Cassie even thought about it, they had gone three laps around the arena. Cassie pulled on the reins and Godzilla came to a stop. The audience broke into applause.

Cassie smiled and reached down and patted Godzilla on the neck.

"You did great, Dillie. But that's it for today. I don't want to overdo it, remember?"

Cassie tried to turn Godzilla back toward the entrance. But for the first time, the big horse did not follow her command. Cassie tried again, but Godzilla did not move.

"Dillie, people have to get their lessons in. We can't just take up the arena all day."

But Godzilla had other plans. Cassie noticed that he was looking at a jump. His ears were also pointed in that direction.

"Oh, you want to do a jump?" Cassie asked.

The big horse pawed the ground.

"All right," Cassie said. "One jump and then we're done."

Cassie turned Godzilla toward the jump, and slightly touched her heels to his sides. Godzilla was off and smoothly approached the jump. Cassie could feel the horse's confidence as they left the ground. They cleared the jump easily, and the landing was so soft it left Cassie speechless. She pulled Godzilla to a stop and looked back at the jump as people again applauded.

"Dillie! That was, ah . . . so cool!"

People were yelling things like, "You looked great!" and "Do another one!"

But Cassie dismounted and led Godzilla back to the crossties. It had been enough for the first day. But Cassie had learned something important. She now understood why people thought Godzilla was so valuable. He was easily the best horse she had ever ridden, the kind of horse that's worthy of being called a champion.

# Chapter Thirty-Two

Through February and March, Cassie committed herself to both schoolwork and riding. With her riding, Cassie practiced every day on Godzilla and twice a day on Saturdays. Mr. Stanley had decided to open his wallet a little when it came to riding lessons. He figured that if Cassie rode Godzilla in a big show and did well, then there was a chance for a better sale. Cassie knew this in the back of her mind, but did not let it affect her practices.

Cassie and Godzilla made tremendous progress and because the pair shared a common goal, they grew even closer. When they were riding, it was as if they had become one, because both rider and horse knew what the other wanted or needed before the thought or decision was even finished in their minds. Toward the end of March, Linda pointed this out to Henry as they stood watching.

"Look at that turn," Linda said. "The timing was perfect."

"Yes," Henry replied, "they sure look good together."

"It's more than that Henry," Linda said. "Sometimes when I watch them it's like listening to opera. Every note is perfection and there's emotion behind it. It's like visual poetry."

But it was Cassie who was really improving. Godzilla, although a little rusty, was already good. Cassie, on the other hand, moved up quickly to Godzilla's level, and it was hard work that did it. Cassie spent an hour and a half each day practicing in the arena. Then she would spend twenty minutes more beside Linda watching video of her practice sessions. Linda was training Cassie's body, mind and spirit, and Cassie's improvement was dramatic.

When Rebecca Simms noticed Cassie's improvement, she became increasingly jealous. She watched Cassie working with Linda and wondered why her coach didn't act the same way with her. Then she saw Linda and Cassie watching the video. Rebecca was livid and threw a fit, and that night she told her father about Cassie's special treatment.

"You can't believe it, Daddy. Everyone is going out of their way to help her, and they're hardly paying any attention to me. It's like she's the best rider. And she hasn't even won a show."

"This is the girl who's always rude to you?" William Simms asked.

"Yes," Rebecca said, "the girl who wouldn't take care of Starfire."

The conversation resulted in a phone call to Mr. Stanley.

"Listen, Bill," Mr. Stanley said. "There's no special treatment. Cassie just wants the extra work. If Rebecca wants to watch video of her practice, she's more than welcome. We'll set it up for her."

Rebecca came in with her coach for a couple of days and watched the video of her practice. But she quickly tired of the process because she didn't want to miss her favorite television shows. And with this choice, Rebecca knew that Cassie was the harder worker and that she risked losing her competitive edge.

However, Rebecca continued to make life hard for Cassie at school, but she was finding herself increasingly alone in her efforts. Rebecca's friends had taken an interest in Cassie because she had saved Godzilla. It was becoming the hot story around the academy, and everyone grew more interested because they could watch the story unfold right before their eyes every day at practice.

As a result, Cassie was invited to her first party in nearly a year. It was to Clara Thurman's house for her birthday, and Clara delivered the invitation in person.

"I really want you to come," Clara said.

Cassie was so excited. Susan took her to the store and bought her a new dress and shoes, and Cassie spent nearly an hour getting ready.

When Henry and Olivia arrived to drive her, they both commented on how nice she looked.

"Cassie," Olivia said, "I've never seen you look so pretty."

"Yeah," Henry added with a smile, "you don't look like the same girl that cleans up horse poop every day."

Cassie blushed.

Henry and Olivia drove Cassie in Henry's old truck. As they pulled up to Clara's house, they looked completely out of place. All the other cars were Mercedes-Benzes or BMWs or SUVs. Although Cassie didn't notice, Henry did, but he didn't say anything. Cassie got out of the truck and turned to Henry and Olivia.

"Thanks, Henry. Thanks, Olivia."

"Have a good time, child," Olivia said.

"Cassie," Henry said, "if you need me to pick you up early just call."

"Okay," Cassie said.

As fate would have it, Rebecca Simms' father was dropping Rebecca off at the same time. He was driving a Hummer. When Cassie turned to go into the house, she ran right into Rebecca Simms. Rebecca gave Cassie a disgusted look.

"Who invited you?" Rebecca snarled.

Cassie was caught off guard. "Ah, Clara invited me," Cassie stammered.

"You don't belong here," Rebecca said and then marched toward the house.

Cassie waited a moment on the drive, and when Rebecca was a safe distance away, she made her way up the long drive.

Clara lived in a new subdivision in one of the better parts of North Dallas. The house was a large Colonial on an acre of land. Some people might have called it a mansion. It had a rock pool and a tennis court, and it was the biggest house Cassie had ever been in. It was a little overwhelming.

The party was in the backyard, where a tent had been set up on the tennis court. There was a deejay spinning music, and food was set up at one end of the tent. The boys were all standing at the end near the food while the girls were at the other end near the music. Cassie walked in the tent and stood for a moment, caught between the two. She looked for Clara but didn't see her. Then Rebecca walked up with two friends from school Cassie didn't know. It was an ambush.

"Cassie, where did you get your dress?" Rebecca asked.

Cassie knew this was a loaded question. She also knew she was in dangerous waters. This was Rebecca's turf.

"Why?" Cassie asked.

"Well," Rebecca said sweetly, "it looks like it came off the sale rack from some place like Ross Dress for Less."

The two girls standing next to Rebecca snickered, and Cassie felt like dirt. The dress had indeed come from Ross. In fact, Cassie's mom had stretched her budget to buy it.

"And those shoes? I bet those are from Don's Thrift Shop."

Cassie didn't know what to say and felt tears well up in her eyes. Rebecca smiled. She smelled blood and decided to go in for the kill.

"Cassie, your cheap dress and shoes make you look like the trailer park trash . . . "

Just then, someone put an arm around Cassie's shoulder. Cassie turned to see who it was and found Clara smiling at her.

"Cassie," Clara said, "I'm so glad you came. When did you get here?" Clara looked Rebecca in the eye and smiled at her. "Rebecca, it's my birthday and that means everyone is going to have a good time."

"Careful, Clara," Rebecca said. "You don't want to choose sides."

"I'm not choosing sides, Rebecca. I want you to have a good time too. Come on, Cassie. I want you to meet my cousin."

Cassie walked away with Clara. It took her a moment to recover. When she did, she pulled Clara to a stop.

"Clara, why does Rebecca hate me so much?" Cassie asked.

"I've known Rebecca since she was five years old. She's always been super-competitive, and that makes her mean. You just have to know that and don't take it personally. Just forget about it. You're here to have fun."

"Thanks, Clara," Cassie said.

"No," Clara said. "Thank you for coming to my party. Now, I want you to meet my cousin. You kind of remind me of her."

Clara's cousin was thirteen, but she looked much older. That was because she was nearly six feet tall. Like Cassie, she was also pretty.

"Cassie, this is Delanie. I know she looks older, but she's only thirteen."

"Hi, Cassie," Delanie said. "Clara told me about you. She said you're a really good horseback rider."

"Thanks," Cassie said. "Do you ride?"

"No," Delanie said. "I play volleyball."

"She also models," Clara added.

"Really?" Cassie said. "That's so great."

"You two can hang out," Clara said. "I've got to go say hi to some more people. I'll be back."

Clara walked off, and Cassie and Delanie stood for a moment, unsure of what to say.

Delanie turned to Cassie. "You know, I used to feel shy about being this tall. But now that I play volleyball, I'm glad I'm tall."

Cassie smiled. "I think being tall is cool."

"Thanks," Delanie said and smiled back. Cassie had just made another friend.

On the way home from the party, Cassie told Henry and Olivia about the good time she had at the party. She jabbered the whole way home. "Clara's house was unbelievable. It's like a mansion. And the food was so good."

"Did you meet any nice friends?" Olivia asked.

"Yeah," Cassie said, "I met Clara's cousin Delanie. She's a model and a volleyball player. She was so great. We hung out all night."

"How about boys?" Olivia asked.

"The boys were kind of silly. They just stayed in a big group all night. Every once in awhile, this one boy would look over at us. But then he would turn away. It looked like the others were teasing him because they always punched him in the arm. But toward the end of the night, all of us girls danced and the boys just stood there watching us. It was just so fun."

"I'm glad you had a good time, child," Olivia said.

"Yeah, it's definitely the most fun I've ever had at a party."

# Chapter Thirty-Three

Toward the end of April, Linda Flemming began entering Cassie in horse shows. But she made sure the shows were smaller C-class affairs because she wanted to bring Cassie along slowly. This led to some terrible arguments between Mr. Stanley and Linda because he wanted Godzilla in the big shows where he could be seen.

"Godzilla's worth half a million dollars," Mr. Stanley said. "And you have him in some beginner show. It's a waste of time, money, and effort. This is a joke, Linda."

"But Cassie needs to be prepared. Otherwise, neither of them will look good."

"I've seen them in practice. They look good enough. I want Cassie and Godzilla in Houston next week. And that's final."

"No," Linda said. "I won't let Cassie ride in a show like that. She's not ready."

"Who's paying for her to ride!" Mr. Stanley yelled, his face turning red.

"Who's coaching her!" Linda shouted back.

"I want Godzilla in Houston!" Mr. Stanley insisted.

"Fine," Linda said quietly. "He's your horse. You can do whatever you want with him. But you'll need to find another rider because Cassie's not going."

There wasn't anything Mr. Stanley could say to this. He knew that Godzilla wouldn't let anyone else ride him but Cassie. But the arguments continued until a compromise was finally reached. Cassie could ride the smaller shows provided she would be ready for the big championship shows, which started in September. Mr. Stanley wasn't happy about it, but he consoled himself with the thought that six months ago he didn't have anything until Cassie had come to his rescue. At least now he had hope.

Through April and May, Cassie rode in five shows. She always won the jumping events and she began to improve in the riding events as well. Then, in her fourth show, Cassie won every event and was the winner of the entire show. When she repeated her performance of winning every class in her fifth show, the officials said Cassie had to advance to the next level. Parents of the other riders had begun to complain that it wasn't fair.

Henry, Linda, and Cassie were standing with Godzilla when the officials delivered the news. After the officials left, Cassie turned to Godzilla.

"How do you like that, Dillie?" Cassie said. "We've been kicked out."

"Don't worry about it," Linda said. "You've earned enough points for the championships in September. I promise you, they won't kick you out of there."

"Yeah," Henry agreed. "It's all right to be kicked out because you're too good. If it was the other way around, then you would have to worry."

The first week of June brought Cassie's academic year to a close. Henry gave Cassie the week off to concentrate on her final tests. Cassie still got her riding lesson in, but as soon as she was finished, she headed straight back to her books.

When the smoke finally cleared from the flurry of tests, Cassie found that she had done well. Cassie brought her report card home on the last day of school and immediately showed it to Henry and Olivia.

Henry looked at it carefully. He had a frown on his face while he studied the report and, for a moment, Cassie thought there was something wrong. But then he looked up and smiled.

"That's real good, Cassie," he said and handed the report to Olivia.

She smiled, "Lots of Bs and an A in English."

"On my last English paper," Cassie said. "I wrote about the both of you."

"You did?" Olivia asked.

"Yep, I wrote about how you have your garden, Olivia, and how Henry has his horses. I also wrote about what you told me, Henry. About how you raise something up with the knowledge that you're doing it to let it go."

Olivia smiled. "That's real nice, child. We're proud of you."

"Yes," Henry smiled, "and you should be proud of yourself."

Cassie smiled as she thought about how important these two people had become in her life. Now it was clear to her that Henry's and Olivia's opinions mattered and their acknowledgment of her efforts gave her pride in what she had accomplished. Cassie had earned the right to feel good about herself.

# Chapter Thirty-Four

S ummer arrived and Cassie took a job as a camp counselor at the academy. Monday through Friday, Cassie spent her mornings with a group of young girls, teaching them what she knew about horses. It was a great experience for Cassie because the girls adored her and hung onto her every word. It was as if she was the biggest horse expert in the world.

But the thing the kids loved the most was the story of Godzilla. Some of the kids had heard about Godzilla being a mean horse, but that he was a great jumper. Cassie told them how sad Godzilla had been because of the death of his friend Sunny and how it had taken a long time for Cassie to become Godzilla's friend. She also said he wasn't really mean anymore. The kids always wanted to see him. At first, Cassie was reluctant. But the kids begged her so she finally brought him out.

"These are kids, Dillie. So be nice."

Godzilla was the perfect gentleman. He was always calm around the young kids and even let them pet him. It was as if the big horse had developed a sixth sense about who was innocent and who was not.

The camp day would end at lunch and then Cassie would take her riding lesson. The kids found out she was riding after camp, and they began making their parents wait so they could watch Cassie and Godzilla practicing. The kids would sit on the fence along the arena and cheer as Cassie and Godzilla went over a jump. They cheered so loud once that Mr. Stanley came out of the office to see what the noise was. He was glad to see that Godzilla had his own cheering section because he thought it might help the horse's reputation, which would help get him sold.

But there was one little girl named Rowan who was especially smitten with Godzilla. She was seven years old, and would wait patiently until all the children were gone. Then she followed Cassie around asking questions such as "Why are people so afraid of him?" "Did Sunny's death make him mean?" "Do you think he still misses Sunny?" There were so many questions that Cassie began to feel Rowan was pestering her. Even Henry noticed.

"That little girl grills you like a cheese sandwich," Henry said with a smile.

Cassie laughed. "I know. It's like she's everywhere."

But later that day, a sad-looking woman approached Cassie. It was Rowan's mother. "I just wanted to thank you," she said. "It's been a really hard summer for Rowan because her sister died of cancer in April. They were identical twins."

"Oh," Cassie said, "I'm sorry. I didn't know."

"Yes, it's been a hard time for all of us. But it's been especially hard for Rowan. Rowan can't understand why she didn't get cancer too. It's almost like she feels guilty because she's the one who lived."

"I've felt that way before," Cassie said. "My dad died of cancer last summer."

"I kind of thought that you knew something about tragedy. People who have survived tragedy, I don't know, it's like they're more aware somehow. Anyway, I want to thank you. You and Godzilla are all Rowan talks about. It's like she has found something to care about again."

Now Cassie understood why Rowan couldn't get enough of Godzilla. It was because Rowan was drawn to his story just like Cassie had been.

After that, Cassie took the little girl under her wing. She named Rowan her special assistant, and when she asked her questions, Cassie understood why. She told Rowan everything, such as how terrible she felt after her dad died and about taking Godzilla to the horses' graveyard to say goodbye to Sunny. Rowan wanted to see the grave, so Cassie took her. Rowan cried, and Cassie hugged her. Cassie also encouraged Rowan to talk to Godzilla about her sister.

"Rowan, talking to Dillie always makes me feel better. He just seems to understand."

On the Fourth of July, Rowan's parents were having a little party and invited Cassie to join them. Rowan was so excited when Cassie arrived that she wouldn't let Cassie out of her sight. Then, at around seven, everyone from the party walked over to the high school to watch a fireworks show.

This was hard for Cassie. Every time she saw fireworks burst in the sky, she thought of her dad. But somehow, being with little Rowan made the pain more bearable. All through the show, Rowan sat on Cassie's lap saying things such as "Isn't that pretty?" or "That one's gigantic!"

Cassie thought about Henry's words of "missing what was" and finding a way to fill the emptiness with new memories. Being with Rowan on the Fourth of July would be a memory to help fill Cassie's emptiness. It also seemed to help Rowan too. As the family walked home from the high school, Rowan suddenly turned to Cassie.

"I'm glad you came with me, Cassie. If you hadn't, I would have been alone."

Rowan then reached out and took Cassie's hand, and they walked back to the house together. Little Rowan stayed near Cassie the rest of the night.

On the last day of camp, Rowan presented Cassie with a gift. It was a book Rowan had made with beautiful drawings of Cassie and Godzilla. There was also a story that included the horses' graveyard and in the end, Cassie and Godzilla won the championship.

It turned out that Rowan's mother wrote children's books and had helped Rowan put it together. She also asked Cassie if she could send it out because she thought there was a chance it could get published. Cassie said, "Sure." It was a great little book and Cassie especially liked the title, "Cassie and Dillie."

But it was also a tearful goodbye for Cassie and Rowan because Rowan's family was moving to Los Angeles. Rowan cried and didn't want to let go of Cassie. But Cassie promised her she would write and that seemed to help. Rowan's mother took her by the hand. But the little girl broke away and ran to Cassie for one last hug.

"I love you, Cassie," Rowan said.

Cassie felt tears well up in her eyes. "I love you too, Rowan."

Rowan then walked away with her mom and Cassie smiled. Rowan was starting to heal.

Cassie looked at the book again. She decided to show it to Godzilla and walked to his stall.

"Look, Dillie. Little Rowan wrote a book about us. We might be famous."

Cassie held the book up for Godzilla to see, and the big horse immediately tried to eat it. He got a hold of it, and Cassie had to pull it away from him.

Cassie laughed. "So much for being famous." She gave the big horse a hug. "Thanks, Dillie, for being so good to Rowan."

*Chapter Thirty-Five*

In August, the academy organized a horse show just for its own riders. Because there were close to a hundred riders at the academy, it was a fairly large show. All three arenas were used.

Cassie and Henry had a lot of work to do. In addition to preparing the horses, Cassie helped Linda organize all the riders according to skill level. She found she would be competing with Rebecca Simms for the first time. There were also several older riders who were in the same events as Cassie. Even Linda decided she would ride for the fun of it.

"Linda, you're going to be riding against me?" Cassie asked.

"Yes," Linda said, "and you better beat me or I'm going to make you work extra hard next week."

However, when it got closer to the day of the show, Rebecca decided not to ride. She had already won several shows that year and thought the academy show was a waste of time. Instead, she and her family went on vacation to their house in the Bahamas.

That left Cassie as the youngest rider in her class to face down the competition from the best riders at the academy—riders who had won several championships at different times in their careers.

It was a fun day for Cassie. She and Godzilla were in three classes. Two were for riding and one was for jumping. Cassie and Godzilla took a fifth and a third in the riding events. But what surprised everyone was that Cassie and Godzilla won the jumping event in a very convincing manner. They beat some very good riders by such a wide margin in terms of their time that it started the whole academy talking. Cassie and Godzilla were for real.

When Rebecca Simms returned from her vacation, the first thing she heard about was Cassie and Godzilla. All her friends were talking about them, and when they described how Cassie and Godzilla won, they made it sound as if the two were unbeatable. Rebecca began to worry. So she talked it over with her father.

"Daddy," Rebecca said, "there's a girl riding at the academy. She's doing really well."

"Who is she?" Simms asked.

"It's that Cassie girl, the one they gave all the special treatment to."

"You mean the girl who was rude to you?"

"Yes," Rebecca said, "same one."

"Are you worried about her beating you?"

"I wasn't until she started riding Godzilla."

"Godzilla? You mean that horse that went crazy? I thought the horse wouldn't let anyone ride him?"

"He won't let anyone ride him. Just Cassie. It's just that Godzilla is a really good horse. I wouldn't be worried about Cassie except that Godzilla is so good."

William Simms began to ask around about Cassie and Godzilla. The reports he got were that Cassie and Godzilla had indeed beaten all the best riders at the academy. But it eased his mind because the reports also said that without Godzilla, Cassie wasn't that good. Simms was also pleased to learn that Mr. Stanley intended to sell Godzilla the first chance he got.

August also brought Cassie's thirteenth birthday. In the morning, she walked down to work at the academy. When Henry saw her, he smiled. "Happy birthday. I guess I can't call you 'child' anymore."

"I don't mind if you do."

"No. You're not a child anymore. You're a young woman now, and that requires a certain amount of respect."

Cassie smiled at this, but there was a sadness behind the smile. Henry's words reflected what Cassie was feeling this morning. She had awakened to find herself a teenager, and when she thought about it, it somehow made her feel different. As if she was leaving something behind and, after hearing Henry's words, she supposed it was her childhood. Part of the sadness was also the fact that her father wasn't there to share the day with her. He had been such a big part of her childhood, and now that she was a teenager, she felt as if she was leaving him behind too.

At the end of the day, Henry found Cassie with Godzilla. She had just finished feeding him.

"Cassie, it's time for dinner. Olivia's cooked your favorite dish."

"Fried chicken?"

"If that's what it is, then that's what she's cooked."

When Cassie and Henry walked in the trailer door, Cassie was almost bowled over by the sound of "Surprise!"

Cassie couldn't believe it when she saw her mom, Olivia, and Linda standing in front of her. Then she saw two other guests, Clara and her cousin Delanie. Cassie stepped back and laughed.

"For me?" was all she could manage to say. When she recovered, she asked, "Who's responsible for this?"

"I am," Susan said.

Cassie walked over and hugged her mom. She walked around the room and hugged everyone individually and said, "Thank you."

Then Cassie stepped back and looked at the group. She had a big smile on her face and her eyes glistened from tears of happiness.

"I've been so sad all day. But now I'm so happy I could do a cartwheel."

Everyone laughed.

Then Olivia said, "Dinner's ready. So let's eat."

Olivia had put the extra leaves in the table and everyone fit nicely. Cassie sat between Clara and Delanie, and they had a great time talking about horses, riding, and the prospects for a new school year. Henry also enjoyed himself. At one point he made everyone laugh.

"Who would have thought it, Olivia? We started out with nothing but boys in our lives, and now we got nothing but women. It's become a regular sorority house."

At another point, Olivia got a big smile on her face when Clara and Delanie announced, "The fried chicken was the best we've ever tasted."

When dinner was over, Olivia said, "It's time for cake."

"Could we go down to the academy?" Cassie asked.

"Why?" Susan asked.

"Because I want to blow out my candles with Dillie. Maybe it will help make my birthday wish come true."

"We can do that," Henry said. "I'll carry the cake."

"Yeah," Linda chimed in, "I could use a little walk after that great dinner."

So the group walked down to the academy. It was a beautiful night for a walk. The days were still long, and even though it was nearly eight o'clock, there was still plenty of light to find their way on the path. It was also a warm night and the sound of cicadas filled the air.

The group arrived at Godzilla's stall and the big horse came right up to Cassie. Cassie rubbed his neck.

"We have to make a wish, Dillie. You have to help me."

Henry lit the candles and everyone sang "Happy Birthday." Then Cassie closed her eyes for a long moment. She blew out her candles in one breath. Cassie reached over, hugged Godzilla and whispered in his ear. No one could hear what she said, but they all knew what Cassie was wishing for, that Godzilla would always be with her.

"You blew out your candles in one breath," Clara said. "That means your wish will come true."

Cassie thought for a moment. "Last year, I told Olivia my wish and it came true. I want to tell her my wish again."

Cassie walked over and pushed close to Olivia, whispering in her ear. Olivia smiled and nodded her head.

"That's a mighty fine wish, Cassie."

# Chapter Thirty-Six

September brought with it the new school year, and Cassie had entered seventh grade. She wasted no time dedicating herself to her schoolwork, and went to the library every day to do her homework at lunch. Clara was so impressed by Cassie's decision that she started doing it too. Cassie and Clara would sit together studying, and if either of them had a question about the work, the other usually had the answer.

At the academy, Cassie continued to make enormous strides with her riding. Linda was pleased with Cassie's progress and was certain Cassie was going to do well. After beating all the best riders at the academy, Cassie now had the confidence to compete with the best riders in the state. Her first championship show was only a week away.

But on Monday, she went to the office intending to watch a video with Linda. While she was waiting for Linda to arrive, she accidentally heard Mr. Stanley talking on the phone.

"David, you've got to come to the show. Godzilla's back, and I've never seen him so strong. He's a different horse. He'd be perfect for you."

Cassie felt a lump rise in her throat.

"All right," Mr. Stanley said, "I'll see you at the show."

Hearing this conversation changed everything for Cassie. She became afraid, so much so that she felt sick to her stomach. Then Linda walked in.

"Hey, Cassie. Let's look at the tape."

But Cassie didn't want to look at the tape. She didn't want to ride in the show anymore.

"Uh, Linda," Cassie said. "I'm not feeling very well. I think I'm going to go home and lie down."

Cassie left the office and headed for home. As she walked up the path, she broke down and cried. Her worst fear was becoming a reality. Mr. Stanley was going to sell Godzilla the first chance he had. She felt as if she were losing someone again, and memories of her father's death came flooding back.

The remaining part of the week was horrible for Cassie. At night, she couldn't sleep. At school, she couldn't concentrate and her homework went undone. At practice, she did so poorly that Linda became alarmed.

"Cassie, are you all right?"

"I'm okay," Cassie lied.

But Linda was worried. This wasn't the same girl she had been working with for the past year. Linda tried to coax an answer out of Cassie, but she refused to talk.

In fact, Cassie didn't confide in anyone. She was too afraid that if she told someone that she didn't want to ride, then Mr. Stanley would find out. He could get mad and take Godzilla away from her. No, she had a dilemma: If she didn't ride, she could lose Godzilla, and if she did ride, she could lose Godzilla. She didn't know what to do, so she kept her problem to herself. She didn't even tell Godzilla.

When the day of the show arrived, Cassie was distraught. She thought about pretending to be sick. But when Henry knocked on her trailer door, she decided that she had better ride. The people in her life would know she was faking, and that would lead to the truth that she didn't want to ride. Mr. Stanley would be livid because a lot of money had already been spent on entrance fees, not to mention months of free riding lessons.

Henry and Cassie drove down to the academy to get Godzilla. There were several other people there, including Rebecca Simms and her father. When Cassie saw Rebecca, she remembered that she would be facing Rebecca in competition for the first time. Rebecca gave her a dirty look. Then Rebecca pulled on her father's sleeve to get his attention and pointed at Cassie, making her very uncomfortable.

Cassie went directly to Godzilla's stall while Henry hitched the truck to the horse trailer. The big horse seemed excited as if he knew today was a big day. The athlete in Godzilla was ready to compete.

Cassie stood at the stall door and Godzilla came to her. She rubbed his neck and the big horse rubbed his face against hers.

"If I hold you back today, Dillie, just know there's a reason and that we aren't supposed to win."

When they arrived at the Dallas Fairgrounds, there were hundreds of people already there, and more were arriving. It was the biggest crowd Cassie had ever seen. All the best riders from the Dallas area were there.

They parked, and Henry went to find their stall while Cassie unloaded Godzilla. Mr. Stanley had paid for a private stall. He wanted to make sure they had everything they needed to do well. Henry returned, and they headed for the barn.

Cassie started to prepare Godzilla. At their other shows, she would talk to the horse the entire time she worked. It had become their routine. She would say things like, "Today we're going to have fun," or "Rhythm, Dillie, today's about rhythm." Her words served as a form of mental preparation for both Godzilla and herself.

But today Cassie was quiet, and the big horse sensed that something was wrong. He reached over several times and rubbed his face against Cassie's.

"Dillie, it's going to be a hard day."

Cassie had decided that they would do well enough only to be competitive. But they wouldn't win. So she held Godzilla back. In their first class they took sixth out of twelve riders. Rebecca Simms won the class and was all smiles when she realized she had beat Cassie.

In their second class, Linda knew something was definitely wrong. Cassie and Godzilla took ninth. They even missed a fence. Unfortunately, Linda happened to be sitting next to Mr. Stanley when she voiced her opinion.

"What's she doing? Cassie's holding him back when she should be giving him some leg. She never did that in the workouts."

"You don't think she's doing it on purpose?" Mr. Stanley asked.

"Why would she do that?" Linda asked.

But Henry knew what Cassie was doing. Now that Mr. Stanley was suspicious, Henry knew Cassie was going to have a problem.

After their ride, Cassie was walking Godzilla back to his stall when Mr. Stanley approached them. Godzilla's ears went back and Mr. Stanley stepped back.

"Ah, Cassie, I need to talk to you."

Cassie led Godzilla back to his stall and made sure he had everything he needed. When she walked out of the barn, she found Mr. Stanley waiting for her. Henry and Linda were waiting there as well.

"Cassie, what's going on with you and Godzilla?" Mr. Stanley asked.

"What do you mean?" Cassie replied.

"Come on, Cassie. I've seen you in your workouts. You've never looked this bad."

"It's just a little overwhelming," Cassie replied evasively. "There's so many people and the riders are all so good."

"Okay," Mr. Stanley said. "Just try to relax. You and Godzilla can do better than this."

Mr. Stanley walked away, leaving Cassie with Linda and Henry. Linda talked to her about her riding and the choices she had made. Cassie listened attentively, but deep down she felt horrible because there were so many people wanting to help her and she was blowing it on purpose. She felt like a liar.

Cassie's next event wasn't until the next day. She had two more rides on Sunday, and the show would be finished. Cassie was tired and just wanted to go home. She asked Henry to drive her, and as they drove across town, Henry tried to get her to open up.

"Tough day, kid," Henry said.

"Yea," Cassie said quietly.

"Are you afraid, Cassie?" Henry asked.

"No. I just don't want to ride. I feel like I'm only riding because Mr. Stanley wants me to."

Cassie closed down and didn't speak the rest of the journey home. She was relieved that Henry didn't ask her any more questions. When they got home, Cassie went straight to her trailer. She fixed some soup and went to bed. She was exhausted from feeling so bad.

On Sunday, Cassie awoke still feeling horrible, and she felt even worse after her mother told her she had taken the day off from work so she could watch her ride. Olivia wanted to come too.

And when Cassie returned to the fairgrounds, she still wasn't confiding in anyone about her problem. For her first class, she decided she would do a little better, but still not well enough to get noticed. Cassie figured fourth place would do the trick.

But it's hard to hold back and not try your best. Cassie was a very good rider when she tried her hardest, but she wasn't good enough to do less than that, and she miscalculated. She held Godzilla back too much in the wrong places and they knocked down three fences. They placed last in their class.

It was a dismal performance, and Mr. Stanley was livid. Henry saw him look at Linda, his face turning red from rage. When Mr. Stanley rose from his seat and headed toward Cassie, Henry knew he'd better follow.

Cassie had just finished taking Godzilla to his stall and was walking out when Mr. Stanley caught up with her.

"I know you're doing it on purpose. You think that horse belongs to you, but I own him and pay for his feed. If you don't ride better in the next class, I'm going to lock Godzilla back up in the shed and you'll never see him again."

Cassie started to cry just as Henry walked up. Henry took one look at Cassie and then turned to Mr. Stanley.

"What's going on here, Stanley?"

"It's none of your business, Henry."

"Anything to do with Cassie is my business."

"All right then," Mr. Stanley said. The veins were popping out on his forehead he was so mad. "Cassie has one more class. If she doesn't ride like I know she can, then that's it. No more Godzilla, and no more riding lessons. It'll be over."

Mr. Stanley walked away, leaving Henry and Cassie alone. She broke down crying and Henry put his arm around her shoulders.

"Hey, don't cry," Henry said.

"It's just that if I ride him and we win, then someone's going to buy him."

"Hey, hey, hey," Henry said gently. "Remember what I told you about raising something up to let it go."

"I know, it's just too hard."

"Cassie, you got to remember what Godzilla is. He's a jumper and you're a jumper too. It's not fair to either of you to hold back."

"I'm sorry. Everyone's tried to help me and I'm letting everyone down."

"No reason to be sorry about that. You're just trying to do what you think is right for the future. But you can't think about that. We don't know what's going to happen tomorrow. But you owe it to yourself and you owe it to Godzilla to do your best. No matter what. That's all there is. That's all you've got. Just today."

Cassie looked at Henry. She wiped the tears from her eyes.

"You're right, Henry. If I ride my best I might lose him, and if I don't ride my best I might lose him. I better talk to Dillie. I know he's wondering what's going on. I can't believe we knocked down three fences."

Cassie walked off to Godzilla's stall. Henry didn't know what was going to happen, but something told him Cassie would do better in the next class.

When she got to the stall, Godzilla came over and rubbed his face against hers. She stroked him tenderly.

"Dillie, I'm sorry I've been holding you back. I know I tell you everything, but I didn't tell you this. There are people here to see you, who maybe want to buy you. That's why I haven't been trying. But this isn't right. I feel terrible, and you feel like you've let me down. So if you want to really try in the next class, I'm with you."

Try they did. It was the final class of the day and the stands were packed. A lot of people had heard about Godzilla and Cassie. Word spreads quickly at these events about new horses and riders because it's a close-knit group. Expectations had been high for the young girl and the mean horse, but after they had done so poorly, most people had written them off.

But in this last class, Cassie did not disappoint. She rode Godzilla with great speed and skill and proved that the gossip had merit. After the first round, there were three riders left, a sixteen-year-old boy, Rebecca Simms, and Cassie.

As they stood for the final round, Rebecca looked over at Cassie.

"I've been beating you all day," Rebecca said. "And I'm going to beat you now."

Cassie patted Godzilla on the neck.

"Hear that, Dillie? Rebecca thinks she's going to beat us."

Godzilla let out a snort and Cassie smiled.

"Dillie says he doesn't think so."

Rebecca gave Cassie a dirty look and then it was her turn. Rebecca rode well. In fact, it was one of the best rides of her life. She didn't knock down any fences and her time was her best for the entire show. When she was finished and heard her time, she thought she had won for sure.

Next, the sixteen-year-old boy rode. It was a very good ride, but he didn't come close to Rebecca.

Cassie came last. She rode Godzilla as fast as she had ever ridden him. They didn't miss a fence, and when they were finished, people in the stands cheered. Cassie then found out she had beaten Rebecca's time. She let out a little cheer of her own. "Dillie, we did it. Now, that was rhythm."

Cassie rode Godzilla out of the arena to where Susan, Olivia, Henry and Linda were waiting to congratulate her.

"Cassie," Susan said, "I couldn't believe you were my daughter. You were great."

Everyone also chimed in, and for the first time in a week Cassie felt good. Not only because she had won, but because she had done what she loved the way it should be done. There was honesty in her win.

In the stands, Mr. Stanley was fielding questions about Godzilla. Cassie's worst fear was coming true because she and Godzilla had done well enough to get noticed. One man, David Jensen, was in his thirties and rode for a living. He was always on the lookout for new talent, and he had come to the event just to see Godzilla jump. He was impressed.

"When I heard he was jumping again, I was surprised," Jensen said. "The horse has made a great comeback."

"Sure, Godzilla's back," Mr. Stanley said. "If you were on him, he could win the Grand Prix."

"How much did you say you wanted?" Jensen asked.

"Five hundred thousand, and he's worth every cent. Next year he'll be worth more."

"I'll be over on Monday to look at him. My sponsors and I are looking for another horse, and he just might fit."

"Good," Mr. Stanley said. "I'll have him ready for you. Afternoon would be best."

Of course Mr. Stanley wanted David Jensen to come in the afternoon. It was the only time Cassie would be there to show Godzilla. Without Cassie, Mr. Stanley had no idea what the horse would do.

# Chapter Thirty-Seven

On Monday, Cassie finished all of her homework at lunch and was able to go straight to the academy when she got home. As usual, she found Henry at the crossties. But the look on his face told Cassie there was something wrong.

"Cassie, I'm afraid I've got some bad news."

"What is it, Henry?"

"A man is here to look at Godzilla."

Cassie froze. "I knew if I rode well someone would buy him. Why did I do it?"

"Now don't jump to conclusions. The man's just here to look at him, and Mr. Stanley wants you to get him ready."

"I won't do it. Tell Mr. Stanley I went home sick. He can show Godzilla himself."

"Wait a minute, Cassie," Henry said firmly. "Mr. Stanley's been good to you. He's given you a job and riding lessons. I know how much you love Godzilla, but he's not yours. Mr. Stanley owns him, and he can do with him as he pleases. I'm not saying it's right, but you've always known this day could come."

Cassie started to cry. "What if his new owner is mean to him?"

"The man coming to see Godzilla is David Jensen. He's a top rider and a little full of himself. But he's basically a good man and treats his horses very well. David Jensen is the kind of owner you want for Godzilla."

Cassie felt like a three-year-old being told to give up her most-prized possession.

"Cassie," Henry said, "you need to try to make this happen. You need to do it for Godzilla."

Cassie nodded her head. "All right. I trust you. If you think I should do it, then I will."

Henry smiled. "Good girl. Don't worry. Most things have a way of working themselves out."

Cassie turned and walked to Godzilla's stall. As always, the big horse was happy to see her. He greeted Cassie by rubbing his face against hers.

"Dillie, there's a man coming to see you. Henry says he's a good man and would give you a good home. He's also a great rider and could take you to all the big shows. So I want you to give him a chance."

Cassie got a halter from the tack room. She walked back thinking that the day had finally come. She and Godzilla were to be parted. She put the halter on Godzilla and led him to the crossties. Cassie groomed her favorite horse like he had never been groomed before. All the while, she talked to Godzilla as she fought back tears.

"Dillie, this doesn't mean we'll never see each other again. Maybe I could come to some of your big shows. Who knows, Dillie, you might even make it all the way to the Olympics, and I could come watch."

Cassie put the academy's best bridle and saddle on Godzilla, and when she was finished, Godzilla looked very handsome. Then Cassie took the bridle in her hands and pulled it so Godzilla had to look Cassie in the eyes.

"Dillie, I want you to be on your best behavior. This is important."

Cassie walked Godzilla out to the first arena and then called out to Henry. "Henry! He's ready."

"Good job, Cassie. I'll go tell Mr. Stanley."

Henry walked to the offices. A few moments later he returned with Mr. Stanley and David Jensen. Jensen was handsome and slender. He also had an unusual gait, like a man who knew he was good at something. His strides were long and confident. Mr. Stanley and Jensen stopped at the fence to admire Godzilla.

"He sure is a good-looking horse," Jensen said.

"Yep," Mr. Stanley replied. "He's got 'champion' written all over him."

"I'm just curious," Jensen said. "How did he get the name 'Godzilla'?"

"My father named him that. When he was born my daddy took one look at his big feet and said, 'He's going to be huge.' He thought about it for a second, and the name 'Godzilla' popped into his head."

Cassie had never heard the story before, and it made her smile. She leaned over and whispered in Godzilla's ear.

"You hear that, Dillie? You were born with big feet, just like me."

"I want to take a closer look," Jensen said.

"Uh, you go on ahead," Mr. Stanley said. "Ill just wait here."

David Jensen gave Mr. Stanley a curious look. Then he climbed over the fence and strode confidently toward Godzilla. Godzilla looked at him, and his ears went back. Cassie noticed and grew worried.

"Easy, Dillie. Best behavior. Remember?"

When Jensen walked up, he smiled. "You must be Cassie."

"Yes," she replied.

"I've heard about what a great job you've done with this horse."

"Thanks."

Jensen walked around Godzilla admiring his legs and muscles. "How is he to ride? Is he smooth?"

"Very," Cassie answered.

David Jensen put his hand on Godzilla's shoulder. Godzilla's ears went back.

"Easy, boy," Jensen said confidently and rubbed the big horse's neck. Cassie still held the reins, looking Godzilla in the eye. He relaxed a little, and for a moment, Cassie thought everything was going to work out.

"Well," Jensen said, "I guess I should take him for a test drive."

Cassie became alarmed. "Mr. Jensen, I don't think you should try that just yet. You should probably spend some time with him first."

Jensen grimaced as if she had just insulted him. "Nonsense," he said. "Horses love me. There's never been a horse I couldn't ride."

"But Dillie isn't like other horses."

"Everyone says that about their horses. I don't have time to keep coming here. I need to make a decision today. Give me the reins."

Cassie didn't know what was going to happen. She handed the reins to Jensen and then backed away. Cassie walked over to the fence, climbed up, and sat next to where Henry was standing.

"What do you think will happen?" Henry asked.

"I don't know," Cassie said. "But he should have spent more time with Dillie."

Jensen spent a few moments rubbing Godzilla's neck. Then, he moved to the side and climbed on. Once on top, Jensen reached down and rubbed Godzilla's neck.

"There, boy. Easy."

Jensen kicked Godzilla, but Godzilla didn't move. He kicked again. There was still no response. Jensen wondered what was going on. Godzilla's ears went back.

"Uh-oh," Cassie said. "That's not good."

David Jensen leaned over to look at Godzilla. This was a mistake. Suddenly, the horse sprinted forward, catching Jensen off guard. He was thrown onto his back, just barely hanging on. Godzilla tore around the arena with Jensen on his back yelling, "WHOA! WHOA!" Jensen started to recover, but just as he sat up, Godzilla hit the brakes. Jensen was launched in the air and thrown over the top of Godzilla's head. He landed on the ground hard, lying on his stomach, dazed.

But Godzilla wasn't finished. The horse ran up to David Jensen, reached his head down, and bit him hard on the butt. Jensen let out a squeal, scrambled to his feet, and started to run. Godzilla chased him, but Cassie leapt off the fence and grabbed the reins.

Everyone stood for a moment with their mouths open, trying to digest what had happened. Finally, David Jensen looked at Mr. Stanley and said, "Your horse tried to kill me."

Mr. Stanley looked stricken—half a million dollars had just slipped through his fingers.

Cassie looked at Godzilla. "Dillie! That was *not* nice. Not nice at all."

# Chapter Thirty-Eight

Even though Cassie felt bad that Godzilla had thrown David Jensen, the horse's actions served to free her from the fear that someone would buy him. Cassie figured there weren't many people around who could afford to pay half a million dollars for a horse that might not let you ride it. For most people, Godzilla's reputation was just too big of a risk.

Still, Mr. Stanley was hopeful. He approached Cassie about riding in the big show in San Antonio the next weekend. Mr. Stanley knew it would be the best chance he had to get Godzilla sold. Cassie, freed from her fear, agreed immediately. She wanted to find out if they were really good enough to face the best talent around. But Mr. Stanley needed to be sure he was going to get what he was paying for.

"Cassie, I need you to promise me that you'll ride your best because it's going to be very expensive to send you to San Antonio."

"Don't worry about that, Mr. Stanley. Dillie and I won't let you down."

"Okay," Mr. Stanley said. He started to walk away, but stopped and turned back to Cassie.

"Why do you think Godzilla did that to David Jensen?"

Cassie was thoughtful. "Mr. Jensen shouldn't have just climbed on top of Dillie like he was just any horse. If someone wants to buy him, they should try and get to know him first. Dillie needs to feel that they're a good person."

Mr. Stanley listened. He suddenly realized how stupid he had been. This young girl had saved the horse. She knew more about Godzilla than anyone.

"You know," Mr. Stanley said, "I don't know why I didn't ask your advice before. From now on, I will."

At practice that week, Cassie felt really inspired. Linda was pleased because Cassie had worked hard like the Cassie of old. On Thursday, Linda had some advice about the show in San Antonio.

"San Antonio is a huge show, Cassie. There will be people everywhere, and you'll be facing the best competition there is. People even come from out of state to compete. But if you focus on your riding and don't let the size of the show distract you, then you'll do fine."

"I wish you were coming with us," Cassie said.

"I wish I was too," Linda replied. "I love the San Antonio show. You know, I won it one year. But my youngest sister only gets married once, and if I missed that, my family would disown me. Even though I'll be in Denver, I'll be sending you all my good thoughts."

On Friday, Cassie didn't go to school. Instead, she woke up at four in the morning with Henry to get Godzilla loaded in the trailer. They had packed everything they needed the night before so they could get on the road early. Henry wanted to make sure they missed the Dallas rush hour.

After Godzilla was loaded, they drove back to the trailer park to say goodbye to Susan and Olivia. Susan had to work and Olivia said her back just didn't feel well enough for an eight-hour drive. The two women hugged Cassie and wished her luck.

"What an adventure," Susan said. "I wish I was coming with you."

"I wish you were too, Mom,' Cassie said, hugging her tightly.

"Take care of my baby, Henry," Susan said.

"I sure enough will."

"Maybe," Olivia said, "we should be telling Cassie to take care of Henry. I know how you get lost."

The women laughed and Henry smiled.

They soon found themselves on the open Texas highway in time for a beautiful sunrise. Cassie was so excited she talked Henry's ear off. Her fear of losing Godzilla had all but vanished with David Jensen's test drive.

"There's nobody in their right mind who would pay half a million dollars for a horse that won't let you ride it."

"That's true," Henry replied. "Maybe you should approach Mr. Stanley about a partnership. Godzilla's got another good nine years of jumping left. If you keep working on your riding, there could be prize money waiting. Not to mention sponsorships. There's a lot of money at the top levels, and Godzilla could get you there."

Cassie loved that idea and lit up like a Christmas tree. "You really think so?"

"I've seen it happen."

"Henry, you are so smart. How did you get so smart?"

"I don't know how smart I am. But I've learned a few things along the way. I've also read a lot of philosophy."

"What's 'philosophy'? I mean, I've heard the term, but what is it exactly?"

"Well, it's kind of like thinking about the reasons for everything, and after you've learned about the reasons, you choose a set of ideals and beliefs you can live your life by. It was a huge help to me when my sons died."

"Are there rules like in math and English?"

"Sort of. But it's more like creating a map. I've studied a lot of writings, and different philosophers had different ways of looking at life. But I always find myself going back to the source, this guy named Socrates. He was a Greek who lived over two thousand years ago. He said everyone wants to be happy, and the real way to be happy is to simply do the right thing. Now doing the wrong thing might make you happy in the short run, but it won't last. Your happiness will disappear. The only way to be truly happy is to do the right thing."

"I always want to do the right thing. It's just that sometimes it's hard to know what the right thing is."

"That's where life comes in. You're always learning, and the more you learn then the more you'll know what the right thing is."

"The right thing," Cassie said. "I'll remember that."

They arrived in San Antonio at just after 3:00 P.M. and traveled around the city for nearly an hour looking for the fairgrounds. When they finally found it, Henry was relieved.

"Now don't be telling Olivia I got lost," Henry said.

"I'll have to think about it. It might be the right thing to do." Cassie smiled at Henry and he laughed.

Several trailers were there with people unloading their horses. Henry found the official in charge, who directed them to the stall they had been assigned. As fate would have it, their stall was right next to Rebecca Simms's. She was there with her father and mother checking on Starfire as Cassie, Henry and Godzilla walked up.

"Hi, Rebecca," Henry said.

"Hello," Rebecca said coolly. Then Rebecca saw that Godzilla was going to be next door to Starfire. "Godzilla's going to be next to us?"

"Looks that way," Cassie said.

"Godzilla?" William Simms asked. "Honey, isn't he that dangerous horse everyone's afraid of?"

"Yep," Rebecca said.

"I don't want you next to us," William Simms said to Henry.

"I don't have any choice in the matter, Mr. Simms. They just assign the stalls. They probably thought that because we're from the same academy we would want to be near each other."

"I don't want to be next to you," William Simms said. "Is Stanley around? I want to have a word with him. I don't know why he would allow a dangerous horse to enter a show."

"Dillie's not dangerous," Cassie said. "He just doesn't like some people."

"That's not what I heard," Mrs. Simms said. "I heard he tried to kill David Jensen."

"That's not true," Cassie said. Cassie opened the stall door and led Godzilla in. She stepped out and closed the door. The big horse walked up to her and she scratched him behind the ears.

"Dillie's here to compete," Cassie said, "not to hurt anyone."

"You'd better hope so," Simms said. "Because if he tries to bite my daughter or our horse, I'm going to demand that Stanley get rid of you and that horse once and for all."

The Simms family walked away. Henry stood watching them with a disgusted look on his face. "It's funny what money does to some people. For some it's a gift to be appreciated and enjoyed. For others, it just ruins them."

# Chapter Thirty-Nine

That night, Henry and Cassie stayed at Motel 6. Mr. Stanley was paying for the trip, but he wasn't about to pay for the Hilton. Not surprisingly, a lot of other horse people were staying there as well. Horse shows are expensive and most people are on a budget. No expense is spared for their horses, but for themselves, it's Motel 6 and Burger King.

In the morning, Cassie and Henry ate an early breakfast at Mo's Diner and then headed to the fairgrounds. A lot of people were already there preparing their horses for the day's events. When they arrived at the stall, they found that the Simms family had hired a groom for their horse.

"Looks like Rebecca is sleeping in," Cassie said.

"Well, the early bird catches the worm," Henry said.

For some reason, Godzilla's stall was completely closed, both top and bottom doors. Cassie opened the top door and Godzilla walked up to her. She immediately noticed there was a huge welt on his nose where someone had hit him.

"Dillie! Henry, someone hit him."

"What?" Henry asked. Henry walked up to see. The groom who was working on Starfire walked over. "*Diablo loco,*" the groom said and pointed at Godzilla. "*Diablo loco,*" he said again.

"What's he saying?" Cassie asked.

"He's saying 'crazy devil.' "

Just then, another man walked up. "Is this your horse?" the man asked.

"Not exactly," Henry said. "But we're responsible for him. What's happened?"

"A man named Salistino was grooming this horse," the man said pointing at Starfire. "He got too close and your horse grabbed his arm. Your horse wouldn't let go, and I had to hit him with a shovel. Salistino was hurt and had to go to the hospital."

Cassie looked into Godzilla's stall and saw an apple with something sticking out of it.

"What's that?" Cassie said.

She opened the lower stall door. The two men backed away. They were obviously afraid of Godzilla, and when Cassie walked in the stall, their eyes grew wide with surprise. She picked up the apple and saw that there were pills sticking out of it.

"This is why Dillie bit the groom," Cassie said. "He was trying to poison him."

Henry took the apple and showed it to the two men.

"What's this?" Henry asked. "We want to talk to the groom that got bit. He tried to poison our horse."

The man who spoke English backed away and put up his hands defiantly.

"No," the man said, "Salistino's a good man."

"Where is he?" Henry asked.

"I don't know," the man said and walked away. Henry looked at the other man. He shrugged and went back to work on Starfire. Henry looked at Cassie.

"Good man, indeed. William Simms is mixed up in this. I better go lodge a complaint."

"I'll get Dillie ready to ride and see if he's okay."

"Good, I'll be back as soon as I can."

When Henry got to the officials' booth, he immediately got the attention of an elderly man.

"I need to lodge a complaint," Henry said. "Somebody tried to drug our horse."

"Which horse is yours?" The elderly man asked.

"Godzilla."

"Oh," the elderly man said. "Just a moment."

The elderly man walked over and spoke to a woman. She looked over at Henry and then picked up a clipboard. She looked the clipboard over and then walked directly to Henry. "We were just getting ready to come to your stall to tell you that you can't ride in this show."

"Why?" Henry asked.

"Someone's filed a complaint," the woman said. "It seems your horse has attacked a groom, and he's too dangerous to let ride."

"Who filed the complaint?" Henry asked.

"That's confidential," the woman said.

"Well," Henry said, "if it was William Simms, I want to file a complaint against him and his groom."

"For what?" the woman asked.

Henry held up the apple for the woman to see. "This is why our horse bit the groom. We found this in his stall. A groom working for William Simms tried to feed it to our horse."

The woman paused. She looked at the apple with the pills and then at Henry. "This certainly changes things," she said.

After Henry left the officials' booth, he went to talk to Mr. Stanley, who was not having an easy morning. When Mr. Stanley first arrived, William Simms greeted him with the news that Godzilla had attacked his groom.

"Why would you let that dangerous horse come to a show?" Simms asked. "You'll be lucky if you're not sued."

It wasn't until Mr. Stanley talked to Henry that he found out about the apple and the pills. He was almost relieved. Then he grew angry and went up to William Simms and asked him point-blank if he was involved in drugging Godzilla.

"Come on, Stanley," Simms said. "Why would I need to do that? We don't need to drug a horse to win."

But Mr. Stanley was suspicious, and he went to the officials' booth and demanded an investigation. The officials were looking into it, but nobody could find the groom who was bitten by Godzilla. He had disappeared. They also made Mr. Stanley sign a form guaranteeing that Godzilla wouldn't attack anyone else. It had, indeed, been a difficult morning for Mr. Stanley.

# Chapter Forty

C assie took Godzilla to the warm-up arena and walked him around. While they were walking, Cassie noticed people pointing at them. She also noticed that people were giving them a wide berth wherever they went.

"Looks like you got a reputation, Dillie," Cassie said. Cassie rubbed his neck and climbed up into the saddle. "Okay, Dillie. Let's see how you feel."

Cassie touched her heels to Godzilla's sides. But instead of moving right away, Godzilla hesitated and Cassie had to kick a little. Finally, he started moving forward in a trot. He stayed in his trot so she thought maybe he was okay.

Next, Cassie asked Godzilla to go into a canter. Again, there seemed to be some hesitation, but the big horse did start to canter and stayed with it for as long as she asked him to.

Cassie just wasn't sure if he was all right. The hesitation worried her, but maybe she was just being overly concerned.

When Cassie felt Godzilla had warmed up enough, she pulled him to a stop and dismounted. "How you feeling, Dillie?"

Godzilla came up and nuzzled Cassie's cheek. There were still about twenty minutes before the first event, so she decided to go back to the stall and rub him down a little. When they got there, Godzilla went to his water trough and drank. He drank a lot of water and Cassie went to find him some more.

When Cassie returned, she saw that Rebecca Simms and her father were there to get Starfire for the first event. Rebecca snickered at

Cassie. "Cassie, I'm so sorry you're not going to be riding today. I was looking forward to beating you."

"Not riding?" Cassie asked. "Why do you say that?"

"Your horse is dangerous. Everyone knows that, and now someone has filed a complaint. They'll be down to talk to you soon, I'm sure. Better luck next time."

Starfire was all groomed and ready to go. Rebecca took the horse from the stall, and she and her father started to walk away.

"Hey, Dillie," Cassie said. "Any idea who tried to feed you a poisoned apple?"

Cassie had said it loud enough for Rebecca and her father to hear. She was angry, and wanted to ride just to prove Rebecca wrong. But she was worried about Godzilla. What if the pills *had* been poison? He could be slowly dying right now. She wondered where Henry was, and time was running out for her first class. Should she ride or should she not? Cassie walked up to Godzilla and looked the big horse in the eye.

"Dillie, do you want to ride?"

The horse pawed the ground. Cassie took that as a sign he did.

"All right, Dillie. If you want to, then I do too. Let's go have some fun."

Cassie took Godzilla from the stall and headed for the arena. There were sixteen riders all lining up at the staging area. When people saw Cassie and Godzilla, they began to move away. It made Cassie very nervous. She was relieved when Henry walked up and found them.

"Henry, Rebecca Simms says someone's filed a complaint and they might not let us ride."

"Don't worry. That's been dealt with. Just don't let Godzilla bite anyone."

"He won't bite anyone."

"Is he all right?"

"I don't know. He seems a little sluggish, and then he seems all right. He wants to ride."

"You sure?"

"Yeah, we're going to do our best."

Henry smiled and gave Cassie a thumbs up.

It took a long time before Cassie had to ride. Twelve of the sixteen riders went before it was Cassie and Godzilla's turn. They were lucky number thirteen.

When they went to the starting area, Cassie looked around. It was a big show and the stands were filled. People were watching them closely because the rumors had been flying around the show all morning. Godzilla was a curiosity and Cassie was of interest—the ferocious beast and the young girl who had tamed him. Cassie reached down and patted Godzilla on the neck.

"Okay, Dillie. I'm ready if you are."

But when they started off, Cassie thought Godzilla was not feeling well. He was sluggish at the start, and she had to really pour on the gas to clear the first jump. The next three jumps went better as Godzilla seemed to improve. But after the fourth jump, she knew they were in trouble. There was a turn and Godzilla stumbled. The crowd let out gasps as Godzilla fell to his knees hard. The crowd thought for sure that Cassie was going to be thrown. But her instincts took over and she somehow managed to stay in the saddle.

"Come on, Dillie!" Cassie yelled. "We can do this."

Cassie pulled up hard on the reins, and Godzilla sprang to his feet. To the crowd it looked as if the fall and recovery were one complete movement, a spectacular moment where a rider had saved her horse from a certain fall.

"Three more jumps, Dillie," Cassie said.

Cassie kicked Godzilla's sides and the big horse sprinted forward. When the pair cleared the next jump, the crowd broke into applause. Many were stunned by what they had just seen. When Cassie and

Godzilla completed the last two jumps, many people in the crowd stood to applaud. They had completed the round without missing or knocking down a fence. The legend of Cassie and Godzilla was being born.

Besides Cassie, four other riders advanced to the next round. One rider was a seventeen-year-old girl from Austin named Shannon who had won the show the previous year. Two other riders were sixteen, from New Mexico and the other from Louisiana. The last rider was Rebecca Simms. She was very unhappy because she had seen Cassie pull Godzilla up. Even Rebecca couldn't deny that it was a superb piece of riding.

Cassie's competitors had all ridden against each other before, but they had never ridden against Cassie. Because Rebecca and Cassie were from the same riding academy, Shannon asked Rebecca about Cassie.

"She's not that good," Rebecca said. "She just got lucky."

"She looks pretty good to me," Shannon said.

After the next round there were only three riders left, Cassie, Rebecca Simms, and Shannon. As they sat on their horses waiting for the final round, Shannon suddenly turned to Cassie.

"You're good," she said.

"Thanks," Cassie replied. "So are you."

The girl from Austin smiled and nodded to Cassie.

When Rebecca Simms witnessed the conversation, she was not happy. For one of the few times in her life, Rebecca felt she was the outsider. The only difference was, Cassie had not intentionally acted to make Rebecca feel excluded. Still, this conversation made Rebecca uncomfortable and it threw off her concentration. In the final round, Rebecca knocked down three fences and left the arena in tears.

Cassie rode well and Godzilla did the best he could do. But it wasn't enough to beat the girl from Austin. Cassie had to settle for second place.

Still, Cassie had stolen the show. She was the new girl who had electrified the crowd. Cassie dismounted and made her way toward Godzilla's stall. As she walked through the crowd, people were congratulating her and yelling out "Great riding, Cassie." It was a little disconcerting for Cassie because these people knew her, but she didn't know them. Henry walked up with a big smile on his face.

"Cassie, that was unbelievable. Everyone's asking about you."

"Henry," Cassie said, "we need to find a doctor for Dillie."

Henry nodded and smiled again because Cassie had just made him prouder than he already was. She had just wowed the crowd with her outstanding riding and everyone was congratulating her. But instead of thinking about how well she had done, Cassie was concerned about her horse.

"You're right," Henry said. "We should have checked him earlier. Take Godzilla to his stall and I'll find a vet."

# Chapter Forty-One

The vet Henry went to find was Athena Westin. Henry had known her a long time, and they often saw each other at horse shows. They always talked about horses, and she was the best horse doctor Henry knew. She was also the first person he had called when Godzilla went crazy with grief. Godzilla had been so aggressive toward her, she thought he would never recover. Now she watched Cassie with Godzilla closely, and the horse seemed so gentle it intrigued her. Athena wondered what magical charm had been used to tame the beast in Godzilla. She immediately agreed to help.

Henry told Athena about the pills, and she had seen for herself how Godzilla had stumbled on the turn. When they arrived at the stall, they found Cassie sitting on the ground next to Godzilla. The big horse was standing, but he seemed to be sleeping. Cassie stood.

"Cassie," Henry said, "this is Athena Westin. She's a great vet."

"Hi," Cassie said.

"Hi, Cassie," Athena replied. "That was a great ride you had. I couldn't believe how you got this horse up to finish."

"Thanks."

"So what seems to be the problem?" Athena asked.

"Dillie must have eaten one of those pills."

"The pills from the apple?"

"Yes," Henry said. "There were three of them stuck inside the apple. Part of the apple had been eaten."

"Has he been drinking a lot of water?" Athena asked.

"Tons," Cassie said. "I've had to fill his water trough three times."

Athena stepped inside the stall very carefully. She took a stethoscope from her bag and placed it on Godzilla's chest. She moved it around, listening not only to his heart, but his breathing as well.

Athena looked at Henry. "He probably ate one of the pills. We'd better see if we can find out what they are. I know a doctor who might help us."

Herny looked at Cassie. Her face was filled with fear. "Don't worry," Henry said. "Godzilla will be all right."

"Yes," Athena said, "his breathing sounds good and so does his heart."

"We'll be right back," Henry said.

Henry and Athena walked away. As they headed out of the barn, they passed William Simms and Rebecca walking in with Starfire. Rebecca was still crying.

"Maybe we should call the police," Henry said loud enough for William Simms to hear. "If Godzilla had fallen, Cassie could have been hurt."

"Whoever gave Godzilla that apple should be shot," Athena said.

William Simms ignored them and walked toward Starfire's stall. However, when Simms passed Godzilla's stall, he stopped and looked in. Cassie was seated on the ground next to Godzilla. She looked up into the eyes of William Simms. In that moment, Cassie knew William Simms had tried to poison Godzilla.

"You stay away from my horse," Cassie said.

"He's not your horse," Simms said and turned and walked away.

Henry and Athena found the doctor. His name was John Melbon. They walked to the officials' booth and asked for the apple in the plastic bag. Dr. Melbon took one look at the pills and knew what they were.

"They're Halcyon," Dr. Melbon said.

"What's that?" Henry asked.

"It's a powerful sedative used for sleeping," Dr. Melbon replied. "I think you should call the police."

Henry went to find Mr. Stanley. He was in the stands sitting near Mrs. Simms. Henry told him what the pills were and together they went to call the police. Then Mr. Stanley and Henry walked to Godzilla's stall. When they got there, they found Athena checking Godzilla over in the stall.

"Is Godzilla going to be okay?" Mr. Stanley asked.

Even though Godzilla appeared to be sleeping, his ears still went back when he heard Mr. Stanley's voice. Mr. Stanley backed away. "He can't be that sick if he still wants to kill me," he said.

"The good news is," Athena said, "he's a big horse. It would take a lot of pills before he would die. But he's definitely feeling the effects."

Shortly after, the police arrived. By that time, two show officials had also shown up. It was quite a crowd. The police asked a lot of questions, and Mr. Stanley, Cassie, Henry, Athena and Dr. Melbon all gave answers. The police also asked the grooms questions. But the grooms said they didn't know the name of the man who was bitten by Godzilla and the man had disappeared. This made Mr. Stanley happy because he knew he wasn't going to be sued. A report was taken, but the police said that without the man who had been bitten, there wasn't much they could do.

Cassie stayed with Godzilla the entire afternoon. Henry brought her some lunch and watched the horse while she went to the bathroom. Otherwise, Cassie did not leave his side all day.

Their next event was at four o'clock. At about three, Cassie took Godzilla out and walked him around. Henry and Athena went with her. The horse still seemed drowsy.

"I think we shouldn't ride," Cassie said. "He seems better, but I just don't want to chance it."

"That's probably a good idea," Athena said.

"We'll just concentrate on tomorrow," Henry said.

Cassie took Godzilla back to the stall and sat by his side. Rebecca Simms and her father came and got Starfire for the event. They didn't say a word to Cassie.

About an hour later the Simms clan returned. Cassie could hear Rebecca jabbering away as they approached. She was really excited.

"I can't believe I took second," Rebecca said. "Maybe I can still win the show."

"You're doing great, honey," William Simms said. "My blue-ribbon girl."

Cassie wanted to throw up or at least yell, "Cheater!" But she didn't say a word. She just had to sit there and listen to Rebecca go on and on about how well she had done. It was a difficult moment.

The Simms family left and Henry returned. He saw that Cassie was upset.

"What happened?" Henry asked.

"Rebecca Simms was just here bragging about how well she did."

"Forget it," Henry said. "They're not worth it."

"I know. But I'm just so mad they tried to hurt Dillie, just so they could feel good about themselves."

"You'll find that people will do almost anything to feel good about themselves. But just remember Socrates. When you do the wrong thing, you never feel good in the long run."

Cassie nodded. "I'm going to always remember that, Henry."

"Good," Henry said. "Now, what do you want to do?"

"I'm going to stay with Dillie tonight. I don't want anymore poisoned apples coming into this stall."

"Okay," Henry said. "I'll go back to the motel and get some blankets. And I'll bring you some dinner."

Henry went back to the motel and gathered up what they needed. Then he went to a Mexican restaurant and bought a nice meal to go. He returned, and Cassie, Henry and Godzilla all had dinner together.

Henry rolled out a blanket, and they sat outside Godzilla's stall eating their tacos, rice and beans.

"It's like a picnic," Cassie said,

"Yea," Henry said. "It's more fun eating like this than in a restaurant."

Cassie was quiet a moment. The only sound was Godzilla munching on his feed. "Thanks, Henry," Cassie said.

"I'm glad you like the food," Henry said.

"No. Thanks for everything. Thanks for bringing me down here so I could ride. Thanks for making me do my homework. Thanks for teaching me about horses . . . " Cassie started to cry.

"Hey, hey," Henry said gently. "There's no need to cry. If you want to know the truth, I'm the one who should be thanking you. You've changed Olivia's and my life. I never knew I could feel such pride. Knowing that I helped make you a good horse person . . . I mean, when I saw you ride today and watched you pull Godzilla up, I felt like part of me was helping you do that. It was like you were my own grandchild or something. That's a gift that I thought was lost with my sons." Henry smiled and patted her hand. "Thank you too, Cassie."

# Chapter Forty-Two

Cassie curled up for the night inside Godzilla's stall. She felt safe next to the big horse and fell asleep quickly. Around midnight, however, Godzilla reached down and nudged her gently on her cheek with his nose.

"What is it, Dillie?"

Godzilla walked to the stall door and pawed the ground.

"You want to go out?"

Godzilla pawed the ground again.

"Okay."

She opened the stall door and was surprised to find Henry sleeping next to the door. She smiled. She had thought that Henry had gone back to the motel. But there he was, looking out for her as always. Cassie and Godzilla quietly stepped past him and Henry stirred.

"More ham, Olivia," Henry said in his sleep. "The boys want more ham."

Cassie giggled as she followed Godzilla down the barn corridor. The big horse led the way because he knew where he wanted to go. They left the barn and soon found themselves at the gate to the arena. Godzilla wanted to go inside. Cassie unfastened the gate and they entered.

There were some lights along the back of the stands. But the arena seemed so empty without the people. It also seemed smaller to Cassie. Almost without thinking, she took Godzilla along the path they would take in tomorrow's competition. They stopped at the first fence.

"Diilie, let's picture ourselves going over each fence."

They stood at the fence. Cassie, with her eyes closed, rehearsed her movements. She pictured herself and Godzilla going over the fence smoothly and landing on the other side.

"Dillie, can you see it?"

The big horse reached over and rubbed his face against Cassie's. Then they walked to the next fence, where they stopped and rehearsed in their minds the same way. They walked to the next fence, and the one after that, until finally, they had walked through all the fences picturing in their minds successful jumps and landings. Cassie was excited and so was Godzilla. They couldn't wait for tomorrow to come.

"Dillie, tomorrow's about rhythm and about fun."

They stood looking at the course for a long time in the cool night air until a voice broke them from their dream.

"Hey, you. What are you doing out there?"

Cassie was startled and looked over toward the fence. It was the night watchman.

"Just practicing," Cassie said.

"You can't be in there," the watchman said. "You need to take your horse back to its stall."

"Okay," Cassie said. She put her hand under Godzilla's jaw and led him out of the arena. When they got to the gate, the watchman met them.

"Are you alone?" the watchman asked.

"No," Cassie replied. "I'm with my horse."

"No?" the watchman said with exasperation. "I mean, is there an adult around?"

"Yes," Henry said.

Henry had awoken at the sound of the watchman's voice. When he saw that Godzilla's stall door was open, he immediately got up to investigate. He walked up to speak to the watchman.

"Why are you both out here in the middle of the night?" the watchman asked.

"We're staying with our horse," Henry said. "Someone tried to poison him yesterday."

"Oh," the watchman said, "well, horses aren't allowed out of their stalls at night."

"We won't do it again," Cassie said. "We're going back to our stall now. Come on, Dillie."

She reached under Godzilla's chin with her hand and led the big horse away.

"Goodnight, officer," Henry said.

"Good night," the watchman said.

Henry quickly caught up with Cassie. "What were you doing out there?"

"I don't know," Cassie said. "Dillie led me out to the arena and we started rehearsing our rides for tomorrow. It was fun. I think we're ready."

"Strange way to get ready," Henry said. "But I guess nothing you and this horse do would surprise me."

Cassie smiled and, if a horse could smile, Godzilla was smiling too. But the main thing that had happened was that Cassie's and Godzilla's minds were filled with images of success. The day's events of poisoned apples and stumbles on turns had been erased by positive expectations for tomorrow's competition. Cassie and Godzilla were mentally prepared.

# Chapter Forty-Three

Activity started early Sunday at the San Antonio Fairgrounds. The grooms arrived at 5:00 A.M. to prepare the horses. This awoke Henry and Cassie. Although she had slept on the hard ground, Cassie felt rested. Henry on the other hand was a little stiff.

Henry hired a groom to stay with Godzilla for an hour so he and Cassie could go back to the motel and take showers. The groom's job was to stand guard so no more poisoned apples would appear in Godzilla's stall. After their showers, they grabbed a quick breakfast and returned to the fairgrounds. All was well, and Henry gave the groom fifty dollars out of his own pocket for watching over Godzilla.

Cassie immediately went to work preparing Godzilla for competition. She gave him a bath at the wash rack, and then started to groom him. She combed out his tail and braided it. She also braided his mane. All the while she spoke to Godzilla.

"This is our day, Dillie. We're going to throw it up for grabs and have fun."

Henry smiled as he stood outside the stall listening to Cassie talking to Godzilla. He smiled even wider when he watched Rebecca Simms and her father walk up to check on the groom preparing Starfire.

"We've been working hard for this, Dillie," Cassie said. "You're ready. I'm ready. We're going to make every jump and we're going to make them fast. Rhythm, Dillie. We're going to have rhythm."

Rebecca had a look of terror on her face. She did not want to lose to Cassie again. Rebecca's father took one look at his daughter's face and he felt his blood boil.

"Don't worry, Rebecca," Simms said. "You're going to win." He had said it loud enough for Cassie to hear.

Cassie paused a moment, shook her head and smiled. "Today is our day, Dillie. Nobody can beat us because we're going to have the most fun."

William Simms's face turned red from anger. "Just get Starfire and let's go warm up," Simms said to his daughter.

Rebecca Simms took her horse from the groom, and she and her father walked away. But as they headed out of the barn, they could hear Cassie still talking to Godzilla.

"Rhythm, Dillie. Speed and rhythm. You and me."

The first class was at nine o'clock. The sun was shining, and the dew from the night before had already evaporated on the surface of the field. Conditions could not have been more perfect.

There were twenty-two riders in the competition for the seventeen-and-under age group. It was important to do well in this class because the top ten finishers would compete in the afternoon for the championship.

Cassie's first ride was perfect. She and Godzilla had easily cleared all the fences, and when the round was over, there were fourteen riders left.

Rebecca Simms had cleared all the fences as well. She had ridden the course early on and felt confident when she had finished that nobody could do it better. But when she saw Cassie and Godzilla complete their round with such strength and speed, her confidence wavered. She was becoming obsessed with how her rival was doing.

But surprisingly, Cassie had found the secret for achieving a peak performance. She simply did not think about how her competition was doing. She was motivated by her competition, but didn't focus on it. She focused only on doing her personal best.

To this end, Cassie and Godzilla completed the next round without any mishaps. This round was also for speed, and when the field had finished, Cassie and Godzilla had the fastest time.

The fastest five advanced to the final ride in the class. The seventeen-year-old girl from Austin advanced along with two twin boys from Houston. This was the Houston twins' first event of the show because their car had broken down the day before. They were both very good riders. The last rider to advance was a sixteen-year-old girl from San Antonio.

Rebecca Simms had not advanced. She had become so focused on Cassie that she had lost concentration. Between the third and fourth fences, Rebecca missed a turn and lost precious time. Rebecca Simms finished eighth.

She was so upset that she just handed Starfire's reins to her mother and ran off crying. Her father followed her and that left Mrs. Simms holding the horse alone. Now, Mrs. Simms didn't know a thing about horses. Moreover, she was deathly afraid of horses and Starfire sensed this fear in her, but he didn't understand why. Starfire began to back up.

"Stop!" Mrs. Simms said.

Starfire backed up some more.

"Starfire, stop!" Mrs. Simms yelled. She panicked and the horse became scared. Starfire backed up even more and Mrs. Simms let go of the reins.

"Bill! Help!" Mrs. Simms screamed. "Starfire's going crazy!"

The horse started to bolt just as the crowd turned to look. Luckily, Cassie was standing nearby and quickly grabbed Starfire's reins. The horse reared up and Cassie found herself holding both Godzilla's and Starfire's reins. But Cassie didn't panic. She stayed calm.

"Easy, Starfire," Cassie said. "Easy, boy, you're safe."

When Starfire saw it was Cassie, he calmed down. But Godzilla didn't like Cassie holding another horse's reins and immediately tried to bite Starfire. Starfire jumped away and nearly pulled Cassie over. But Cassie still remained calm. With one hand she jerked Godzilla away from Starfire and with the other she held Starfire tightly.

"Dillie, you stop that," Cassie said. "Starfire, easy, boy."

Starfire started to calm down again just as Henry ran up. Cassie saw him and quickly handed him Starfire's reins and pulled Godzilla away.

"Cassie, you need to ride," Henry said. "I'll take Starfire back."

"Thanks," Cassie said.

Henry walked Starfire back to his stall and Cassie rode. When Henry returned, she was finished. He was very sorry he had missed it because he heard about it everywhere. Cassie had won the class.

Cassie was surrounded by people who were congratulating her when Henry walked up. She spied Henry and threw her arms around him.

"We won!" Cassie squealed. "We won!"

"Way to go, girl," Henry said, beaming.

Some people around them began to applaud. The story of Cassie and Godzilla was now more than just gossip. It had the ingredients of legend and Henry was a part of it.

A reporter and a photographer walked up to them.

"It's Cassie Reynolds, isn't it?" the reporter asked.

"Yes," Cassie replied.

"We're from the *San Antonio Sun*. We'd like to get a picture of you and Godzilla for our paper and ask you a few questions."

Cassie stood next to Godzilla as the photographer took some pictures. Godzilla rubbed his face against Cassie's and the photographer shot that as well.

"That's great," the reporter said. "Now, we understand your horse has a nasty reputation. Some people even think he's dangerous."

"Dillie's not nasty. He's a sweetheart."

Henry was smiling as he watched Cassie rub Godzilla under his chin. But his smile quickly disappeared when he happened to glance over to see William Simms watching Cassie as well. William Simms did not know Henry was watching him. Otherwise, he would have shielded his face from Henry. For Henry saw in William Simms's face malice, anger, and the kind of hatred that makes one shudder.

# Chapter Forty-Four

It was definitely not the big payday weekend Mr. Stanley had hoped for. In addition to the problem of Godzilla biting the groom, the story about Godzilla trying to kill David Jensen was following him around. It seemed to Mr. Stanley that everywhere he went people wanted to ask him about Godzilla. But during every conversation, the other person always said something like, "Of course Godzilla's a great horse. But he won't let anyone ride him but that little girl." Even after Cassie and Godzilla had won the morning class, people still said "no way" after he casually mentioned Godzilla was for sale. His hopes for a half-million-dollar payday were diminishing quickly.

On the other hand, everyone was asking about the academy. Word had spread that Cassie had been riding for only a year and that bolstered the academy's reputation. Mr. Stanley was quite pleased with the recognition Cassie was receiving, but he was well aware that it would take a lot of student riding lessons to make up for the loss of half a million dollars.

Mr. Stanley was sitting in the stands thinking about his losses when he was approached by William Simms.

"Say, Stanley," Simms said. "Can I talk to you in private?"

"What about?" Mr. Stanley replied.

"About Godzilla."

Mr. Stanley grimaced. "Are you going to confess that you tried to poison my horse?"

"Fine," Simms said. "If that's how you feel, then I guess you're not interested in selling him." Simms started to walk away. But this was the first interest anyone had expressed in Godzilla since David Jensen,

and Mr. Stanley's greed got the better of him. He was not going to let
this opportunity slip.

"Wait, Bill. If you're interested in Godzilla, I'm willing to listen."

Mr. Stanley stood and followed William Simms out of the stands.
When they got to the bottom, they stopped in the corner where no
one could hear them.

"How much are you asking?" Simms asked quietly.

"Around five hundred thousand," Mr. Stanley said hopefully. "But I
wouldn't put Rebecca on him. Maybe if you got Cassie to help . . . "
Mr. Stanley paused. He saw what Simms was going for: Simms wanted
to buy Godzilla to keep Cassie from competing with his daughter.
Without Godzilla, Cassie didn't have a horse that could come close to
Starfire.

"I see," Mr. Stanley said. "Rebecca's having a tough day?"

"Yes, she is. I don't know why that girl Cassie throws Rebecca's
confidence, but she does. Maybe it's because that Cassie's always rude
to her and she isn't used to it."

"But buying up the competition won't help Rebecca become a better rider, Bill."

"I'm not worried about her riding. This is something different. Her
confidence is the problem, and I've made a huge investment in
Rebecca's dream and I want to see her succeed. I've never seen her
cave in like she did today and now she's even talking about quitting.
I won't let that happen without doing everything I can to help her,
and I don't want that Cassie in Houston next week."

"But the price is half a million dollars," Mr. Stanley said.

Simms smiled. "I'm hoping to do a little better than that. I know no
one else will touch the horse. I'll give you seventy-five thousand in
cash for Godzilla and another ten thousand if you fire Cassie."

"Fire Cassie?"

"Yes," Simms said. "Either she goes or we leave the academy. I
don't want my daughter around that kind of trash."

"Bill, I don't know. I may sell you Godzilla, but Cassie stays. Horses can be sold, but people can't."

"Everything has its price, Stanley."

"That's where you're wrong."

Mr. Stanley walked away. This made William Simms very unhappy. People simply did not walk away from him and get away with it.

# Chapter Forty-Five

After her morning competition, Cassie stayed at Godzilla's side for the rest of the day. She didn't trust Rebecca Simms and her family.

At noon, Henry brought Cassie some lunch. They set out the blanket again and sat in front of Godzilla's stall eating hamburgers and French fries.

"I checked the standings," Henry said. "You're in sixth place overall. Missing the class yesterday really set you back. I don't think you can win the show, but I do think you have a shot at second."

"Second would be good," Cassie said. "But I'm not going to worry about it. Dillie and I are just going to go out and do our best."

"Good girl," Henry replied.

After lunch, Cassie started getting Godzilla ready for their final class. They had developed their ritual and the horse started to get fired up as she talked to him.

"Dillie, we're going to have big fun. We'll find our rhythm just like in practice. Every jump will be easy and smooth."

Rebecca Simms had just barely made the final event as well. Her hired groom was preparing Starfire as the Simms family arrived to check on him. Once again, Rebecca heard Cassie talking to Godzilla.

"Dillie, we're going to ride like we're the only ones in the arena. Focus on what we're doing. Did I also mention that we're going to have fun? It's competition day, Dillie, and that means fun."

When William Simms saw the fear in his daughter's face, anger welled inside of him. It was the misdirected anger of a parent who wanted to give his child everything. Instead of being happy that his daughter faced strong competition, Simms wanted to knock the bar down for his daughter so she could be the winner.

The trouble for Rebecca was that she was so used to winning that she had never learned how to lose. Everything had been given to her. Her father had bought her the best horse he could find. He had bought Rebecca the best coaching that money could buy, and he placed her in as many situations as he could in which the outcome was controllable and Rebecca could emerge victorious. What this produced was a paper tiger, someone who appeared strong but backed down when life got a little tough. In Rebecca's case, she didn't have the perseverance to stand up to the challenge Cassie presented.

Cassie's perseverance came from her love of riding. She loved competing, and she loved to work hard to make herself better. But, it wasn't just about winning. That was just a way to measure your accomplishments. Cassie had found the true joy of sports, which is really about the journey. It was about reaching deep down inside and finding the best you had to give. It was about the ride more than it was about the ribbons.

This was why Cassie and Godzilla were ready for the final event and Rebecca wasn't. It was also why Rebecca completely gave up after she heard a conversation between Cassie and Shannon, the girl from Austin, just before the final class started.

"You know," Shannon said, "you're the first rider to beat me this year."

"Really?" Cassie replied.

"Yeah," Shannon said. "By the way, are you really only thirteen?"

"Yes."

"I'm glad I'm turning pro this year. I'd hate to face you in a couple of years."

"I'm glad you are too."

Rebecca Simms's final ride was a disaster. She knocked down two fences and completely missed the final gate. She took last.

Cassie and Godzilla battled hard, and when it was over, they had taken second place behind Shannon. They had lost by less than a second.

Afterward, Shannon went up to Cassie and thanked her for competing against her. "That was a great ride," Shannon said.

"Thanks, Shannon. Yours was too. Dillie and I tried our hardest to beat you."

"I know you did. I had to make one of the best rides of my life to beat you. Are you coming to Houston next week?"

"I don't know," Cassie said. "I'll have to check."

"I hope you come," Shannon said. "It's fun competing against you."

"Likewise, and congratulations."

"Thanks," Shannon said. She walked away and was surrounded by friends and family. She had won not only the class, but the show as well.

For Cassie, there were well-wishers too. As Cassie made her way to the stall, people called out to her, "Good job, Cassie!" and "Nice ride, Cassie."

Cassie had been noticed and her story was a good one. People loved it. Poor girl from the wrong side of the tracks makes good. Young girl with a dangerous horse beats the odds. Unknown rider breaks in and wows the crowd. Take your pick—the stories were everywhere. But Cassie didn't know any of this, and that's why she was surprised and a little embarrassed when a group of young girls asked her for her autograph. She blushed as she signed her name. It was one of the best days of her life.

# Chapter Forty-Six

When Cassie got back to Godzilla's stall, there was another scene taking place. Rebecca, eyes red from crying, was yelling at her parents. "The only reason Cassie beat me was because she has a better horse! Starfire sucks!"

Cassie was just walking up with Godzilla. Rebecca's outburst made her a little angry. Not because Rebecca was trying to insult her—she was used to that—but because she knew Starfire was a great horse. Most kids would be so thankful to have him as a horse they wouldn't be able to see straight. Still, she felt sorry for Rebecca because she was so miserable.

However, when Cassie got to Godzilla's stall her feelings changed. Rebecca glared at her as she walked up, making her feel very uncomfortable. "What are you looking at?" Rebecca snarled.

"Nothing," Cassie said. "I just want to put my horse in his stall."

"Your horse? Yeah, right," Rebecca continued.

Cassie opened the door and led Godzilla in, but she was not about to leave him alone with the Simms family. Cassie stood at the door and the horse came up and rubbed his face against Cassie's.

"It was a great day, Dillie," Cassie said. "Thank you."

"You just got lucky," Rebecca croaked.

Cassie turned to look at Rebecca. Her parents stood behind her. "Maybe that's true. Everyone has good days and bad days. You'll do better next time."

When William Simms heard this, he exploded. "Who are you to say that to my daughter!" he screamed.

"What?" Cassie asked.

Cassie had thought she was being nice, but Simms was staring at her with such hatred it scared her.

"You're just trash," Simms hissed. "You're always rude to Rebecca and that's why she rode poorly. It's because of you."

Cassie was scared. She was all alone and a grown man was screaming at her. She started to cry. "What did I do?"

Henry happened to be walking in the barn when he heard Simms yelling. He started running to Cassie. He could see that Simms was in her face.

"Go ahead and cry. Rebecca's been crying all day."

"Hey!" Henry yelled as he arrived at Cassie's side. "That's no way to act toward a young girl. Who do you think you are?"

Simms looked at Henry and lost what control he had left. He walked up to Henry and pushed him so hard that Henry fell to the ground.

"You stop!" Cassie yelled and got between Simms and Henry. Godzilla went berserk in his stall. The big horse was rearing up and coming down hard on the stall door trying to get to Simms. It wasn't a question of if but when Godzilla would be through the door and on top of Simms. Simms looked at Godzilla and he started to back away. His senses were returning.

"Rebecca," Simms said, "go find the groom and get Starfire loaded. I've got someone I have to talk to." He walked away as Cassie helped Henry to his feet.

Henry smiled. "I've got some good news. You took second place in the show."

When Rebecca Simms heard this, she put her face in her hands and ran off. Mrs. Simms walked off after her daughter, leaving Cassie and Henry alone. Henry turned to Cassie.

"There's an awards ceremony," Henry said.

"Never mind that," Cassie said. "Are you all right?"

"I'm fine. People can get pretty ugly at these shows sometimes. I guess I should have warned you about it."

"Yeah," Cassie said, "that was pretty ugly."

"You can't let it bother you. You rode great today and you deserve to get your award. Don't let William Simms get in the way of that."

"I can't leave Dillie alone. No telling what that idiot will do."

Henry smiled. "Take Godzilla with you. After all, he won second too."

The awards ceremony was short and sweet. First through third place won trophies. Cassie was all smiles when she was handed her trophy for second. It was a really big trophy.

Henry was watching with a big smile on his face. He was just about bursting with pride. But he happened to glance up into the stands and saw something he knew was wrong. Dead wrong. Mr. Stanley and William Simms were sitting on the very top bleacher. They were off by themselves and huddled together in what looked like a very serious conversation.

In an instant, Henry's heart sank. It wasn't because of what had happened. He knew anything William Simms said would not affect him with Mr. Stanley. Henry had known Mr. Stanley since he was a boy and Henry knew they were joined. But Godzilla was another matter. Henry knew that the conversation was about Godzilla and that Cassie's world was about to come crashing down.

It was Cassie who broke Henry's concentration on the stands.

"Henry," Cassie said, "look at our trophy."

"Well, that's a mighty fine trophy. Won't Olivia and your momma be proud when they see that?"

Maybe it was the sadness in Henry's voice or maybe it was the lack of excitement, but Cassie sensed something was wrong.

"Are you all right?"

"I'm fine," Henry said. "But we got a long drive home. You take Dillie back . . . "

"Hey," Cassie said.

"What?" Henry asked.

"You called him Dillie. That's the first time anyone but me has called him Dillie."

"Huh," Henry said. "I guess because I've spent so much time with the both of you it's starting to rub off on me."

"That's good. Because deep down inside that's who he is. Dillie."

Henry smiled. "Then from now on it's Dillie. But we need to head for home. So take Dillie back and gather up our stuff. I just need a minute to talk to someone and then I'll be right along."

"Okay," Cassie said and she turned to walk off. But she stopped and looked back at Henry.

"Henry," Cassie said, "today was a great day."

"It sure enough was," Henry replied. "But you go on now. We'll be leaving right away."

Cassie nodded and led Godzilla away, leaving Henry with a sad smile on his face.

# Chapter Forty-Seven

Henry made his way to the foot of the grandstands, where he watched William Simms and Mr. Stanley talking. He could see that a negotiation was taking place. Simms was writing something down on a piece of paper, and after some hand-waving by Simms, Henry saw Mr. Stanley sign the paper. Then, Simms produced his checkbook and wrote out a check and handed it to Mr. Stanley. Henry knew the deal was done. Godzilla had been sold to William Simms.

Simms stood and made a couple of final gestures. He pointed at Mr. Stanley a couple of times, and Mr. Stanley sat there shaking his head. Simms shrugged, turned, and walked away.

As Simms walked down the stairs, he passed Henry standing at the bottom. Henry looked Simms in the eye, but when Simms saw him, he just looked away. He walked past Henry without even acknowledging him.

Henry walked up the stairs to where Mr. Stanley was sitting. Mr. Stanley saw Henry coming, and he knew what Henry was there for. It had not been a good weekend for Mr. Stanley.

"Now, Henry," Mr. Stanley said, "I've agreed not to talk about it."

"How much?" Henry asked.

"A lot," Mr. Stanley said. "And he's paying me another five thousand to keep it confidential. What happened between you two anyway? He offered me another twenty thousand if I'd get rid of you and Cassie."

"What did you say?"

"What do you think I said? The guy's a jerk. A jerk with a lot of money and that's the worst kind. They think they can buy anything."

"Have you thought about just keeping Godzilla? You and Cassie could form a partnership. A champion horse can bring in a lot of money with sponsors and prizes."

"Yes, I was considering that. But Cassie and Godzilla are a long way off from becoming champions, and horse shows are expensive. I would be putting out a lot of money with only the possibility of a return. Besides, Godzilla hates me. Every time I walk around the academy, the first thing I have to do is figure out where he is. It's unsettling."

"Maybe I can buy him instead," Henry said.

"No, Henry. It was a lot of money. I know you've got some money, but this was a lot. At least you can be happy with knowing that the Simms family is leaving the academy. He said that if I didn't get rid of Cassie and you, he was gone. That's when I knew he was going to pay a lot for Godzilla."

Henry was quiet. He had no idea what he was going to tell Cassie.

"What's he planning to do with the horse?" Henry asked.

"Probably destroy it," Mr. Stanley said. "We both know that Godzilla won't let anyone near him but Cassie, and it costs a lot of money to keep a horse. No, my guess is he'll get rid of it and destroying it is his best option. He wants to make sure Godzilla never competes again."

"This is just wrong, Stanley."

"I know it is. But I remember what my daddy used to say: Horse people are crazy. You have to be a little crazy to love a sport that breaks your heart most of the time."

"I don't know what I'm going to tell Cassie," Henry said sadly.

"You can't tell her anything. First, it would break her heart and, second, I signed a paper saying this sale is completely confidential. Simms says that if I tell anyone, he'll sue me for everything I own. I only told you, Henry, because you're too smart to be lied to and I'm too smart to try."

"All right," Henry said. "I think that's the best way to play it anyway. As much as I hate a liar, I think a lie is the best way to break it to Cassie."

Henry turned and started to walk away. Mr. Stanley called out to him.

"Tell Cassie she rode great. We'll find her another horse."

## Chapter Forty-Eight

Henry and Cassie left the San Antonio Fairgrounds at just after six-thirty that night. Henry calculated that with stopping for dinner and gas along the way, they would arrive home sometime after two in the morning. Most of the drive would take place at night and Henry was thankful for that. He had some thinking to do.

Cassie was so excited to be getting home. She couldn't wait to show her mom her trophy.

"We'll just have to wake everyone up when we get there," Henry said.

"Yeah," Cassie replied. "I can't wait. Henry, this was the best weekend of my life."

It was a hard drive for Henry. Cassie was so happy and full of life. She jabbered the whole way, talking about their adventure. "Henry, do you think Dillie and I could make it to the Olympics?"

Henry bit his lip as his heart sank. He didn't know how or when he was going to tell Cassie about Godzilla.

"That's a mighty fine goal, Cassie. I think if you work hard enough you could get there."

They stopped for dinner at Denny's, and Cassie had a hamburger and a shake. She talked about their adventure some more. Then she brought up the subject of William Simms.

"You know, I felt really bad when Rebecca's dad yelled at me. He was trying to make me feel like I had done something wrong. But then I remembered about Socrates saying that if you do the right thing, you don't have to feel bad. I had done the right thing at the show. I hadn't tried to hurt anyone."

"Yeah, Socrates says that if you try and do the right thing, you can look yourself in the mirror and know. Then you don't need to feel bad about people like William Simms. Mr. Simms would do well to read a little Socrates himself."

After dinner, Henry called Olivia and told her they would be home after two. Olivia sensed something in Henry's voice.

"Is everything all right, Henry?" Olivia asked.

"Something's happened, but we'll have to talk about it later. Tell Susan when we'll be home and that Cassie did just great."

Before they got back on the road, Cassie unloaded Godzilla from the trailer and walked him around in the parking lot. Henry stood by the trailer and watched as Cassie and Godzilla walked in the cool night air. Cassie stopped and gave Godzilla a hug. The big horse rubbed his face against Cassie's and she rubbed his neck.

It made Henry sick to his stomach thinking that William Simms now owned Godzilla. Then he nearly started to cry as he thought that Simms probably just intended to destroy such a beautiful animal. Nobody had a right to do that. It was a sin in Henry's mind.

Henry also wondered why money had to determine the ownership of an animal. Cassie didn't own Godzilla in a legal way, but spiritually Cassie was his true owner. The souls of this horse and this young girl were joined. That was true ownership.

Henry felt anger well up inside of him. He felt as if he had to do something. At first, he thought he and Cassie should just steal Godzilla. But he knew that was wrong. Then, suddenly, a real plan entered his mind. Henry checked his thinking with what Socrates might say. Was it the right thing to do?

"Yes," Henry said to himself. "Socrates would approve."

Cassie walked Godzilla back and she loaded the big horse into the trailer, and they were quickly back on the road. Cassie talked for another hour or so and then she suddenly said, "You know. Henry, I think I'm kind of tired."

Cassie laid her head against the seat, closed her eyes, and fell asleep so fast it made Henry smile. It had been quite a weekend.

For the next six hours, Henry did nothing else but think about his plan and drive. The wide-open Texas roads were good for thinking and, by the time he got them home, he had his plan pretty well thought out. He didn't know if his plan would work or if it would lead to some places he didn't intend it to go. But at least he had a plan. If he didn't do anything, Henry wouldn't be able to live with himself.

# Chapter Forty-Nine

Henry pulled his old Ford truck into the academy at just after two-thirty in the morning. It took about twenty minutes to unload Godzilla and put him in his stall. After Cassie did so, she gave the horse a big hug.

"Dillie, it was a great show. We sure make a good team."

It was close to three when they arrived at the trailer park. Olivia and Susan awoke to greet them, and the two women couldn't believe how big the trophy was. Afterward, Cassie wanted to tell them everything. At first, Susan wanted her to go to sleep because there was school the next day, but she quickly realized that her daughter needed to talk. Once Cassie started talking, Susan wanted to listen as she learned about the poisoned apple and Henry being pushed to the ground. When Cassie finished talking and closed her eyes, it was just after four. Obviously, Cassie was going to miss another day of school.

Henry, on the other hand, had gone straight to bed. His mind was tired because he had been thinking so hard about his plan, and he knew that he needed to be up early to put it into action. By the time Olivia came in, he was asleep.

It was 7:00 A.M. when Henry awoke. He took a shower and dressed and then went into the kitchen and made some coffee. He was just finishing his cup when Olivia came in. She took one look at his face and knew something was wrong.

"Why are you up so early?" Olivia asked.

"Because something's happened and I need to try and fix it."

"What's happened?"

"This ugly man has bought Godzilla, and I think he intends to destroy him."

"Destroy him? Why would somebody do that?"

"So Cassie doesn't have a horse to compete with against his daughter."

"Oh, Henry," Olivia said. Olivia sat down in the chair across from Henry. "First her father and now her horse. Does she know?"

"No," Henry said. "And don't tell her. Don't tell Susan either. If I can't fix it, Cassie must never know. It would break her heart, and she would always blame herself for doing so good at the show."

"This is terrible," Olivia said. "What are you going to do?"

"To start with, I'm going to see Mark."

"Your nephew?"

"Yes."

"But you haven't seen him in twenty years. What do you think he can do?'

"I don't know," Henry said. "Maybe nothing. But I have to start somewhere."

"Yes, you do."

Henry picked up his keys and headed for the door.

"Wait," Olivia said. She walked over and gave Henry a kiss on the cheek. "You're a good man, Henry Williams."

"Let's just hope I'm good enough to fix this."

# Chapter Fifty

Henry drove to downtown Dallas. He had called Information and got the phone number and address for KTTU Dallas. He found a parking spot in the parking structure across the street and headed for the building. He knew his nephew would be there because he was on the morning show every weekday. Henry just hoped he wasn't sick.

Henry walked up to the security guard at the front desk.

"Can I help you?" the security guard asked.

"Yes," Henry said, "I'm here to see Mark Sinclair."

"Do you have an appointment?"

"No," Henry said, "but he's my nephew. I think he'll want to see me."

"Name?"

"Henry Williams."

Mark Sinclair was sipping coffee and looking over his notes for his show when a secretary came in.

"Mark," the secretary said, "do you have an uncle named Henry Williams?"

"Yes."

"He's downstairs asking to see you."

"What?" Mark Sinclair nearly spilled his coffee. He set his cup down and got to his feet. "My uncle's downstairs?"

"Yes," the secretary confirmed.

Mark went to the mirror in his office. He straightened his shirt and smoothed his hair. The secretary looked at Mark curiously.

"He's just your uncle," the secretary said. "It's not like you're going on the air yet. You still have an hour."

"This is not just any uncle." Mark made his way down to the front desk. When he saw Henry standing at the security guard's desk, he almost didn't recognize him. The man he remembered was much younger. Mark called out to Henry as he walked up to him.

"Uncle Henry. To what do I owe this honor?"

"I need your help, Mark."

Mark frowned. "You need my help?"

"Yes," Henry said.

Mark was about to say something, but then he looked down and saw the security guard watching them. "Follow me," he said.

Mark led Henry to the elevator. They didn't say a word to each other. But as they rode up, Mark turned to Henry. "Is Olivia all right?"

"She's fine."

"This isn't about Olivia?"

"No."

Mark shook his head. The elevator doors opened and Mark led Henry down the hall to his office. Once inside, Mark closed the door and turned to his uncle. The frown was still on his face.

"You need my help," Mark said. There was anger in his voice. "Well, don't that beat all. You take care of my mother and me all the while I was growing up. You pay for me to go to college and graduate school too. You even buy me my first car. The trouble is, I never see you. Oh, I see Olivia sometimes. But not you. What is it? You just don't like me?"

"No, Mark. I've always liked you."

"Then why did you just cut me off from your life?"

"Mark, you deserve an explanation."

"Darn right I do."

Tears began to well up in Henry's eyes.

"What is it, Uncle Henry?" Mark asked.

"I'm just not good at talking about it. But to say it as simple as I can, when I see you it just hurts too much."

"Why?"

"You and my boys were like three peas in a pod . . . "

"And you were like the father I never had. Danny and Mike get killed in that stupid war and then that's it. You just stop talking to me."

"I know. But it's more than that. When I see you, Mark, it makes me think of what might have been. I've always been real proud of you. Not just your success, but proud of the man you grew to be. I like to think my sons would have been half as good."

Mark looked at his uncle. Tears came to his eyes too.

"But I loved you," Mark said. "When I was young you were everything to me. Why did you stop loving me?"

"It's not that I stopped loving you. I just knew you couldn't be around me, missing what might have been. I was like a black hole swallowing up all the happiness around me. You wouldn't have understood why I was sad, and I didn't have the courage to tell you. It's taken thirty years for me to tell you now. But I never stopped loving you."

Mark began to cry and Henry reached out to his nephew, and Henry held him as he wept. He was surprised at how strongly Mark was reacting. Henry never knew that the selfishness of his own pain had caused so much pain in Mark. In the middle of downtown Dallas, two men were hugging each other, reconciling their pain that had existed for over thirty years, and Henry was glad he had come.

# Chapter Fifty-One

William Simms was feeling satisfied with himself. He had just called his accountant and told him to transfer $255,000 into his checking account to cover the check he had written to Mr. Stanley. Godzilla was bought and paid for. Now Simms could do what he wanted with the horse.

Next, Simms called a man name Freddy Lava who worked for Simms collecting money from people who had bought cars and didn't pay their loans on time. Simms called him an associate, but the correct term was "henchman." Rumor had it, Freddy Lava wasn't above breaking an arm or two in the service of William Simms. Freddy Lava was not a nice man. In fact, if he had been a little smarter, he might have even been considered evil.

"Freddy," Simms said, "how would you like to make the easiest thousand dollars in your life?"

"Sounds good," Freddy replied. "What do you need, Bill?"

"I need you to get a horse trailer and go pick up a horse. Then I want you to drive it out somewhere, kill it, and bury it."

"Sounds pretty easy," Freddy said. "Where do I find the horse?"

"At a place called The North Dallas Riding Academy. It's out on Oak Grove Drive. I'll tell the owner you're coming this morning. But under no circumstances are you to mention my name, and if anyone asks, tell them the horse is yours."

"Okay," Freddy said. "Anything else I should know?"

"Yeah," Simms said. "The horse is kind of dangerous. Supposedly it's tried to kill people, so take a couple of guys with you when you pick it up."

"Why don't I just kill it first?"

"No," Simms said. "There might be kids around or something. People would ask questions. I just want the horse to disappear."

"Okay," Freddy said.

"Oh," Simms said, "if it all goes smoothly, I'll pay you an extra thousand. That's two thousand if you do it today and you do it right."

"Sounds good," Freddy said.

When Simms finished talking to Freddy, he walked into his kitchen with a smile on his face. But there was a surprise waiting for him when he sat down at the breakfast table with his daughter and wife. The family was eating and watching the morning show on KTTU, and as luck would have it, Mark Sinclair's sports report was on. Mark talked about the Mavericks and the Cowboys. Then, he talked about something else.

"Lastly, I want to highlight a sport that we don't talk about too much and that's equestrian jumping. There's a story about a young girl named Cassie Reynolds and her amazing horse, Godzilla. Tonight on our evening sports show, we're going to feature Cassie and Godzilla, and I know their story is going to touch your hearts. And just wait until you see them jump. See you tonight."

But Henry had miscalculated. Instead of scaring Simms, it just made the man more determined to get rid of Godzilla, especially after Simms saw his daughter's face when Mark had reported on Cassie. When his daughter left the room in tears, Simms went to the phone and called Freddy Lava again.

"Freddy, it's Bill. How's it coming with the horse thing?"

"Good. Got a trailer."

"Do you think you can get the job done by noon?"

"Maybe. It'll be tight, though. I'm still rounding up some guys."

"Well, if you get it done by noon, I'll throw in another thousand. That's three thousand dollars cash if it all goes smoothly."

"Three thousand if it's done by noon. Consider it done."

# Chapter Fifty-Two

If Henry had known Simms was going to act so quickly, he would have altered his plan. But Henry didn't know how ruthless Simms could be when he wanted something. So Henry was still moving forward and he had one more meeting before his plan would be in place. This part of his plan involved his childhood friend Chester Johnson.

Henry and Chester had been next-door neighbors while growing up. They had been best friends until they reached high school. There, Chester went left and Henry went right. Chester became a gangster and had somehow survived. Henry, thanks to summers on his grandfather's horse farm in Oklahoma, got a job with the railroad, met Olivia, and started a family.

Chester made a life for himself on the streets and became known as The Negotiator. It helped in negotiations that Chester was a huge man, who stood six foot seven and weighed nearly three hundred pounds. But what really set Chester apart was a trademark steely stare that was both scary and crazy. On the street, it was said that Chester could stare down a lion, and he was known to have stared down many of the toughest gangsters of his day.

Chester was now in his seventies, semiretired and living alone in the same house he had grown up in. He did an odd job now and then, but his gangster days were pretty much over. Henry wanted to use Chester's steely stare, and also his loyalty, to try to save Godzilla. Chester was the best negotiator Henry knew and he wanted to sic him on Simms.

Henry pulled up outside of Chester Johnson's house. He saw Chester's baby-blue Cadillac parked in the driveway and knew Chester was home.

But Henry paused for a moment to look at the house next door— the house he had grown up in. The image of himself as a young boy playing baseball in the front yard flashed through his mind, and for a moment, he found it unbelievable that the young boy he remembered would be on this street some seventy years later trying to figure out how to save a horse. The future is always full of those kinds of tricks, he thought. You pass through a place you've been before and you are always a little surprised at the person you've become.

After the memory passed, Henry got out of his truck and walked to Chester's front door and knocked. There was no answer so Henry knocked again.

"Who is it?" a voice finally bellowed.

"Henry Williams."

"Who?"

"Henry Williams."

"Not the little Henry I knew that left his neighborhood behind to live among the rich people?"

Henry shook his head and smiled. "Yes," Henry said. "It's the same little Henry."

The door flew open and Chester Johnson stood there smiling. He had aged, but his massive size still cut an imposing figure. He gave Henry a hug that nearly broke Henry's back.

"Well, what do you know?" Chester roared. "Fresh from the land of Wonderbread walks Henry Williams."

"Hey, Chester."

"Hey, yourself," Chester said and then he laughed. "And what could possibly drag Henry Williams down to the old neighborhood?"

"I need your skills, Chester."

"What do you need me for? You're rich."

"I need you to help me buy a horse."

"A horse?"

"Yeah, a horse. There's money in it for you."

Chester Johnson smiled. "In that case, step into my office."

# Chapter Fifty-Three

When Cassie had gone to sleep, everything had been right with her world. But she woke up in tears from a nightmare that Godzilla was gone. She bolted out of bed and threw on her clothes. She headed out the door to the academy and didn't even stop to eat. Something told her she needed to see Godzilla.

As Cassie walked from the trailer, she saw that Olivia was watering some plants along her driveway.

"Cassie, how are you doing this morning?" Olivia asked.

"I had a bad dream that Dillie was gone. I'm going down to check on him."

"Wait a moment, Cassie," Olivia said quickly. "I'll go with you."

"No need. Isn't Henry down there?"

Then Cassie heard a sound and Olivia heard it too. It was the terrible sound of a horse screaming. She knew immediately it was Godzilla.

"No!" Cassie sprinted in the direction of the academy. She ran so fast that she fell and skinned her knee. But she was quickly back on her feet, racing toward the academy.

When Cassie arrived, she couldn't believe her eyes. There were four men with ropes on Godzilla and they were dragging him toward a rusty old horse trailer. The men also had yellow hoses about sixteen inches long, and when Godzilla would rear up or try to bite or kick, the men would beat on him hard. The big horse had several welts on his face, neck, and body. The men were trying to beat him into submission.

Mr. Stanley stood watching the men from a safe distance, but he never expected to see Cassie.

"What are you doing!" Cassie screamed.

"Cassie," Mr. Stanley called. "These men have bought Godzilla. He's going to his new home."

Cassie saw that Godzilla was still struggling. When the men hit him again, she ran and got between the men and Godzilla. The big horse saw that it was Cassie, and he immediately settled down. She threw her arms around him.

"He's not leaving!" Cassie yelled to Mr. Stanley. "I'll buy him. I'll work the rest of my life for free. Don't sell him to these men."

"These men own him now," Mr. Stanley said. "He's bought and paid for. You have to let him go, Cassie."

"No, I won't!"

"That's enough of that," Freddy said. After all, he was going to make three thousand dollars if he got the job done by noon. He wasn't about to waste time on a young girl who loved a horse.

Freddy walked up and grabbed Cassie by the back of her shirt and tore her away from Godzilla. She fell to the ground and Godzilla went after him. But Freddy was too quick for the horse and hit Godzilla right between the eyes. The squeal of pain Godzilla let out made Cassie cry out as well. The big horse was stunned. Cassie lay on the ground and cried as Freddy's men began beating him with their hoses again.

"Stop it! Stop it!" Cassie screamed. "I'll put him on the trailer for you."

Freddy stopped and looked at Cassie. "You can do that, girlie?"

"Yes!" Cassie yelled. "I can do it."

"Then do it," Freddy said, "or we'll beat the tar right out of him."

Cassie slowly got up. Tears were streaming down her face. Had she known the true intentions of these men, she would have been fighting. But she didn't know they were taking Godzilla away just to kill him. All she wanted was for the men to stop hitting him.

Cassie walked up to Godzilla and saw that he was scared.

"Easy, Dillie. These men have bought you. You have to go with them. But I promise I'll come find you."

"Just put him on the trailer, girlie," Freddy said. "We don't have all day."

Cassie looked at Freddy and he held up the rubber hose.

"Come on, Dillie."

She led the horse toward the trailer. As always, Godzilla followed her and the men looked at each other because the horse that had tried to kill them followed Cassie so easily.

"Well, will you look at that," one of the men said. "That horse follows that little girl just like a lamb."

"Yeah," Freddy said, "the lamb to the slaughter."

The men laughed and luckily for Cassie, she didn't hear their remarks because this was easily the hardest thing she had ever done in her life. She was taking Godzilla, her Dillie who trusted her, and she was putting him in a trailer for some men who would just as soon beat him as care for him.

When they got to the trailer, Godzilla hesitated. He didn't want to go in. Cassie looked back at the men. Freddy again lifted up the yellow hose and hit it in his hand.

"Dillie," Cassie said, "you have to get on the trailer or these men are going to hit you. Please, Dillie. Do it for me."

Godzilla stepped forward and climbed into the trailer. Then Cassie climbed in the trailer too. Once inside, she hung onto the big horse's neck.

"Hey, little girl!" Freddy yelled. "Get out of there. We gotta go."

"I'm going with you."

"No you're not!" Freddy yelled. "Get out of there."

All of Freddy's men gathered around the trailer and were watching him order Cassie out.

"I said get out of there!" Freddy yelled again. He reached inside the trailer and grabbed Cassie by the back of her shirt. He started to yank her out. That was his first mistake. Wham! Freddy went to his knees. It was Olivia. She had a shovel in her hands.

"You touch that child again," Olivia yelled, "and I'll kill you!"

One of Freddy's men circled around Olivia and snatched the shovel out of her hands.

"You men stop now," Olivia said. "Stanley, you tell these men to stop."

"Hey," Mr. Stanley said lamely, "you can take the horse, but leave the girl alone."

Freddy Lava had recovered from being hit by the shovel. He reached in the trailer and grabbed Cassie by the foot.

"Hey," Mr. Stanley yelled, "I said keep your hands off the girl!"

But Freddy yanked Cassie's foot hard and she fell to the ground. After that, Freddy was able to drag her out. He picked Cassie up and he threw her toward Olivia, where she landed in the dirt.

Then Freddy stood on the ramp and looked at Olivia. "If I ever see you again, old woman, you'll regret it."

That was his second mistake. Godzilla reared up on his front legs and kicked out with his back hoofs. One hoof caught Freddy Lava in the square of his back. The impact sent Freddy flying and he landed on his face in front of his men. His men started laughing.

"Hey, Freddy," one man said, "we better get out of here before you get killed."

Freddy picked himself up. His face was scratched and he had trouble talking for a moment, but he was not about to make a third mistake. "Close up the trailer and let's go," Freddy said.

The men did as they were told. Then they all climbed in their trucks and started them up. Cassie just sat in the dirt crying as Olivia held her.

"There, there child," Olivia said gently. She was crying too, and she looked over at Mr. Stanley. "Stanley," Olivia said, "if your daddy were alive, he'd kick your butt." Then Olivia returned her attention to Cassie. "There, child," Olivia said. "Henry will be home soon. He'll know what to do."

But there was nothing Olivia could say that would help Cassie, whose cries were desperate. The men pulled away in their trucks, and Cassie cried even harder as she watched her beloved Dillie disappear down the driveway.

# Chapter Fifty-Four

When William Simms arrived at his kingdom, the Blue Ribbon Auto Mall, he passed a banner that read: Everyone's a Winner. It made Simms chuckle. "Not everyone," he said to himself.

Simms's glee could be directly attributed to the phone call he had just gotten from Freddy Lava. Freddy had told Simms that a young girl had put the horse in the trailer for them and that she had been very upset. Simms knew it was Cassie, and he was glad that she now felt as bad as Rebecca did. Moreover, Freddy had assured Simms that the job would be done by noon. That was less than an hour away.

"Yes," Simms said to himself, "some people are winners and some people are losers."

But when Simms saw six-foot-seven Chester Johnson walking confidently toward him, it made him pause. Chester had on his best black silk suit and a red tie. On his head was a black hat and Chester was giving Simms that stare of his, the kind of stare that makes one shudder. Simms was shuddering.

"William Simms!" Chester said loudly. His baritone voice carried easily across the parking lot. Simms looked around nervously. He wondered if he should run.

"I said, William Simms," Chester bellowed again.

Chester was ten feet away and closing fast. Simms began to back up.

"You bought a horse named Godzilla," Chester said.

"No, I didn't," Simms said nervously. "What makes you think that?"

"You're pathetic. You bought the horse from Stanley and now I'm going to make you one offer. I'm going to pay you ten thousand for the horse and that's more than you deserve."

"I don't know what you're talking about," Simms said and started walking away.

"You better not walk away, Simms, or the world's going to know about you buying a horse just so your little daughter can keep appearing on billboards."

Simms stopped. If nothing else, Simms was a smart businessman. If the world found out about Godzilla it could be bad for business. People could stop coming to his kingdom for their cars. Simms looked at Chester, and he knew the big man was serious.

"I'll be back at four with a contract and ten thousand dollars. I'll have some friends with me, too. You're going to sign the contract because that horse doesn't belong to you," Chester said.

Chester turned to walk away. Then he stopped and looked at Simms hard. "Nothing better happen to that horse."

## Chapter Fifty-Five

Freddy Lava was in a good mood. He and his cousin Benny were heading down the highway at seventy miles an hour. They had left the Dallas suburbs and had found themselves in the open countryside. Freddy figured they were about a half-hour to the turnoff to his private shooting range. It was the place where Freddy and his redneck friends spent their Sunday afternoons drinking beer and blowing holes in the empty cans. Freddy turned to his cousin and smiled. "This is the easiest three thousand dollars I've ever made."

"It wasn't that easy," the cousin said. "The old lady hit you with a shovel, and the horse kicked the snot out of you."

"No big deal," Freddy replied. "I'll take a shovel hit for cold, hard cash anytime. Besides, it'll be fun when we get to blow away the horse."

"Yeah," Benny added. "Maybe we should let the horse make a run for it before we blow it—"

Wham! The truck swerved. Wham! The truck swerved again.

"What was that!" Freddy yelled.

Wham! The trailer nearly came off its hitch. Freddy slowed down.

"It's the stupid horse," Benny said. "It's kicking the trailer."

Wham! Freddy had to swerve or he would have lost control.

"Let's just shoot the horse now," Freddy said.

"Nah," Benny replied. "If we shoot it now we'll just have to drag it out of the trailer. It's a big horse, Freddy."

Wham! The trailer and truck swerved again. Freddy slowed and pulled to the side of the road and stopped.

"We're going to shoot it now," Freddy said.

"Maybe you're right," Benny agreed. "Otherwise we might never get there."

"And I can call Simms and tell him it's done. Heck, we don't even have to bury it. We'll just leave it on the side of the road and let the county deal with it. It's not like it has a name tag or anything."

Freddy reached in the back of the truck and pulled out his shotgun.

"Maybe we should find a dirt road somewhere," Benny said. "We don't want anyone to see us."

"There's no law against shooting a horse," Freddy said, "especially one that's tried to kill people. Come on."

The two men got out of the truck and walked around to the back.

"Open the trailer and I'll shoot it," Freddy said.

Freddy raised his shotgun and Benny walked up and undid the latches. Benny carefully began to lower the door down. Wham! Godzilla hit the door with everything he had. The door flew down knocking Benny right into Freddy. Freddy fell back and the shotgun went off, blowing a hole in the side of the trailer. Godzilla bolted. He ran toward the fence on the side of the road and jumped. The big horse easily cleared the fence and was running through the fields before Freddy could get up. He got off one last shot but it was too late. His three-thousand-dollar payday was nearly out of sight. Godzilla was free.

# Chapter Fifty-Six

What do you mean he got away!" Simms screamed. "I don't know how it happened," Freddy stammered. "One second we were going to shoot him, and the next second he was gone."

"Well, where's he gone?"

"I don't know," Freddy said. "He took off across a field and disappeared."

Simms's mind was racing. On top of losing the horse, he had Chester Johnson on his mind. Then an idea popped into his head. It was one of those ideas that strike you, and had Simms thought it through, he might have seen the risks involved. But he could only see that he wanted to be rid of Godzilla once and for all.

"Okay, Freddy," Simms said. "I want you to call the police."

"The police?" Freddy asked with fear in his voice.

"Just calm down," Simms said. "Call the police. Tell them that your horse tried to kill someone, and it's extremely dangerous. Tell them you think it has a brain tumor or something and that you were going to destroy it. Tell them that the horse went crazy and nearly killed you. This way the police will kill it and you'll still get some money. Okay?"

"I don't like anything to do with the police," Freddy said.

"You got nothing to worry about. Just tell the police you're a concerned citizen worried about the welfare of other people because the horse is extremely dangerous. I mean, you were with it. Wouldn't you say that horse is dangerous?"

"Yeah," Freddy said brightly. "I had three guys with me and we were still scared of it."

"Well," Simms replied, "there you go. Just tell the police what happened when you tried to move the horse. How it nearly killed you and three of your friends. The police will be happy you called them."

"Right," Freddy said, "how much will I get if the police shoot the horse?"

"Freddy, if you really sell the fact that the horse is dangerous and the police kill it, I'll give you the whole three thousand."

"I'll do it," Freddy said. "After I'm done, the police will call out the SWAT team."

"Good," Simms said. "Now go get on it."

Simms hung up, feeling pleased with himself. The police would get near Godzilla and he would act dangerous toward them. Then they would feel justified in killing it. If Chester Johnson showed up he would just say, "I didn't kill Godzilla. The police did. It was just one big misunderstanding."

# Chapter Fifty-Seven

If we could know what was in Godzilla's mind, he would have told us it was simple. He was headed home to Cassie where he would be safe. His instincts had told him that the men he had been with were bad men. Now that he was free he was going to stay away from bad men.

The distance Godzilla had to travel was twenty-eight miles. He was on the outskirts of town and whenever he saw someone, he tried to stay as far away as he could. But soon, he couldn't avoid human beings because he had reached his first housing subdivision. He jumped the six-foot wall and found himself in a backyard. The next thing Godzilla knew, he heard screams coming from inside the house. He quickly ran alongside the house and jumped another fence. He found himself on a street lined with tract homes. He headed down the street in the direction he thought was home.

Peekaboo Sue was the neighborhood busybody. When Peekaboo and her husband moved into the Liberty housing tract, she had decided it was her job to keep track of all the comings and goings on the street to make sure everything was normal. On this particular morning, Peekaboo was sweeping the sidewalk while her two young sons rode tricycles nearby. She was content in the belief that all was right in her world.

Although Peekaboo had heard a newsflash about a dangerous horse, she supposed that the horse had been miles away. So imagine her surprise when she looked up to see Godzilla trotting toward her at just after one in the afternoon. She immediately panicked.

"Help!" Peekaboo screamed. She ran to her sons and yanked them both off their tricycles. The children, sensing their mother's fear, began to scream bloody murder. Peekaboo looked back to see Godzilla still coming down the street. He was less than thirty feet away.

"It's a monster!" Peekaboo yelled.

Peekaboo frantically dragged her two young sons toward the safety of their house. When she got to the front door, she looked back to see if the horse was coming after them. But Godzilla was gone. Still, Peekaboo immediately went inside, called the police, and reported that Godzilla had come after her and her children. She said, "The crazed horse was trying to kill them."

The police were alarmed. Freddy Lava had already sold them on the story that Godzilla was sick and capable of killing someone. Now the police had Peekaboo Sue's story that Godzilla had indeed gone after a woman and her children. To the police, this meant that the public's safety was at risk. Something had to be done, and quickly.

A helicopter was mobilized, the SWAT team with their sharp-shooters was put on standby, and a bulletin was sent to every car in the field. A sick, dangerous horse was on the loose and all officers were commanded to shoot it on sight. William Simms's plan was going to work after all.

## Chapter Fifty-Eight

Henry had just come from the bank, where he had transferred ten thousand dollars from his savings into his checking account. Henry had given a check to Chester Johnson to give to Simms for Godzilla, and Henry wanted to make sure the check was good.

Henry climbed into his truck and headed for home. He figured he would know by the end of the day if his plan had worked. He turned on the radio and immediately heard the news report about a loose horse.

"The horse is sick and extremely dangerous," the announcer said. "So please, if you see it, stay away from it."

Because Henry didn't know that Godzilla had already been taken, he had no reason to suspect that it was Godzilla. Henry was more worried about how Chester Johnson's meeting with Simms had gone. He hoped that it had gone as planned.

But when Henry arrived home and saw Olivia walk out from Cassie's trailer, he knew something had gone terribly wrong. Olivia's face was filled with such grief that it reminded him of the time his sons had died. Henry stepped out of the truck as fast as he could.

"Olivia, what's happened?" Henry asked.

"They came and took him."

"Took who?"

"Godzilla."

"What?"

"There were four men, Henry. They were beating Godzilla and then Cassie got between them and they started beating her."

"Is she hurt?"

"Not physically, but she's hysterical. She's been crying and moaning for over two hours. I've tried everything I can think of to console her, but she's beyond consoling. I've called Susan to come home. This is terrible, just terrible."

"That son . . . " Then Henry paused. "It couldn't be . . . "

"What?" Olivia asked.

"Okay," Henry said quickly, "stay with Cassie. I've got some calls to make. Godzilla may be running loose, but don't tell Cassie. I don't know how this is going to end."

# Chapter Fifty-Nine

Godzilla found himself in the middle of a busy Kmart shopping center. People saw him coming and started running in all directions. Cars were slamming on their brakes as Godzilla ran between the lanes. It didn't help that the police were there with their loudspeakers warning people not to get near the horse. But the police had trouble getting into the parking lot because of the traffic jam.

Godzilla was scared. He knew the direction he had to go, but there was a building in his way. He stopped for a moment in the middle of the sidewalk. He was breathing hard. Behind him, the police had abandoned their cars and were proceeding on foot with their guns drawn.

Then Godzilla took off down the sidewalk. He got to the end of the building, where there was a driveway between the Kmart and a Costco. Godzilla ran down the driveway toward the back of the buildings.

"We got him!" a policeman yelled. "There's a ten-foot fence in back. He'll never get over that."

"Don't shoot the pretty horse!" a nine-year-old girl yelled as the police ran past her.

Four policemen turned the corner and stopped. They could see Godzilla at the end of the drive looking at the fence.

"We've got him trapped," a policeman said. "He'll never get over the fence and this is the only way out."

"The order is to shoot on sight," another policeman said.

A helicopter flew overhead. It was a news chopper and the policemen knew they were on television.

"Hey," another cop said, "I've got a daughter that loves horses. I don't want to be the cop on the news that shot the pretty horse. Call animal control. Let them deal with it."

"Good idea," the first cop said. He pulled out his walkie-talkie. "Dispatch, we have the horse cornered behind the Kmart. Can you send animal control . . . " The police man's mouth fell open.

Godzilla bolted toward the fence. There was a flatbed truck parked next to the fence with the cab facing toward the fence. Godzilla leapt onto the back of the truck, ran a few feet, then jumped again onto the roof of the cab. With a mighty spring, Godzilla flew off the roof and over the ten-foot fence. He landed on the other side and fell to the ground. Before the police could react, Godzilla was on his feet and running through a vacant lot behind the building. The big horse was gone in seconds.

A voice came across the walkie-talkie. "The order is to shoot on sight."

The policeman with the walkie-talkie looked at the other three. "I think we're in trouble."

## Chapter Sixty

Henry turned on the television and watched spellbound and shocked as Godzilla cleared the ten-foot fence. The helicopters were following the horse as he jumped over fences into backyards. Henry ran to the phone and dialed 911.

"911 operator," a voice said.

"Yes, my name's Henry Williams. The horse the police are chasing is not dangerous. It belongs to . . . me. Let me come get it."

"Is this an emergency?" the operator said.

"Yes! The horse is named Godzilla. We'll come get him. He's a valuable animal . . . "

"Sir, are *you* injured or in danger?"

"No," Henry said. "Not directly. But they can't hurt the horse . . . "

"Sir, if you're not hurt or in immediate danger you have to call the police business line. This line is for emergencies only."

"But the horse is in danger!"

"Sir, do you know how many calls we've had about the horse? Dozens. Now please clear the line."

Henry hung up. For a moment, he was frozen, not knowing what to do. He looked at the television. Godzilla was jumping over another fence behind a house. Henry grabbed his car keys and left the trailer.

Henry ran as fast as he could to Cassie's trailer and walked inside. He went directly to Cassie's room. She was lying on the bed crying, and Olivia was sitting next to her rubbing her back. Olivia looked up at Henry when he entered.

"Cassie," Henry called, "I need you to come with me. We need to try and get Dillie."

Cassie turned over and looked at Henry. "What?" Cassie asked. Her eyes and face were red from crying.

"We need to go and try and get Dillie," Henry repeated.

Cassie jumped up immediately. "Where is he?"

"I don't have time to explain now. I'll explain in the truck. We need to hurry because I don't think there's much time. Come on."

Henry yelled to Olivia as they headed out the door: "Call Mark and tell him the game is still on! Chester Johnson is expecting to meet him at four o'clock. Got it?"

"Okay," Olivia said.

"Also have him call every reporter in town and tell them that Godzilla is the horse on TV."

"Dillie's on TV?" Cassie asked. "I want to see."

"We don't have time!" Henry said. "We have to hurry or it might be too late."

Cassie headed for the truck.

"Good luck!" Olivia called.

"Thanks," Henry said. "We'll need it."

*Chapter Sixty-One*

Godzilla was getting very tired. He had entered an old neighborhood and jumped a fence. The backyard was littered with broken-down cars and dirty, old refrigerators and stoves. Godzilla paused here to take a much needed rest. As he stood breathing hard, he looked around for a drink of water.

All around the neighborhood, Godzilla could hear sirens blaring, and overhead, the helicopters were circling. Instincts were telling Godzilla to run, but he was so tired and thirsty. Water was all he could think about. Then the horse heard a voice behind him.

"Do you need some water, beautiful horse?" the voice said.

Godzilla spun around to see a ten-year-old boy carrying a large bowl of water. The bowl made the boy look small, and it took all of the boy's balance and strength to carry it.

At first, Godzilla's ears went back. But then he saw the water and sensed that the boy was not there to harm him.

At the Blue Ribbon Auto Mall, William Simms was watching the images of the boy carrying the water to Godzilla on television. The announcer felt inspired to comment.

"This boy is taking his life in his hands. The police have reported that the horse may have a brain tumor, which makes it very erratic and dangerous. The horse already tried to kill two men earlier today and then tried to attack a woman and her children."

But the images showed the young boy setting the bowl of water in front of Godzilla. The big horse leaned down and began gulping the water.

"Amazing," the announcer said. "It looks like the horse is drinking."

William Simms started to worry. He had never expected the story to get this big. It was capturing the imagination of the entire city. He began to sweat. If the truth were to come out, Simms' empire could come crumbling down. For the first time, Simms began to question the choices he'd made.

On television, the news helicopters showed two police cars pulling up in front of the house. Four policemen jumped out of the cars and headed toward the backyard.

When they got to the side fence, they broke through the gate, startling Godzilla. He bolted, accidentally bumping the young boy and knocking him down. The boy was unhurt and got up quickly, but on television it looked as though Godzilla had tried to run the boy over.

The announcer commented, "See, that's why the public needs to stay away from this animal. The police have said that the horse is dangerous. That boy could have been killed."

Simms smiled. His hopes returned for a resolution in his favor. Namely, that the police would kill Godzilla and if it came out that he owned the horse, Simms could just claim it was a big misunderstanding. It would all blow over, because the public's memory was short. But those hopes were quickly dashed with a knock on the door.

"Come in," Simms said.

A secretary walked in with a worried look on her face.

"Mr. Simms," the secretary said, "there's a news crew outside. A reporter by the name of Mark Sinclair says you'd probably like to talk to him before he does a story on a horse named Godzilla."

Simms paused. He knew this was not going to be good. "Ask him in," he replied.

A moment later, Mark Sinclair entered the room. But he was not alone. He had the big bad bear with him. When Simms saw Chester Johnson, he knew he was in trouble. Simms had completely forgotten that Chester said he would be back at four. Simms didn't even stand up to greet them.

"What do you want from me?" Simms asked.

"We want the horse," Chester said. "I have a check for ten thousand. That's a fair price. All things considered."

"What makes you think that I have the faintest idea what you're talking about?" Simms said.

"Cut the baloney, Simms," Mark said. "We know the truth, and I promise you that if it gets out it will not be pretty. What kid in this city would let their parents buy a car from the horse killer?"

Simms gulped.

"Because," Mark added, "if I do my story that's what it's going to look like."

"I'll sue you for slander," Simms said quickly.

"The truth isn't slander," Mark replied.

Simms gulped again.

"Here's a contract," Chester said, "and I've got the check. Sign the contract, and we'll leave you alone."

"I don't sign contracts without my lawyer looking at them first," Simms said.

"You signed a contract last night without your lawyer," Mark said. "Just take the ten thousand and we'll go away. If you don't, I'm going to go right outside and do my story. And I'd like to do my story. It's a reporter's dream. A scoop like this. Who knows? It might even win me a Pulitzer Prize."

Chester Johnson held out the check and the contract. Simms hesitated for a moment until he looked into Chester Johnson's eyes. Chester's steely stare convinced Simms that he had better sign the contract because he realized that if he didn't, everything that he had spent his life building could disappear. Simms reached out and took the check and contract. He signed the contract and handed it back.

Then, Simms looked at the check. Simms was surprised at the name on the check.

"Henry Williams?" Simms asked. "That field hand? He's behind all this?"

Mark and Chester looked at each other and smiled. Simms grew angry.

"That field hand?" Simms asked. "Where did he get ten thousand dollars?"

"That field hand," Chester said, "has probably got more money than you."

Chester stood up and then Mark did too. Chester looked at Simms hard. "You better hope that horse doesn't die."

# Chapter Sixty-Two

Henry's truck was old, but it was dependable. Still, Henry was a little worried because he was pushing it so hard. He and Cassie raced through the streets of Dallas to where the news reports said Godzilla had been seen. It was difficult to know exactly where to go. People were calling in from all over the city saying they had seen the killer horse, and even though the reporters had the television coverage to refer to, they were still getting confused.

Meanwhile, Mark Sinclair had gotten a call from Olivia and was doing everything he could to try to stop the police from shooting Godzilla. But he had two big obstacles. First, the story was so big it had acquired the kind of momentum that feeds on itself. The producers and reporters had gone with the killer-horse story and were very reluctant to change their angle because they didn't want to be wrong. Mark was just a fellow reporter and didn't have the authority of the police to decide whether Godzilla was dangerous. They also had the footage of the young boy being knocked down to "prove" that he was.

The police were proving to be an even bigger obstacle. As far as they were concerned, Freddy Lava was the horse's owner and he had given them the right to shoot Godzilla. They also had the report from Peekaboo Sue that the horse tried to attack her. The police weren't about to listen to some reporter when the public's safety was at risk. By the time Henry and Cassie had gotten close enough to Godzilla to see the helicopters circling, the police command remained stubbornly intact: "Shoot on sight."

Godzilla was now in a wealthy neighborhood. He was still jumping and running through backyards. But instead of running around abandoned cars, the big horse was avoiding swimming pools. The houses were near a golf course, which was built along the side of a large lake. Godzilla was running through the estate-sized backyards of houses that backed up to the golf course. Godzilla was only a few miles now from the academy.

Henry and Cassie turned onto Hampton Drive. People were out on the street watching the helicopters circling. Henry slowed to look up at the sky just as a police car zoomed by. A little farther ahead, a police car blocked the road. Henry pulled to a stop, and both he and Cassie ran up to the policeman who was standing by his car in the street.

"Road's closed sir," the policeman said.

"Officer," Henry said, "the horse belongs to us. If you let us through we'll get him and take him home."

The policeman laughed. "You know how many crackpots are saying the same thing? The phone's ringing off the hook down at the station house."

"No, really!" Cassie pleaded. "I just rode him yesterday in a big show."

"Look," the policeman said, "if he's really your horse, call the station. My job is to keep the road clear for police cars. Now move your truck so the police can do their job."

Cassie began to cry. "But he's my horse."

"I can't help you," the policeman said.

Henry and Cassie got back in the truck and turned around. They headed back up the street. Suddenly, the helicopters were circling in front of them. A police car zoomed by Henry and Cassie again. Its lights were flashing and its siren was wailing. Then, about a block down, Cassie saw Godzilla. He had appeared from behind the houses lining the street. For a moment, he was on the front lawn of a house.

"It's Dillie!" Cassie yelled.

Henry saw the horse, but there was a police car ahead of them and it raced toward Godzilla. The horse saw the police car and started to run. The police car drove onto the lawn and looked as if it was going to try to run Godzilla down.

"No!" Cassie screamed.

But Godzilla was too fast and ran back between the houses. The policemen jumped out of their car and pursued. By the time Henry and Cassie got there, Godzilla was gone. The policemen were walking back to their car. Cassie flew out of the truck and ran at the policemen.

"He's not dangerous! He's not dangerous!" Cassie was yelling.

Cassie ran so fast that the policemen were caught off guard. One officer grabbed Cassie and held her. She was hysterical.

"He's my horse," Cassie sobbed. "He's not dangerous."

Henry arrived and the policemen looked at Henry for an explanation. "The girl's telling the truth," Henry pleaded. "The horse belongs to us."

The two policemen looked at each other.

"Miss," the policeman said, "settle down."

"Just let me get him!" Cassie yelled.

"You're telling the truth, aren't you?" the policeman asked.

"Yes," Cassie said.

Over the radio a voice crackled, "The horse is on the golf course. SWAT team report to the golf course. All other units stand by."

"There's not much I can do," the policeman said. "We're in a tactical alert so I can't use my radio to help you. But if he is your horse, I'd get to the golf course as fast as you can. Tell them Officer Wooters sent you."

"Thanks," Henry said.

Cassie and Henry ran to the truck. At least now they had some hope. Somebody finally believed them.

# Chapter Sixty-Three

Godzilla was standing on the green of the fifth fairway. He was tired, hot, and spent. He was also very scared. The police had chased him and shot at him, and he just didn't understand why. To a horse, it all meant he had to run. Panting for air, mouth foaming, sweat pouring off of him, Godzilla just couldn't run anymore.

The sun was setting and the nearby woods were throwing long shadows onto the green. Godzilla wondered if he could just stay where he was. The helicopters were still circling, but there were no police cars coming after him.

Godzilla rested for about ten minutes as the police cast their net. The more he rested, the longer the police had to corner him. Godzilla had been moving so fast, the police had been unable to do anything but chase him. Now they were closing in.

The first sound he heard was a bang and a whistling past his ear. Godzilla looked to his right. There were two golf carts coming toward him. He looked to his left. There were three golf carts coming from that direction. He looked in front of him. There were men coming over the fence. There was another bang and more whistling. This time the bullet had come closer. He looked behind him and saw the woods, and beyond that, the lake.

Godzilla gathered what strength he had left and ran for the woods. There was another bang and Godzilla felt a stinging in his neck. It wasn't a direct hit, but the pain and the fact that he was tired made him stumble and fall. There were more bangs and more whistling as bullets flew past him. For a moment, Godzilla just lay there. Then, the big horse heard Cassie's voice in his head, "We can do this, Dillie." Godzilla picked himself up, and with everything that he had left, he ran to the woods and disappeared into the trees.

# Chapter Sixty-Four

Henry drove to the golf course as fast as he could. He actually drove a little too fast, but since all the policemen were on standby for Godzilla, Henry wasn't too worried about a ticket. Still, it took Henry a little longer than he would have liked because they had to stop twice and ask for directions to the golf course entrance.

When they finally arrived, it was getting dark. They pulled into the entrance and found that a policeman was stopping the cars from entering. Henry pulled up to the officer and stopped. Henry rolled down the window.

"The golf course is closed, sir," the policeman said.

"We were told to come here," Henry said quickly. "The horse you're chasing belongs to us."

"Who told you to come here?" the policeman asked.

"Another policeman. His name was Wooters."

"Wait a second," the officer said. He stepped away for a moment and talked into a walkie-talkie. Then, he came back.

"It's too late," the policeman said.

"You mean they killed him?" Henry yelled. "They killed our horse?"

"I'm not sure what they meant," the policeman said. "They just said it's too late."

"It can't be too late," Henry said and he hit the gas. He sped by the first cop and proceeded up the long driveway. The cop was yelling and waving his arms, and Henry saw him talking into his walkie-talkie in his rearview mirror.

When Henry and Cassie reached the top of the drive, they saw several police cars parked and what looked like an armored truck.

Several policemen were running toward them waving their arms. Henry left the drive, bounced over a curb, and headed up the fairway. He could see the police helicopter's spotlight in the distance.

"Cassie," Henry said. "I don't know what else to do."

"Just get us there," Cassie replied between her tears.

Henry was driving as fast as he could, but it was a little tricky. The old truck was slipping in the grass, and Henry had to really concentrate to keep from spinning out. Cassie sat in the seat next to Henry, crying.

"Cassie," Henry said, "you have to be strong. You have to be strong for Dillie."

Henry saw the lights of the helicopter and he knew that that was where they would find Godzilla. But when he pulled up and stopped, three cops rushed the truck and pulled Henry from the cab and threw him to the ground.

"Stay on the ground!" the policemen yelled.

"Cassie," Henry yelled, "run to Dillie, girl. He's in the woods. Don't stop until you get there."

Cassie leapt out of the truck, catching the policemen by surprise. She ran in the direction of the spotlight shining down on the trees.

"Halt!" a policeman yelled. "You might get shot."

"Then tell everyone not to shoot!" Henry yelled.

But it was too late. From the woods came the sound of gunfire and all the officers' walkie-talkies crackled with the sound of voices.

"Did you get him?"

"I think so."

"Yeah, you got him."

"But he jumped in the lake. I don't see him anywhere."

"He's probably sunk to the bottom."

Cassie fell to her knees and screamed. "But he's my horse. No! Please no!" She lay on the ground and curled into a ball.

# Chapter Sixty-Five

Henry got into some trouble at first for not obeying the commands of the police and for driving onto the golf course. But then a call came from somewhere and the police quickly changed their attitude. Henry and Cassie were immediately released. Later, Henry found out that his nephew had gotten through to the Dallas police chief. After listening to Mark, the chief realized his department had made a serious mistake, and was now worried about a public backlash. The police had acted recklessly. Apparently, they had killed an innocent horse.

Now the police were looking for someone to blame. Investigators were sent to talk to William Simms and Freddy Lava. The two men were in big trouble, because it was a crime to file a false police report. Godzilla was not sick and did not have a brain tumor.

Cassie had not said a word since she had fallen to the ground on the golf course. In her mind, there was nothing to be said. Her best friend was dead and she was in so much pain she was numb. She felt she would never recover.

Henry drove Cassie home. He was worried because he had expected Cassie to be crying, but she was silent. Henry tried to think of something to say but nothing came to mind that would help. So they rode in silence and Henry knew Cassie was in real trouble. First her father and now Dillie.

When Henry pulled up at home, Olivia and Susan came out of Susan's trailer to meet them. They had seen the television report that said the killer horse was dead. They both walked to Cassie and tried to give her a hug.

"Bed," was all Cassie said.

Susan walked Cassie into the trailer, leaving Henry and Olivia alone in the dark.

"What happened is terrible," Olivia said. "But you can't blame yourself. You tried everything you could think of."

"I know," Henry said. "It's just that it all ended in the worst way possible. It would have been better if I hadn't done anything."

"Henry Williams! Don't you say that. Mark called and that man sold them the horse. That was your plan and that worked. The rest is just something you had no control over. That part was up to God."

"I'm tired of God making choices in my life. I always come up short."

"Maybe not," Olivia said. "There might be a reason for it all that we don't see yet. There's a reason for everything."

"The only reason I can see is heartache. I'm going to bed too."

Olivia watched her husband shuffle off to the trailer. She knew that the two people she loved most in life were in terrible pain.

# Chapter Sixty-Six

Henry awoke in the middle of the night. He quietly climbed out of bed and dressed. Then he got in his truck and drove away. He couldn't sleep because he kept thinking about the policeman saying that Godzilla had jumped in the lake. He didn't know why he kept thinking about that. He guessed he was hoping against hope that Godzilla was still alive.

But when he drove along the lake, his hope began to wane. The lake was so black and the night so dark that it sucked the hope from his spirit. Henry parked alongside the road and looked out across the still black water. The longer he looked, the sadder he got. Soon, he found himself crying. He cried for Godzilla. He cried for Cassie. Then Henry cried for the sons he had lost some thirty years ago.

"Why, God, or Creator, or whatever you want to be called these days, do you always take from me? I don't understand. I'm an old man and you're still taking from me."

Henry stared out across the lake. On the distant shore were the lights from houses.

"God, I'm asking for a miracle. Don't let Dillie be dead. Take something else. But don't take Dillie. Cassie needs him too much."

Henry sat in silence for a long time. He was hoping that Godzilla would just climb out of the water. But when nothing happened, Henry felt foolish.

"What good is a prayer anyway?"

Henry started his truck and drove home.

# Chapter Sixty-Seven

C assie had hardly slept all night. Toward dawn, the pain she was feeling had finally worn her out and she fell off to sleep. But she slept fitfully, and awoke again with the rising sun. Then she curled up in a ball and moaned quietly.

Outside, the sun had just risen over the horizon. It was going to be a beautiful day, and a stream of morning sunlight was shining on the wall above Cassie's bed. Cassie lay curled there looking at the stream of light shining on the wall. At the bottom of the light beam were two shadows pointing up. They reminded Cassie of horse ears and she remembered how Dillie's ears always went back when Mr. Stanley was around.

Cassie felt such a powerful wave of grief run through her that she gritted her teeth and closed her eyes. The pain came like a wave pounding the seashore. It rolled up on her soul with such force that it made her shake. Then as quickly as it had come, the feelings rolled away, leaving her numb. After a moment, she opened her eyes and saw that the shadows were gone.

Cassie closed her eyes again and thought about how much she was going to miss riding. She knew she would never ride again because it would just hurt too much. Riding and Dillie, the two things that had gotten her through her father's death, were now lost to her forever. She had no idea how she could go on.

Cassie opened her eyes to find the shadows had returned. She watched the shadows, wondering what had happened to Dillie's body. She wanted to bury him in the horses' graveyard next to Sunny. She needed to see her horse one last time to say goodbye. Cassie blinked. The shadows moved. She blinked again and the horse-ear shadows moved across the wall as if they were dancing on the beam of light.

"Dillie?"

Cassie rubbed her eyes and looked and the shadows were gone. Then, suddenly, the shadows appeared again. Cassie leapt out of bed and ran to the window.

It was Godzilla. The big horse looked tired and spent, and at the top of his neck there was blood. But it was Godzilla, and when Cassie saw him she screamed. Only this time there was joy in her screams. Her horse, her partner, her best friend had come home to her.

"Dillie!" Cassie screamed again and she ran to the door.

Cassie's screams had awakened Susan. She jumped out of bed and ran to the hall. Cassie and Susan collided in the center.

"Cassie! Cassie! It's just a dream, sweetheart."

"No, it's not, Mom. He's right outside." Cassie ran past her mom and headed for the front door. She burst from the trailer screaming, "Dillie! Dillie!"

Cassie's screams woke Henry and Olivia, and they leapt out of bed too. They came out of their trailer in their pajamas to see what was happening. They couldn't believe their eyes as they saw Cassie running to Godzilla.

Cassie threw her arms around her horse and cried. But these were tears of joy, and the pain she had been feeling was being cried away.

"Dillie!" Cassie yelled. "You're home! You're home!"

Cassie looked over at her mom. "See, Mom, Dillie came home."

Susan had tears in her eyes. "Yes, sweetheart, your horse came home."

"Dillie, my Dillie," Cassie said and she started kissing the big horse on his nose.

Henry couldn't believe his eyes. He was so surprised he couldn't talk. Olivia had to speak first. "Will you look at that."

"Well, I'll be damned," Henry finally said. "It's a miracle. God, thank you for your miracle."

"You see, Henry," Olivia said, "things happen for a reason."

Henry walked over to Cassie and Godzilla. He walked slowly around the big horse. He examined Godzilla's neck and saw that it was only a flesh wound. The horse had scratches and cuts, but for the most part, he was in good shape.

"It's a miracle, Olivia," Henry said. "From this day forward I can say I believe in miracles."

Cassie suddenly stopped crying and looked to Henry. There was panic in her voice.

"Henry, help! We have to hide him! They'll come for him. They'll take him away!"

Henry smiled. His plan had worked after all. "No, Cassie, Dillie belongs to us now. You'll never have to worry again."

"What?"

"He's half yours."

"What do you mean?"

"I bought him from Simms yesterday, and I'm going to give you half, provided you'll ride him. I'll pay for his feed and the shows, and you ride him. When you become a champion, we'll split the profits fifty-fifty."

Henry stuck out his hand. Cassie smiled and shook it.

"Smart girl," Henry said.

"I guess I'm smarter than you because I would have ridden him for free."

Henry laughed and then Cassie gave Henry a big hug.

"Thank you. Thank you for everything."

Cassie pulled back and looked at Olivia. Susan and Olivia were standing together smiling and hugging each other. Tears were streaming down their faces.

"You're my good-luck charm, Olivia," Cassie said. "Every time I tell you my birthday wish, it comes true."

Olivia laughed. "Only the first part came true. We'll have to wait a little while on the second part."

"Don't worry," Cassie said happily. "Dillie and I will take care of the rest."

Cassie gave Godzilla another hug. The big horse reached over and rubbed his face against hers. He was happy to finally be home. Cassie looked at her horse and smiled.

"I love you, Dillie."

# Chapter Sixty-Eight

The equestrian field was surrounded by poles with flags from different countries, and in the center was a large flag with several circles. The field was also surrounded by grandstands, and every seat was filled. Most of the people looked different from Cassie's earlier shows. Many of them were Chinese.

Henry, Olivia, and Susan were sitting together in the stands, waiting for the competition to begin. They had smiles on their faces, and when Cassie and Godzilla arrived at the entrance to the arena, Olivia turned to Susan and hugged her. They looked at each other, crossed their fingers, and hugged again.

Cassie sat on top of Godzilla, she was proud to be representing her country and proud of what they had accomplished. She could feel proud because she had earned the right to be. It was the culmination of perseverance, hard work, and talent, not to mention a little luck.

Back in the United States, a crowd of people had gathered around a big screen television set up outside the offices of The North Dallas Riding Academy. About a hundred people were there including Mr. Stanley, Athena the vet and Linda Flemming, Cassie's first coach. The crowd started yelling and applauding when Cassie and Godzilla appeared on the television screen. An announcer's voice could be heard over the image.

"Next up for Team America is young Cassie Reynolds and her amazing horse, Godzilla. This is their final appearance here in Beijing, and it's just unbelievable what these two have accomplished. The quest for gold is in their hands. It's one of the truly great stories of these games."

"Yes, it is," the second announcer replied. "Seventeen-year-old Cassie Reynolds is riding the meanest horse that's ever been ridden in equestrian competition. And just maybe the finest horse as well."

"It's really a love story, isn't it?" the first announcer asked.

"Yes, it is," the second announcer replied. "A love story that just might win Olympic gold."

Cassie had blossomed into a beautiful young woman. For luck, she reached down and rubbed Godzilla's scar, the one made by the bullet that could have killed him. Since that time, Cassie had always called it Godzilla's lucky scar. Not only for him, but for herself as well. Rubbing it reminded her of just how lucky they were.

"This is it, Dillie," Cassie said. "We're seven thousand miles from home and the only thing that matters is that we're together. But let's make this one special. We'll ride this round for Sunny, and we'll ride it for my dad. Let's make them proud."

Godzilla snorted and Cassie knew it was time. Cassie took a deep breath and smiled. She touched her heels to Godzilla's sides, and the big horse and Cassie began to fly.

Praise for
## *Riding Godzilla*

"A great story about perseverance and never giving up. *Riding Godzilla* artfully dramatizes what it takes to achieve your dreams.
> — **George Morris**
> Chef d'Equipe of the USA equestrian team,
> Olympic Silver Medalist

"*Riding Godzilla* is a sensitive portrayal of a young girl's special bond with a horse. It is full of practical examples of natural horsemanship."
> — **Neecy Twinem**
> Children's book author and illustrator

"Here is a courageous and inspiring story to remind children and adults to never give up under any circumstances. Teachers will appreciate this story for the wonderful opportunities that it presents for discussing valuable life lessons in the classroom. *Riding Godzilla* is a must have for every school library."
> — **Ruben Martinez**
> McArthur Foundation "Fellows Award"
> Recipient, 2004

"*Riding Godzilla* is an easy-to-read story with a supremely important message: *Only love has the power to heal grief and loss, and turn us into champions.*"
> — **Othello Bach**
> Author, ***Whoever Heard of a Fird, Cry into the Wind*** and other best-sellers for children and adults

"Amid danger, tragedy and grief, **Riding Godzilla** gives way to a grand adventure as young Cassie learns to ride Godzilla, the meanest horse ever. The timeless passion of youth and the unbelievable power of a most angry animal fill every page of this charmed story. Forged from sadness and sheer willpower, two souls bond an unbreakable love. P.S. Foley has created one of tomorrow's truly great horse classics . . . today."

— **Jim Great Elk Waters**
Shawnee author, **View from the Medicine Lodge**


"Usually, horse tales are about the love between man and his horse. **Riding Godzilla** is an unforgettable story of love between a girl and her horse. A great read!"

— **Pat Schroeder**
President and CEO, Association of American Publishers


"Inspiring!"

— **Jason Lezak**
U.S. Olympic Gold and Silver Medalist